Praise for *Pentimento Mori*

"An intriguing plot you can't put down." *Il Secolo XIX*

"[Corciolani] glories in art and exposes the artistic codes and details hidden in that art." *La Repubblica*

"An often ferocious, yet hopeful, satire." *Bruno Morchio, best-selling author*

"Readers, from amateurs to experts, cannot help but be enthralled by the way Corciolani, with infinite expertise and real passion, introduces fascinating ideas, curiosities, and anecdotes." *Thriller Nord*

"Corciolani opens the door to an unexpected world of art admired not only for its beauty but for the meaning behind it." *Le Recensioni della Libraia*

"*Pentimento Mori* is a classic mystery filled with irony. Written for art lovers, it is detailed with perfect precision." *Solo Libri*

"The writer serves us on a silver platter an abundance of details that are historically accurate, and at the same time intriguing and satisfying." *Milano Nera*

"This novel has everything: information on medieval painting, on colors, on their uses and their meanings, on alchemical beliefs, on the history of religion and its myths." *La Libraia Virtuale*

"A brilliant mystery blending elements of art, religion and history with truly elegant mastery." *Viaggi e Libri*

"Brilliant dialogue and descriptions, lively pacing and a carefully constructed and entertaining plot." *Ginodeilibri*

Pentimento Mori

Valeria Corciolani

Kazabo Publishing

Garamond MT Std 12/16
ISBN: 978-1-948104-29-6
P01

Chapter One

Yellow.

Everything is dry and yellow.

He rocks slowly, moving forward a little, to get a better look. It's been a dry summer, yes, but not unlike last year and the years before, because now it's always like this and the heat beats down from the sky to split your skull open.

But this time it's different. He can feel it.

He still advances on the branch and moves his head in small nervous jerks, with his round eyes peering among the broad leaves of the holm oaks, in search of the juicy green he likes so much. But no joy – the grass is scorched, with large bare patches, stiff and straight as needles.

Everything is dry. Dry and yellow.

And he doesn't like yellow. Lemons are yellow.

Dead leaves are yellow.

Marlena, whose voice scratches the air like a bulldozer and frightens him stiff, has yellow hair.

Even that van that almost ran over Berta the other day was yellow.

Yellow, like the sulfur of hell.

Because yes, yellow is bad, and no, he doesn't like it at all.

And a dry summer has nothing to do with it. Because this time it's different. He can feel it.

And then there is the matter of the kite.

It's been a long time since a kite was seen around here. And this, too, is a sign.

And even though the man who's always saying "Oh My God," and that he has now nicknamed OMG, says that the only things that bring bad luck are the bad thoughts in our head, he is not so sure of it, because the earth sometimes speaks.

In its own way, but it speaks.

He moves again on the branch, craning his neck to find a way out of all this evil yellow, before it strikes him too.

But perhaps it's too late, because the branch cracks, opening a void underneath him.

But it's no problem, he thinks, as he immediately spreads his wings.

Which, however, don't open as they should, and in fact with a dull thud he crashes on Marlena's chicken coop, dragging under again that unfortunate hen, Berta, poor thing, who had escaped the wheels of the yellow van only to see almost land on top of her one hundred and eighty pounds and six feet of useless wingspan, in a mess of feathers, eggs and chicken poop.

Berta squawks away, ruffled and offended, while the bulldozer scream of Marlena rends the air.

And he remains there, his back on the ground, his wings still wide open and his eyes staring at the sky.

An exceptionally yellow sky, *ça va sans dire*.

Chapter Two

"Things like that," she says, her slender hand, weighed down by countless bracelets, gracefully twirling in the air and encompassing with a gesture all things she considers useless and too boring to mention.

How is it possible that wrist of hers, which is thinner than a bread stick from Turin, has not yet crumbled apart remains, for Edna, a deeper mystery than the third secret of Fatima. But Zara Guglielmi, aka the widow Silvera, looks at Edna with a stubborn obstinacy. Although almost eighty, with a lemur's physique and encroaching osteoporosis, nothing can alter her unshakeable habit of adorning herself like a Madonna in procession. And this, despite the fact that she will, in all probability, never set foot outside the house, and the only ones to marvel at the sight of her trappings will be herself and Kalina.

Actually, after today, maybe not even Kalina. And this is the heart of the matter.

"Listen, Mom," Edna exhales, forcing herself to focus on the issue, because her mother has the power to burn through her already-limited supply of patience with a single incendiary word, "you have to admit that calling Kalina an illiterate…"

"And a nincompoop," points out the sharp voice of Kalina from the room next door, "plus the beating," she adds through her copious tears.

"A beating, oh, come now… the usual exaggeration," Zara rolls her eyes.

"Yes, a nincompoop and a beating. With a bottle. Three times!" repeats the voice from the other room, but with fewer tears than before and many more sharp edges.

"Did you beat her with a bottle?" hisses Edna, "Have you completely lost your…"

"It was a plastic bottle," huffs her mother. "And it was empty."

Edna stares at her, eyes narrowed and arms crossed. She has the air of someone who, at 8 o'clock in the morning, has already seen her entire daily allotment of patience reduced to ashes. This figurine, as slender and elegant as Limoges porcelain, who swings her leg in woolen periwinkle trousers with the blasé detachment of an aristocratic who at the cry of "Madame, the palace is on fire" sighs "Oh, I just had the curtains redone," is now causing Edna to reconsider the possibilities of a bottle as a blunt instrument. And not in plastic… or empty. She quickly regrets the thought. As she well knows, her mother, with an almost surgical precision, always manages to draw out the worst in her. She's known this for almost fifty-seven years, essentially from the moment the beautiful twenty-one year old Zara Guglielmi popped her out and delivered her to an endless succession of nannies and au-pairs without a second thought. Nothing could be allowed to hinder her return to charming audiences with her precious cello and her capricious beauty.

A choice that Edna did not personally condemn; every woman has the sacred right to choose her own life and her own career. Motherhood should never become an obstacle. Indeed, growing up knowing that the person who carried you in the womb for nine months pays you about as much attention as she would to an odd sock stuck in the back of a dresser is the kind of thing that either kills you or makes you stronger.

And here, in all probability, genetics comes into play. The egotistical determination transmitted from her mother to Edna is counterbalanced by the radiant enthusiasm of the Silvera family and by her father in particular. As a result, Edna often goes her own way, not unlike an eighteen-wheeler or an aircraft carrier, barreling ahead in a straight line without too much concern for failed hopes and missing hugs.

To be honest, even her father was never the king of doting affection, especially when she was a little girl. But as soon as she became interesting and began to exhibit a keen intelligence and a lively curiosity, he began spending more time with her and even treated her as something of an equal. Though spending your days in a doctor's office is not typically a young girl's highest aspiration, she could not have asked for anything better: all that human variety fascinated her in the same way it enchanted her father.

Observing both people and Art – with a capital A – were the two great interests that Giuseppe Silvera transmitted to her both by nature and by nurture. Though her upbringing left her life resembling Swiss cheese, these twin passions allowed her to fill those holes.

So all things considered, despite an unpromising start, she has turned out pretty well. She is not a serial killer. She does not require a steady diet of anti-depressants. She has pursued a regular course of study she loves and that has given her great satisfaction. Sure, there have been a few bumps along the way. At thirteen, she set fire to her mother's cello, a priceless instrument created by Giuseppe Guarnieri in the eighteenth century. At fifteen she set off with a backpack and a Eurail pass, leaving behind only a page ripped hastily from a notebook with a scrawled message: "I'm touring Europe. I'll be back when I'm back."

But these were typical adolescent rebellions, perhaps slightly enhanced by her naturally unyielding disposition. Because, yes, her personality is hardly accommodating and, no, she's not easy to get along with, but only because she has always cared little about the approval of others, freeing her from the need to be popular and allowing her to say, almost always, what she likes. In fact, forget the "almost."

Just as her mother has also always done, after all.

But for now, Edna takes a deep breath and tries to smile benignly, waiting for an acceptable explanation to justify the name-calling and bottle-beating of the new housekeeper, or, at the very least, a plausible lie.

But Zara Guglielmi, aka the widow Silvera, just does not get it. Musical genius she might be, able to stride the most famous stages in the world and mingle with kings and peasants alike. But she has never had the slightest understanding of what makes her daughter tick.

And so, she continues her tirade: "That woman had the face to say that it wasn't her fault, that I didn't explain properly," she goes on undeterred. "What was there to explain? I asked for a simple dessert, a Norwegian Omelet… everyone knows what that is!" she continues as she taps her small foot on the precious Bokhara rug.

Edna raises an eyebrow. She's not so sure "everyone knows" that Norwegian Omelet is another name for Baked Alaska, and she has the sneaking suspicion that her mother intentionally set a trap for poor Kalina.

"And what does she do?" Zara asks dramatically. "She serves me an omelette filled with smoked salmon! As if that could possibly be a dessert! Clearly, one loses one's patience and…" she twirls her hand, wrist clanking, to illustrate the unavoidable consequences.

"So, let me get this straight," sighs Edna; "you beat Kalina with a bottle, called her an illiterate…"

"And a nincompoop!" adds a sharper voice from the other room.

"A nincompoop, yes," sighs Edna once again, because separating her from Kalina's room is a salon larger than the hangar for a Boeing 747, and so at the moment she not only risks seeing the umpteenth housekeeper disappear, but one with hearing that would qualify her for her own superhero comic book. "In short, you mean to tell me that you've beaten and insulted her over a matter of culinary linguistics."

"There was a valuable lesson for her to learn: fish is not a substitute for ice cream. I can appreciate that this might not be immediately obvious to an illiterate nincompoop…"

"For God's sake, stop it!" hisses Edna, glancing nervously at the wall of the salon that separates her from Kalina's room. "Can't you hear yourself when you talk?"

"What a fuss," exhales Zara, shrugging her shoulders. Then she fixes Edna for a long moment with her deep-green eyes, still brilliant and sharp as a shard of crystal. "Beating sense into fools has a long and historic pedigree. I believe Greek schoolmasters were famous for it. That gentle chastisement with the bottle was purely pedagogical."

Edna raises the other eyebrow.

"Very well, very well," concedes her magnanimous mother, plucking non-existent lint from her pale-blue sweater. Perhaps the beatings were a trifle enthusiastic and I can't deny they gave me some momentary satisfaction. Nonetheless, my main intent was expository and I had her best interests at heart."

Edna sighs for the third time and collapses on the rather uncomfortable embroidered ottoman. She carefully positions herself so she cannot see her mother. Merely being in the same room with her has chemically transformed the ashes of her patience into something highly volatile. Even a glance at the object of her daughterly devotion might result in an unfortunate series of events which, not to put too fine a point on it, would culminate in direct confrontation necessitating medical intervention. In short, Edna was ready to kill her.

"Have you combed your hair this morning?" This was not helping. Her mother, as emotionally oblivious as usual, rises quickly out of her chair and plants herself directly in front of Edna for a better look. It is a wonder she has survived as long as she has.

"Let's forget the fact that ever since you stopped teaching regular classes at the university you dress like a gym rat. But now you've given up on basic hygiene. Remember, at your age, a slender figure and a fine pair of eyes no longer suffice. And stand up straight, for God's sake; gravity is already doing a fine job, you don't want to help the process." She accompanies this advice with little tinkling slaps here and there, as though Edna were a particularly uncomfortable pillow that needs fluffing up.

Edna dodges in desperation and passes her hand across her face. She is tired. Dead tired. She lifts her head, and the massive Rococo mirror reflects the image of a thin and lanky woman with her mother's high cheekbones and feline eyes, and her father's straight, elegant nose. The image is altogether consistent with the track suit she's wearing: hardly new and slightly frayed, but still presentable. In short, the same Edna as always. Her face looks pale and crumpled. So would yours if you'd been dragged out of bed at 6:15 a.m. to have a bizarre conversation involving Baked Alaska and empty bottles, during which, between sobs and a clatter of foreign consonants, an unspeakable horror has slowly dawned: Kalina wants to leave and she, Edna, has landed right back in it once again.

She plants her fingers in her short blonde hair and throws another musing glance at the mirror. No, she hasn't combed her hair this morning. But the angry call from Kalina had her jumping into the car and taking the curves on the highway as if she'd suddenly remembered she was supposed to be at a bank robbery. All things considered, her mother should be thankful she wasn't wearing pajamas.

Kalina appears in the doorway completely dressed, and holding a cast iron frying pan in one hand. "Here are the keys," she says, dropping them on the side table with a thud. "This frying pan is mine. It is necessary to make proper *palacinkas*, Romanian pancakes. I only mention this because I don't want *someone* to accuse me of stealing pots." She elaborates, throwing a scornful look at Zara.

As she wheels her suitcase towards the door, she looks back over her shoulder, "Signora Edna, it's been a pleasure knowing *you*. Best of luck."

"Kalina! Wait! Let's try to…" Edna jumps to her feet, but the door is already banging shut behind the slender brown nape, the frying pan, and the suitcase. The sound echoes dolefully with a finality that cuts off any possibility of reconciliation.

"*Porca miseria*, Mom," Edna snorts wearily as she plops down on the ottoman again. "Kalina is the sixth housekeeper you've chased away in five months. The sixth! Do you realize that?"

Zara Guglielmi sighs and spreads her tinkling arms wide, the blameless victim of circumstance. Edna knows that it's pointless to try and make her mother see reason.

The clock on the mantle whirs softly and tolls eight crystalline notes; Edna realizes that she's been up for less than two hours, and that she'd be less exhausted if she'd dragged a locomotive up the local mountainside for her morning exercise.

Shit. She takes a deep breath.

Shit. Shit. Shit.

"Well!" Zara crosses her periwinkled legs, looking around with the satisfied air of someone who has just enjoyed a bravura performance at the theater.

"Well my ass, Mom," Edna snarls, as she flails about in the quicksand of practicalities created by this disaster. Given the choice between finding a new housekeeper and miraculously inventing a time machine that would unwind the last two hours and restore Kalina, with her frying pan, her suitcase, and her sharp consonants, she'd go for the time machine. It would be easier.

But extraordinary events and miracles have never been a big part of Edna's life, leaving a lot of room, instead, for chaos and lunacy. And in these devastating situations, which seem to be replicating with the increasing frequency of a Fibonacci sequence, only one hope remains.

"Where are you going?" asks her mother with casual indifference.

"I'm going to hell," Edna growls, pulling out her keys.

"That's nice," Zara nods as if her daughter had just announced her intention of nipping out to the pub down the road and not plunging into the depths of the underworld.

And there it is, sighs Edna to herself. Her mother is the mental equivalent of those Christmas lights that flash on and off, alternating between glittering light and total darkness. Light and darkness, that she herself has absolutely no intention of managing.

And so, she opens the door, steps quickly up two flights of stairs, and rings the doorbell of The Only Salvation.

Chapter Three

Silence.

Edna presses the doorbell, harder and harder. She is determined to gain access to the apartment if she has to crawl through the keyhole.

Because now she needs the only person in the world capable of taming Zara. There is only one man impervious to her mutant annoyance field, a superhuman ability that turns anyone who enters her dazzling, tyrannical orbit into a screaming, gibbering ball of rage. The problem is that recruiting him becomes more and more difficult each time.

She rings again.

There is a light but unmistakable creak.

Edna puts her ear against the door. Silence.

But this time it is the dense and palpable silence of a six-foot-one, two-hundred-and-forty-pound man, wrapped in a shiny Japanese kimono and holding his breath.

"I know you're in there." Edna raps the wood with her open palm, "I wouldn't be here if I had any choice so you might as well open up. I'm not going anywhere until you do." Silence.

"I'll give you anything you want, I swear, just help me out."

Silence.

A loud harrumph, rather like the sound an annoyed whale might make, echoes off the marble stairs. There is a soft clack and the door finally opens.

"The Negri, the engraving by Pietro Negri," says The Only Salvation, blocking the entire width of the door with his massive figure.

"The Negri?!" Edna plants her hands on her hips. "You are demanding a 1668 engraving from the tenebroso school just for spending some time with an old woman? I would call that extortion. Don't you think you're exaggerating?"

"To compensate me for having to spend days or, God forbid, weeks with your mother I ought to be asking for a Caravaggio and even that wouldn't be enough. As you know better than anybody. So I'm being more than generous. It was that damned loose plank that gave me away, wasn't it? I've got to get that fixed. You might as well come in, you look like someone in urgent need of coffee." He examines her from head to toe, stroking his short chin-strap beard pensively. "Well, looking at you better, I'd pass directly to the active principle of the infamous Marian wine of Pius XII, but let's proceed step by step," he tightens the belt of his dressing gown and leads the way.

Edna follows his huge back wrapped in shiny golden silk, and if it weren't for the fact that this morning she's not in the mood for jokes and even less humor, she would compare her friend Ottavio Battiston, the highly esteemed musicologist and music critic (as well as her potential Only Salvation) to a giant Ferrero Rocher. She giggles without much conviction, because the mud slide that fell on her this morning has perhaps subsided a little, but it's still up to her knees, ready to raise to her throat and suffocate her.

"Are you amused or is that the grin of someone about to have a massive stroke?" he glances at her from the glass door of a display cabinet.

"And what, pray tell me, am I to find so amusing, struggling in this NIGHTMARE since a quarter past six this morning? What about you? Did you pile more crap in here since my last visit or am I wrong?" she asks, carefully wading through the profusion of statues, paintings, ancient musical instruments and extravagant objects, which give the long, gloomy corridor the bizarre aspect of a Diagon Alley shop.

"Let me think," he looks around, pirouetting his wardrobe-size body gracefully through the narrow passageways, "perhaps the little fortepiano you see over there, a real gem. The tuner is coming the day after tomorrow to put it in shape, but it's already wonderful. Now sit there and I'll tell Flora to make you a coffee, and in the meantime you can tell me what is going on."

Once the coffee arrives, Edna breathes in its smooth aroma and takes a long sip of the black and hot beverage, prepared just the way she likes. "What can I say? Kalina took her frying pan, her trolley, and her consonants, and left."

"I figured, otherwise you wouldn't be here. Tell me what I don't know." Ottavio peeks at her from over his pipe, stretching his legs on the carpet.

"She called her an illiterate and a nincompoop. And then she hit her with a bottle. Over a semantic matter having to do with desserts and smoked salmon, it seems," she takes another sip and then lowers her eyes. "With those lizard-colored slippers and all that smoke around you, you really look a lot like the caterpillar in *Alice in Wonderland*, are you aware of that?"

"Ha ha" he laughs coughing, rather amused. "I wish I could have been there, although all my sympathy goes to poor Kalina. And yet," he leans forward blowing the smoke in two perfect circles, "for someone who has come here to beg for help, calling your potential savior an insect doesn't seem like a very wise move to me. Are you aware of that?"

Edna raises an eyebrow as if she might even agree with him, but certain mental associations are sometimes so powerful that they can't be censored by one's brain, let alone by one's common sense.

"What else are you not telling me? Because what I have in front of me is an Edna Silvera who is still looking pretty good, I admit, but is scrambled like an omelette: Is there something else?" Ottavio presses on, pushing the bowl full of Kipferl cookies in front of her nose that he has sent to him directly from Vienna.

"The fact that my mother scares away housekeepers more effectively than a horde of Huns doesn't seem enough to you?" she mutters, munching on one of those cookies, each loaded with what seemed a half-pound of butter.

"Perhaps. How's it going at the university?"

Edna jerks her head up and stares at him with narrow eyes.

"Did she say something to you?" she spits drily.

"Who, Zara?" he calmly puffs out two circles of smoke, "No. I just took a guess, and judging by your face I'd say I guessed right. So?"

"So nothing. It has been a year since I left teaching, slamming the door behind me, and they still force me to hold seminars and bullshit like that, and only because that moron Schiaffino claims that 'I draw an audience.'" she air quotes. "Can you believe it? Artistic techniques and cultural anthropology are measured based on an audience, like a TikTok video!"

"Everything is now subject to the laws of the market, my dear, art above all. You should know that. And what's wrong with that? Your lectures are a wonder, and depriving your students of something capable of stimulating their spongy brains, I personally consider it a crime against humanity. This is why the vice-provost Schiaffino won't let you go." Then he watches her slyly from over his pipe. "Well, besides the *other* reason, of course."

"What *other* reason, pray tell?"

"Oh, blessed woman!" exclaims Ottavio, rolling his eyes, as if this were clear even to a Lapland caribou, "Vice-provost Edoardo Schiaffino, as charming as a mature Pierce Brosnan, has had a thing for you for years!"

"Schiaffino?" Edna bursts out laughing, "If it weren't for the legal consequences, he would gladly set me on fire with napalm! He had his intense and extremely fleeting opportunity thirty years ago, he played his cards badly and the whole affair ended then and there both for him and for me. So no, believe me, he keeps me chained there for some obscure reason, perhaps for the simple pleasure of annoying me. Not to mention that Schiaffino now has a wife who is twenty years younger than him, and consequently also twenty years younger than me. Honestly, Ottavio. Would an almost sixty-year-old man lose his head for a woman his same age, who on top of that is also a supreme pain in the ass? And for the second time? Come on, do you hear yourself when you speak?" she concludes, dropping another half pound of butter into her mouth.

"Trust me. He has a crush. A crush as large as the Taj Mahal. And how is it that you eat like a Tyrannosaurus and still keep your figure?" Ottavio sighs with mild envy. "I've been on a diet since April and I've gained twenty pounds."

"Lost, you mean."

"Gained, my dear, gained!" Ottavio spreads his arms, to show evidence of the crime. "Months of a diet worthy of a Soviet orphanage in wartime and not only do I not lose a pound, but I gained twenty!"

"Mmh," she ponders skeptically, "perhaps a few mistakes here and there or a little snack too many in between meals, like these cookies with a ton of calories per bite…"

"Are you joking? By now I feed only on their aroma, because Flora is watching me like a KGB agent." He approaches and whispers into her ear, "She checks everything, I am convinced that she measures the slices of bread with a caliper and inventories the contents of pantry, fridge and freezer hourly. The other day she frisked me because she was missing a plum, which, as it happened, had just rolled behind the sideboard. As you can see, under Commandant Flora, I'm basically living in a prison camp. And yet…" he shakes his head passing his hands over his belly, "It might be a case of oneiric metabolism."

Edna stops chewing and stares at him blankly.

"I mean to say that I dream, darling. I dream of salmon en papillote, hares in fricassée, noodles with venison ragout, timbales, zuccotto and Saint Honoré, I dream of their smell, their flavor, their velvety texture on my tongue and palate. And in the dream I eat them. All of them. And every night. The next morning I weigh myself and bam, I've gained weight as if I really did eat them. A mental disorder, and it happens right there, in the dream universe and out of the reach of my housekeeper."

"A compelling theory," admits Edna, "but what strikes me even more right now is Flora's unwavering devotion. You wouldn't let me borrow her for a while, or at least until my mother…"

"Stop it right there!" Ottavio raises his big hands in front of him. "I won't give up Flora, not even in exchange for the entire contents of the Musée d'Orsay, so resign yourself to your fate. But take heart, we'll find a solution for Zara. In the meantime, for now, I am that solution, in exchange for the engraving by Negri, as agreed," he smiles seraphically, over the stem of his pipe, "so you have time to get organized. But this time I want to be present at the selection of your mother's new housekeeper, first of all because two extra eyes don't hurt, and also because I am convinced of the truthfulness of the saying 'leave haste to the hares', and let me tell you, my dear, that in these matters you are always in a hellish hurry, and in fact…"

"Look, someone that suits my mother, or tough enough to survive her, hasn't been born yet, so haste has nothing to do with it."

"Allow me to disagree, my dear. Look at yours truly, for example. Your mother just adores me. The right person just has to know how to handle her. This excludes *in primis* you and all the people who oppose the Zara Guglielmi universe."

"You've just excluded the entire human race except, apparently, you".

"Come on, my dear, I sense a hint of negativity in you. Wallowing in negativity only attracts more negativity. So, be positive! Because life smiles at you if you take it with a smile."

"Now I'm sorry I ate all those cookies. I think I'm going to be sick. Just so you know, it's quite hard to give such profound wisdom all the respect it deserves when it comes from someone who looks like a two-hundred-and-forty-pound Ferrero Rocher. Seriously, where did you get that dressing gown?"

"More like two-hundred-and-sixty-five, alas," sighs Ottavio melodramatically, touching his golden paunch. "And sure, you just keep on throwing rude remarks at your Only Salvation, and then let's see who has the last laugh. When you bang your head on my door, clutching your useless 1668 tenebroso school etching, I'll be a thousand miles away from here, relaxing in a Turkish bath in Marrakech."

"What is this, blackmail?"

"No, I'm teaching you the basic concept of not biting the hand that feeds your mother, my dear. See that you also apply it with regard to the Art History Department and that saint of a vice-provost Schiaffino. Remember, on your next birthday you'll turn fifty-seven and perhaps it's time you learned something useful. Now you go home and tidy yourself up. I'll take care of Zara."

"Are you going to visit her dressed like this?" Edna raises an eyebrow, taking in the golden dressing gown and the curly slippers.

"No, my dear, let me remind you that you showed up at my house before dawn. So as soon as you lift your early-rising ass off that sofa and leave, I'll tidy myself up, too," he says, looking at her with patient condescension. "Although I'm sure that, unlike you, your mother would have the artistic sensibility to find me enchanting just as I am. Now go, shoo, you're in my way. I'll call you later."

Well, perhaps Ottavio is right, sighs Edna carrying her early-rising, and yet exhausted, ass down the stairs. She is in fact a bit rigid and not very accommodating. Not to mention, almost completely tactless, but only in relation to the list of ever-increasing annoyances that plague her life.

She climbs into her car, unzips her jacket and puts her hands on the steering wheel.

Ok, she nods, glancing at her reflection in the rear-view mirror which resembles nothing so much as a tragic mask in Greek drama. What is it that Ottavio said? Ah, yes, negativity invites negativity. Considering that it's not even nine in the morning on an ordinary Tuesday in mid-September, she certainly has enough trouble already without having to attract other disasters. So she breaths in and twists her lips, in a lame attempt at a smile, an apotropaic effort to exorcise new troubles and annoyances.

The cell phone peremptorily vibrates from the seat next to her. She rolls her eyes.

Oh no. It's him.

Vice-provost Schiaffino.

She inserts the first gear and merges into the lazy morning traffic without the slightest sense of guilt.

Chapter Four

"Seven messages. Seven," he sighs, as a red hen strolls across the lawn with mild indifference and positions itself beneath the large stone table to peck at his shoelaces.

"Seven messages, along with an unspecified number of phone calls," he says, looking at her earnestly, pressing his foot against his calf to conceal the laces. "Tell me what to do, Edna. Tell me."

"I had some trouble with my mother. She dragged me out of bed at an ungodly hour," she grumbles, yanking her straw hat off her head and slamming it onto the table. "And I'll spare you the rest. Look, Edoardo, I don't know why you're so insistent on keeping me at the department, but as you can see, I'm completely unreliable and too busy with other things."

"Other things like… this?" Vice-provost Schiaffino leans under the table, pointing at the red hen. Unfazed by his feeble attempt to hide his shoelaces, the hen has now started pecking at his other shoe with impudent persistence.

"Yes, this too," Edna replies dryly. "Along with the research work I started twenty years ago and never had the time to finish, for instance."

"Still researching that Bosch stuff?"

"Yes, *still researching that Bosch stuff,*" she mimics him, "and spare me that look of shock as if you've stumbled upon a *Playboy* centerfold under the priest's mattress, because with just a whistle towards the henhouse, I can unleash the other six birds onto your precious English shoes."

"Listen, Edna," he exhales, placing his palms on the table, "I reluctantly indulged your unreasonable decision to give up both professorships, but I think—"

"Ah! Unreasonable decision, that's a good one," Edna interrupts sourly, crossing her arms.

"Unreasonable, indeed. If you believe that over a trivial difference of opinion, one should throw away—"

"For Pete's sake, he manipulated the assignment of doctoral degrees!" she cuts him off. "While referring to me, in turn, as a paranoid witch, someone who thinks with her uterus, and a madwoman driven by menopausal hormones. He even suggested I take up knitting, a pursuit he considers fitting for women, especially after the age of forty. Pardon me, but I wouldn't call it a 'trivial difference of opinion.'"

"And you called him a chauvinist jerk," Schiaffino sighs.

"De Cesaris *is* a chauvinist jerk, and you know it."

"Now, let's not exaggerate. I admit that De Cesaris might not be what one would call a supporter of—"

"He eliminated three highly qualified candidates to replace them with three imbeciles with the imagination of a redwood tree trunk and the IQ of a poisonous mushroom, solely because they were women!" Edna shouts, her face just an inch away from his nose. Reluctantly, she has to admit that Ottavio might not have been entirely wrong. The years seemed to have eroded his pretty-boy looks and left him with a rugged charm and a certain resemblance to a mature Pierce Brosnan. Nevertheless, she still has the urge to eradicate that smug, half-amused, half-satisfied smile with a weed whacker.

"'Poisonous mushroom?' I have to write that one down," he chuckles. "And while I acknowledge that De Cesaris may have displayed unpleasant and possibly sexist behavior, it doesn't justify covering his car (which was barely three months old) with manure, both inside and out… It was a bit much, don't you think?"

"I wouldn't know anything about it," Edna stares at him unwaveringly.

"The manure was of avian origin," he sighs, nudging away the hen that is pecking at his shoelaces with a gentle movement of his foot.

"What's that supposed to mean? As if I were the only person in the world who raises chickens! It could have been anyone. I don't see why I should be implicated," she shrugs, leaving the impression that she was indeed involved and quite proud of it.

"Yes, of course," he says again, that same half-amused, half-satisfied smile still on his face. "In the end, he had to return the car because the stench couldn't be removed from the leather seats. It wasn't all that easy to remove it from him, either. Sharing an elevator with him was like being in a chicken coop. And besides, by leaving the department, you made it seem like De Cesaris had won."

"Thanks to you and your damned refusal to leave me alone, I'm still stuck with the honorary professor and researcher roles, if I'm not mistaken. It's a shame you're always there, asking me to do things and never giving me the time to pursue my research. And what the hell do I have to do with Dante, for heaven's sake? There are plenty of literary experts who would be thrilled to share their knowledge."

"Ha! 'Refusal to leave you alone!' 'Always there!' You never answer your phone and rarely show up, unless we send someone to physically drag you into the office. But joking aside, Edna, this Siestri matter is truly important."

She leans back in her chair and stares at him, not uttering a word.

"It will be a quick affair, you'll see," Schiaffino continues, trying to shoo away a second hen with the tip of his shoe. "It will be over in just half a day. It's about Dante's journey through Liguria on his way to Milan..."

She looks at him as if she already knows all of this and can't comprehend why he bombarded her with countless messages and phone calls within the span of an hour. And above all, she wonders why on earth he is sitting at the stone table in her garden, invading her space, and skillfully avoiding birds, insects, and Cagliostro, her cat, who is, at this very moment, casually marking his territory on Schiaffino's trousers.

"Your cat, unlike you, is inexplicably friendly," Schiaffino remarks, completely misunderstanding Cagliostro's intentions as he reaches out to pet the cat's arched black back. But Cagliostro skillfully avoids his hand, raising his tail for one final mephitic spray.

"Yes, yes, very friendly," Edna smiles grimly, imagining with satisfaction the moment when Schiaffino will finally catch a whiff of that affectionate aroma while driving along the sharp bends of the state highway.

"Getting back to us," he shoots her a serious look, "in the village of Siestri mentioned in the nineteenth Canto of the *Purgatory*, there will be celebrations to commemorate the seven hundred years since Dante's death. Grand celebrations. Very important celebrations. With national TV coverage, authorities, representatives of the Ministry of Culture, specialized journalists, and the press... In short, the department wants someone to represent us. *Andwethoughtitshouldbeyou*," he finishes in one breath.

Edna narrows her eyes, turning them into sharp, lethal blades of green. "Oh really?" she nods, surprisingly calm. "Then listen carefully because I won't repeat it: no. NO. And with that, the discussion is closed. We can say goodbye. I wish I could say it was a pleasure to see you, but truth be told, I've learned to associate your presence with an enormous headache. I prefer to hear and see you as little as possible. So, goodbye, and please convey my regards to your young wife."

"She's in Bali," he replies.

"Excuse me?"

"My wife. She's been in Bali for the past three weeks."

Edna shrugs. First Lady Schiaffino could be taking a foot bath in Samarkand for all she cares. A ghost of annoyance for how things could have turned out differently nearly thirty years ago flickers through her mind. But she promptly exorcises it.

"Returning to the matter of you in Siestri, Edna…"

"Did you just suffer one of this ministrokes I've been reading about? There is no 'me.' And even less of a 'me in Siestri.' Send someone else, De Cesaris, for example. I can easily envision him envisioning himself there." She rises from her seat, trying to remember where she had put the shovel in case she needs it to chase him off.

"They enlisted two of your former students to organize the event!" he exclaims, bringing out his heavy artillery as a last resort.

Edna freezes, struck by his words.

"*Those* students," he elaborates with deadly precision, scoring a direct hit.

Edna exhales and slides back into her seat, all thoughts of the shovel forgotten.

"Well," Schiaffino smiles, satisfied. "Now that I have your undivided attention, let's discuss the details of your visit to Siestri next week."

Chapter Five

Bad coffee. A beverage that can deceive your taste buds with its initial sip, only to later slide down your esophagus and into your stomach like an espresso cup full of acid.

Nando Folli, feeling the corrosive effects of the coffee he has just drunk, hastily loosens his trouser belt and grimaces as his heartburn rises burning his throat. Leaning over the passenger side of his van, he rummages through pencil stubs, a measuring tape, rags stained with solvent and crumpled papers, desperately looking for the Maalox. He always keeps it within reach, whether on his nightstand, his workshop table, or in his "new" second-hand van, purchased at a bargain due to its eye-watering yellow color that was visible even in the dark and possibly from space.

Distracted by the flashing blue light – an ambulance, perhaps? – among the helm oaks near Marlena's henhouse, Nando glances through the windshield. Meanwhile, he continues rummaging until his fingertips recognize the bottle he so desperately seeks. With a disturbing yet liberating creaking sound, he stretches his vertebrae, reaching out over the gear lever to finally claw the bottle toward him with two fingers.

"I knew I shouldn't have accepted that damned coffee," he sighs, chewing the Maalox tablet. "How could I have imagined that old Mrs. Scopelli, who looks like someone who can barely make canned soup, would have any clue about making a proper espresso?"

Even at the time, Nando had lamented the absence of a comforting biscuit or slice of cake to go along with the hell-brew now eating its way through his esophagus. But Mrs. Scopelli seemed the type to skimp on ice cubes. Perhaps, however, his suffering was not in vain because he had stumbled upon something intriguing amidst the clutter of her cellar.

Jumping out of the van, Nando opens the large poisonous-yellow hatch. Its hideousness works to his advantage, as the van could be spotted easily from anywhere and miles away – a lemon-colored flash standing out like a daffodil amidst the monotonous flow of traffic. Just last week, in the vast parking lot of Famagosta in Milan, he had no trouble identifying it after another coffee incident with one Carlo Kowalski had marked yet another successful deal. A deal that was quite possibly the most profitable one in the past decade, if his instinct proved correct.

Nando Folli is a divvy. He possesses an exceptional nose, capable of sniffing out potentially valuable items among a sea of worthless junk. Similarly, he can assess the toxicity of a cup of coffee based on the person offering it. Kowalski, of Polish descent but a Lombard by adoption, was clearly someone who had never tasted a decent cup of coffee in his entire life.

Nando lifts the shutters of his workshop and continues unloading the van. Despite the constant annoyance of his sliding trousers, he chooses to prioritize relief for his burning stomach over maintaining whatever minimal sex appeal he had left.

He turns on the lights and begins to arrange the merchandise, moving items that need "restoration" in the back while placing things that are ready for sale in the public area in the front. He is looking forward to the influx of potential customers who will flood the valley in less than a week, to commemorate the seven-hundred-year anniversary of Dante's departure for a (hopefully) better life. A chuckle escapes Nando as he reflects on Dante and imagines the poet shuffling off the mortal coil and finding himself facing a blank white screen with "THE END" written on it, instead of the expected circles, crowds, and purgatories. For someone who built a literary career dealing with lost souls, such an experience would have been the ultimate insult. A fitting retaliation (or as the illustrious poet himself would have called it, *contrappasso*) for the agonies that Dante inflicted on high school students around the world. Pushing aside a big chest of drawers in order to make more room, Nando reflects that Dante would also make an undrinkable coffee.

The upcoming festival to commemorate Dante's death provides an opportunity for Nando to dust off and display anything related – no matter how tenuously – to the Divine Poet. These events attract tourists who will stumble upon his shop. Nando loves tourists. Even if they later realize they have just bought a piece of junk, they won't make a special trip back to the store and ask for a refund. And it is certainly going to be a piece of junk, because Nando is not going to sell his good stuff for a few hundred euros so that some weekend visitor can have a souvenir.

He adjusts his trousers once again and picks up a wooden panel, unwrapping it to reveal a painting depicting two anonymous figures, possibly monks, dressed in brown robes and executed by a mediocre painter. Although the figures themselves aren't remarkable, Nando's interest is piqued by the background landscape, the attempt at perspective, and the angular rocks in the painting. He runs his hand over the thin layer of paint and turns the panel over, examining the undoubtedly very old wood. He examines it sideways, testing it with his fingernail. But the age of the wood doesn't mean much. When you want to create old documents, you only need to find a batch of paper from the right period and you can make an excellent forgery. While the age of the wood alone doesn't hold much significance, something intangible, a tingling sensation at the base of his neck, caught Nando's attention when he discovered the piece in the dusty attic of the Polish-Lombard, Kowalski. So Nando purchased it along with half-a-dozen worthless paintings. These "decoy purchases" prevent a seller from suspecting the presence of something truly valuable and allow Nando to appear as a well-intentioned individual doing the seller a favor by taking them off his hands. This wasn't Nando's first rodeo.

Nando carefully rewraps the wood panel and hides it among the other pieces, visible enough to be almost invisible, and giving himself time to decide what to do with it. His cell phone lights up and vibrates in his pocket. He examines it and finds it is yet another call from his girlfriend, Franka. Nando has always avoided commitment and the complications of relationships but, nonetheless, finds himself entangled with Franka, the human equivalent of superglue. While she is extremely beautiful, he finds her to be too free-spirited, uninhibited, and indifferent to her husband. Nando could almost feel sorry for him except that the poor man was a consummate ass to marry someone like Franka. How could he not have known what he was getting into?

Franka's clinginess frustrates Nando. She constantly seeks his presence, inquiring about his whereabouts and lamenting their brief separations. Recently, she even gave him an anniversary gift, to which Nando responded with confusion. "Anniversary?!" he had asked, rolling his eyes. "Anniversary of *what*?" What a scene! During the ensuing argument, he discovered that it had been three months since they had first slept together.

The thought of Franka invokes disquiet in Nando, as he compares her to the obsessive character in the movie *Fatal Attraction*. His cell phone goes silent, but the respite is short-lived as the phone calls are replaced by a barrage of text messages. Franka seems unusually trigger-happy tonight. Nando shudders, recalling the movie and wondering if Franka's trigger-happiness extends beyond text messages. He silences his phone and contemplates ghosting her, a tactic he often employs when he grows tired of his current companion. Nando believes that letting things fade away naturally yields the desired outcome with less energy wasted and fewer problems.

Satisfied with the state of his shop, Nando turns off the lights, lowers the shutters, and pulls up his trousers yet again. He returns to his van and glances through the windshield, noticing that the blue light by Marlena's henhouse has vanished. While mildly curious about what happened, the thought quickly dissipates as he starts the van, reverses, and drives away, forgetting the incident after a couple of turns.

The road stretches ahead under the hazy mid-September sun, with only the shadow of a large kite flying free and circling over the yellow van. As he contemplates whether to take another Maalox to soothe the acidity caused by Franka's relentless messages, he loosens his belt another notch.

Chapter Six

What a drag!

Edna, feeling frustrated and fatigued, throws her straw hat onto the coat rack and collapses into an armchair, rebelliously extending her legs onto the rosewood coffee table. She reflects that if Ottavio were present, he would be furious about the potential harm to the delicate inlays. However, enjoying the freedom of living alone, she disregards such concerns. Lifting both legs onto the table, Edna revels in the ability to do as she pleases without answering to anyone.

Nevertheless, she laments that, one way or another, there always seems to be someone invading her space and managing her time. And that someone is often Schiaffino. She closes her eyes, trying to ward off the encroaching migraine. If she had the strength, she would get up and pour a glass of Vermentino to alleviate her discomfort.

She is far from happy about the upcoming week. She can hardly believe that Schiaffino had the audacity to visit her house and coerce her into yet another of those tedious performances as a university representative. This time, it's to commemorate the seven-hundredth anniversary of Dante's death in the middle of nowhere, aka Siestri. She will have to endure a two-hour drive each way on winding roads only to be faced with even more annoying tasks once she finally arrives. In short, it will be a day from hell which, she was forced to admit, was oddly fitting.

Despite her reservations, she had accepted the request. She runs her fingers through her hair and scoffs at her own foolishness. "How could I be such an idiot?" But she knows that the primary reason she agreed was her concern for her students, who will be lambs to the academic slaughter, especially if she is replaced by De Cesaris.

Secondly, Schiaffino always manages to convince her, and Edna cannot resist his influence. She puts her feet back on the floor and stands up, contemplating whether she should reconsider the idea of having some Vermentino. Well, now that she is up… She opens the fridge, retrieves the bottle, and while pouring herself a glass, acknowledges that her inability to refuse Schiaffino is not due to his charm or rhetorical skill. It's not due to anything, really. It's simply that she cannot say no to him, just as she couldn't thirty years ago.

Taking a generous sip, the flavors of grape, cedar, and sun dance on her nose and palate, enveloping her in a gentle enchantment. However, the wine also stirs up memories, bringing forth other buried emotions. Sensations of lapping waves, lowered sails, sunsets, and salty skin flood her thoughts. Perhaps the Vermentino was not such a good idea after all. She sighs and places her glass on the slate shelf, acknowledging the futility of escaping her past.

Cagliostro, momentarily distracted from licking his paw, glares at Edna with annoyance before stretching out, turning his back to her, and settling back into his chair. He emanates an air of someone hoping not to be bothered by any further disturbances. Edna envies him and contemplates how simple it would be if she could adopt the smooth egotism of a feline. Or pee on Schiaffino's leg. Perhaps that would finally get rid of him.

Squinting her eyes, Edna realizes that her migraine shows no signs of relenting and continues to dig its claws into her frontal lobe. It could be the result of the wine and the resurfacing memories, or perhaps it's her anger. The mere thought of De Cesaris makes her choke. She privately admits that instead of handling the situation with tact and diplomacy to protect her students' interests, she indulged herself by telling that macho misogynist exactly what she thought of him. That had a certain satisfaction but it also had consequences – and not just for her.

Alternatively, her migraine might be caused by her self-loathing for being unable to say no to Schiaffino. Now she's obligated to endure yet another official event in a small town, accompanied by mayors, councilors, and the entire line-up of officers, all dressed to impress the television cameras. Sarcastically congratulating herself, she sighs, grabs an apple from the fruit bowl on the kitchen table and takes a bite.

Reflecting on her life, Edna admits that it has always been characterized by an unwavering love for her studies and an innate intolerance for the bureaucratic and social formalities associated with teaching. She describes herself as an angel in the auditorium and a demon in the dean's office. Patience has never been her strong suit, and that's precisely why she chose a career as an art restorer – to find solace in the serene and satisfied solitude of underground niches or perched atop scaffolding.

All she wants is to remain here, surrendering herself to the comfort of her armchair, in this rural hermitage within the warm simplicity of her home – a spacious stone structure that exudes a cheerfully shabby charm. She cherishes her chickens, the veranda overlooking the silvery olive trees, and the sea close enough to see and smell but far enough to keep away the tourists. She surveys the room, taking in her furniture, salvaged from old abandoned farmhouses or acquired from trustworthy junk dealers. Her gaze then settles on the enormous bookcase designed by Pepe Tanzi, brimming with books – the only piece from her old bedroom that has faithfully accompanied her through every move.

Edna caresses the white walls with her eyes, critically observing the arrangement of paintings and antique prints she had discovered in obscure galleries or on Portobello Road. Her gaze eventually lands on a messy heap of packages and folders stacked on an industrial counter, which would serve as a desk if it were visible. Despite its initial minimalist Nordic style, her decor has evolved into a pleasant and lively mess – a reflection of her moods, passions, and ever-changing self. She prefers to keep a room empty until she finds the perfect piece to fill it, rather than settling for anything to occupy the space. This philosophy extends to her social relationships as well, allowing her to live peacefully in her secluded sanctuary, surrounded by seven birds and an independent cat, where she can choose who to meet and when.

However, in a period of less than twenty-four hours, she has found herself entangled in a double predicament. First, the disappearance of her mother's housekeeper, and then the ambush by Schiaffino! Thankfully, the ringing phone interrupts her pity party. Without opening her eyes, she reaches out and fumbles for the receiver.

"Hello." she says, employing the vocal equivalent of icy barbed wire.

"Goodness. Put that thing down or at least point it somewhere else. Been having a bad day? Are you alone?"

Just when she thought things couldn't get worse. Edna opens her eyes. "Please, Ottavio, who do you imagine might be here? Of course, I'm alone."

"I'm just calling to let you know that I'm here with Zara, and we're cooking a delicious shrimp and vodka risotto," Ottavio replies.

"Should I remind you that my mother no longer has the stomach of a twenty-year-old, and you, if I'm not mistaken, are on a diet?" Edna retorts.

"Your mother is in better shape than both of us combined, and I trust in the principle of reverse metabolism – I eat and therefore lose weight. I'll tell you all about it later. Now cheer up and remember to be positive! Anyway, it's mostly vodka." Ottavio concludes before hanging up.

Edna sighs as she gets up to prepare something for herself. Despite her reservations about seeing Zara again so soon, she admits that a shrimp and vodka risotto doesn't sound bad at all. Especially the vodka. Ottavio was right again.

Chapter Seven

"I was hoping you'd reconsider, Edna, thank you!" Schiaffino sighs in relief. "This event in Siestri is really important for the department. I just spoke on the phone with the guy that De Cesaris has decided to put in charge of it…"

"And you'd like to douse him in gasoline and offer to light his cigarette," Edna concludes for him, holding the phone against her shoulder while she throws the last forkfuls of cold pasta into the trash bin and drops her dish in the sink. "I know exactly how you feel."

Of course, it was all quite predictable: Every big event is like feeding time at the zoo for the sort of idiot that likes to see themselves in the spotlight. In this case, the chief idiot is Pierpaolo Santi Niboni, who, apart from having a ridiculous name, is the head of the national association called Amici di Dante. She has never met him in her life, and had hoped to continue her streak. But based on the unreasonable demands just described by Schiaffino, he fits perfectly into the category.

"Thanks again, Edna. I'll find some way to make this up to you, you'll see…" continues the vice-provost, but she's no longer listening. She has just dropped the phone into the wood basket and abandoned herself in the wicker chair on the veranda, stretching her legs out with a sigh. She is definitely not looking forward to driving on a winding road for sixty miles (each way) and having to deal with an academic idiot.

An apocalyptic roar pierces the air of the quiet afternoon, followed by a stampede of feathers and felines. The residents of her chicken coop, which just seconds before were quietly scratching around, are now furiously cackling on the lawn.

"WHAT THE HELL…" Edna shouts. Based on the noise, she can only assume a fighter jet is using the road that runs alongside her property as a landing strip. Considering that the road leads only to her house and then stops just after a curve, in front of the former villa of the Dodero family, now uninhabited for at least two years, whatever it is that is making all this noise shouldn't be there at all. The chickens were now piling up around her shins in search of protection, but another rumble, this one much closer than the first, sends them shooting off as if a grenade had burst in their midst. Two of them end up in the middle of the road – not the best move, perhaps, but they are chickens, so what do you expect? And indeed, they end up exactly in front of what turns out to be an enormous motorcycle which, swerving to the right and barely missing a hen, ends up wedged against the chicken coop. *Her* chicken coop.

"Hell and damnation," Edna shouts furiously, grabbing the first thing she finds lying about, in this case, an old cast-iron pan. "Hey, you! What's wrong with you?!" she thunders, flying across the yard waving her pan.

The centaur, all sheathed in black leather, barely condescends to turn his head in her direction. With perfect aplomb, he gets off his bike, gracefully disentangles it from the chicken coop, lifts it up on the stand, kneels, removes the feathers stuck between the wheel spokes with his gloved hand, then gets up and stands there for a moment, staring at her. Edna sees herself reflected on the shiny visor of his helmet. In her mind, she was an avenging valkyrie but, in reality, she is just a dishevelled woman waving a pan who looks more like the sort of person you see shouting on street corners. In short, not a pretty sight.

In all likelihood, the centaur agrees with her. He finally opens the chin strap and takes off his helmet. A wise move. It would have been easier to smash him into pieces with her pan if he had kept the helmet on. Because her anger begins to evaporate at the appearance of this young man with eyes like blue lakes and the profile of a Greek god, who is looking at her with an amused air and the sort of smile you can feel in your knees. Not *her* knees, of course. He is young enough to be her son, and she finds the current trend for toy boys and beardless boyfriends slightly repellent. Her temporary emotional displacement is due to purely aesthetic, or rather, artistic appreciation.

"I apologize for inconveniencing you, you seem to be in some difficulty," he says while settling his helmet on the motorcycle saddle and approaching in the hopes of disarming her.

"I can manage very well," she responds, suddenly lowering her arm without thinking of the consequences. But he ducks just in time, narrowly avoiding the falling pan. He retreats to a safe distance and observes her with an air of scepticism.

She returns his gaze, hand on hip, the pan pointed to the ground like a troll's club, and the loving expression of one of Tolkien's orcs.

"Are you mad about the chicken coop? I only damaged the side wall a little, nothing irreparable, and in any case, I managed to avoid your hens. That's the important thing, isn't it?"

"Let me get this straight," she leans forward, eyes narrowed. "You come up like a maniac along this dead-end street, noisier than a freight train, you almost slaughter two chickens, you break my chicken coop, and you have the face to come up with an indifferent 'nothing irreparable'? For your information this is a private road," she straightens up with an unconvincing smile, "so if I see you again, I'll shoot at your tires. All clear?"

"Then you'll have to stock up on a lot of ammo," he smiles back, "because from now on, I think we'll be seeing a lot of each other."

"Meaning?"

"Meaning that I live here now. I rented the house up the street," he gestures with his hand towards the curve behind the chicken coop.

"Dodero's old place? You're renting it? You? With that?" Edna roars, pointing with her chin at the two-wheeled monstrosity glistening in the sun and surrounded by her hens who are now curiously examining it.

"Well, no. I'm renting it with money," he replies with logical exactitude. "But yes, that is my bike." Her visitor now has the distinct air of someone who would gladly burst out laughing but is doing his level best to maintain the social niceties. In fact, he takes off his glove and introduces himself, "Nice to meet you, Leonardo. Leonardo Sacco."

Edna stares at his hand for a long moment, then raises her eyes to the sky, turns around sharply, and with a resolute step (or at least as resolute as allowed by uneven gneiss slabs and a cast-iron pan occasionally bouncing off of her right knee) she disappears into her house.

A dull, almost soft roar, like the purr of a two-ton cat, warns her that her new neighbor is taking himself and his damn motorbike to their new home.

Perfect.

Absolutely perfect.

Definitely, without a doubt, this is a day to forget.

And it's only a quarter past two in the afternoon.

Chapter Eight

The plot thickens.

Nando puts down the phone and scratches his chin, perplexed. Perhaps he had been too hasty. Normally, he moves with the stealth and caution of a hunting leopard, but this time he strolled through the savannah whistling, like a particularly naive gazelle. And that's never a good thing, he reflected, not for him, not for the gazelle.

But he had asked Filipponi for advice and the damage was done. On the other hand, it's also true that he needed to take action. Despite his natural ability and his considerable hands-on experience, he still lacked the technical know-how that comes from years of devoted study and that only an expert in the field possesses. Filipponi may not be the sharpest paintbrush in the box but he does know his paintings. Apart from his ample experience in restoration, he has a very nice side-business creating counterfeit works. Now that he thought about it, planting a seed of doubt in the mind of a dodgy operator like Filipponi might not have been the best idea. But he consoles himself that he hadn't revealed all that much and that there was nothing he could do about it now anyway.

Nando walks over to the window. The days are growing shorter and shorter. On one hand, the harsh sunlight always exposes flaws, and that's never ideal for his work. On the other, in recent years, the mere thought of venturing out into the damp darkness of the evening has made him yearn for the comfort of his home. He had to make a concerted effort to avoid going out to dinner with Franka. He had been looking forward to spending the evening in his armchair, channel surfing on TV, and eating whatever he could find in the fridge. But now, to his dismay, he has to go out after all. Not only that, but he has to take the car and drive up to Gattorna, where his shop-cum-warehouse is located, to retrieve the painting he stashed between the boards beside the chest of drawers. True, Gattorna is only a ten-minute drive away but then he needs to head down to Genoa to meet with Filipponi. Because you have to catch Filipponi when he's available or you don't. So Nando has to abandon his cozy nest and hit the road.

Reluctantly, he takes off his old sweatpants, which he always dons as soon as he crosses the threshold of his house, and sadly examines his increasingly-thin legs under his ever-rounding belly – a truly depressing combination only found in certain beetles and in people who eat too much and exercise too little, in his case, not at all – the exercising, not the eating. Definitely not the eating.

He lets out a sigh and pulls up his jeans, leaving them unbuttoned, knowing he would have to unbutton them in the car before even shifting into second gear. He grabs his keys and briefly hesitates over whether to take the van instead of the car, which probably has a fuller tank and won't require a pit stop for fuel. Then he slaps his forehead and chooses the car. What kind of hunting leopard drives around the savannah in a bright yellow van? Tonight was a night for stealth and blending into the shadows.

He unlocks the car door with a click and slides into the seat, contemplating whether to chew two preemptive Maalox tablets. Perhaps it's better to wait and see how the evening unfolds. Between the poisonous coffee he had at Scopelli's and Franka's incessant nagging, he has already exceeded the daily limit written on the bottle. As he rolls down the window, he realizes that his car still reeks of the anti-fog fluid he spilled in the trunk three days ago. His initial eagerness to embark on this trip is waning. To give purpose to his sacrifice, he hopes that Filipponi will confirm his intuition regarding the potential value of the painted panel. The stench of the anti-fog fluid is unbearable, he thinks with a grimace, and he can't imagine inhaling these fumes for the rest of the evening. Hoping to avoid climbing the stairs and going back into the house, he sighs and searches for the spare van keys he keeps in the car's glove compartment but he struggles to find them. In his haste, he accidentally drops something cylindrical, which rolls under the seat. Finally, he locates the keys, exits the car, climbs into the van, and wearily settles into the driver's seat. So much for his stealthy hunt.

Nando absentmindedly glances at the empty side street as he pulls out of his parking space and into the road. But the side street isn't empty. As he passes, a battered gray Renault Clio with a dented bumper, parked along the road, turns on its lights and pulls away from the curb, following the shiny yellow van at a discrete distance.

Chapter Nine

Flying is indeed useful, but knowing how to land is also crucial. He lets out a small sigh and walks towards the window. It's closed. He would have preferred to stay, if not perched on the tree, at least seated on the balcony. Unfortunately, it wasn't meant to be. He sighs again and tilts his head ever so slightly. The morning's disastrous landing has left him a little bruised, although he's still in one piece. However, the same cannot be said for Marlena's chicken coop. Clearly, something went wrong, he muses, raising his wings to inspect them, but he quickly lowers them. Partly because his wings are also sore, and partly because if Marlena were to catch sight of him, she would shout at him again with her booming voice. The thought of that voice sends a shiver down his spine. He takes another step towards the window, tilts his head a bit further, and peeks through. Yes. The dry grass is always there, he knows it. Even though the large fig tree leaves in front of the house conceal it, he can sense that all that yellow is still present, just as he can feel that all that yellow has something to do with his bruised wings, the broken branch, the flattened chicken coop, and everything else.

And it seems the matter isn't over yet, he notes with a hint of apprehension, as a yellow van has just appeared up the gray road. He remembers that van because it nearly ran over Berta. Now it has come to a halt. Right here, in front of his nose.

That's not good at all, he thinks, pressing his eye against the window to observe the scene: who enters, who exits, who passes by, who comes and goes. He doesn't miss a thing. Because yellow is bad. And he knows it.

Perhaps even the enormous kite circling above his head knows it too.

Chapter Ten

"A crimson sunset," Edna mumbles to herself, pouring a generous glass of Merlot before donning her glasses, "and hopefully, a tranquil and above all, productive evening." As the notes of Brahms' *Hungarian Dances* fill the room, she settles at the computer with a contented sigh and powers it on. For one reason or another, throughout the entire week, she hasn't been able to delve into her "Bosch stuff," as Schiaffino described it with undisguised disdain, not so much for the Flemish artist himself but for the entire amalgamation of superstition, magic, witchcraft, and alchemy that envelops the world of Hieronymus Bosch.

He was a truly unique *homo medievalis*, carrying with him the enigmatic darkness associated with those peculiar practices, just like many artists who preceded and succeeded him. It's precisely this aspect that purists like Schiaffino or De Cesaris abhor, much like the idea of a rap music concert at La Scala, and perhaps that, in turn, is precisely why she has immersed herself in this monumental research endeavor with such delight and curious amusement. She rifles through her notes, pausing at the recipe for an ointment, which, according to Cardano, the renowned sixteenth-century scientist after whom a Moon crater and an asteroid were named (if she recalls correctly), was required to partake in a witches' Sabbath. She takes a sip of wine and begins typing: "Four parts of darnel, henbane, red and black poppy, portulaca, lettuce. . ."

Lettuce? Edna raises an eyebrow and takes a closer look, suspecting some sort of typo. If there is any vegetable less evocative of demons and magic, she can't think what it is. Next she will be discovering that they were serving celery sticks and ranch dressing at these events. Maybe even medieval witches watched their figures!

She studies the document carefully. It is indeed the sad *Lactuca sativa*, the necessary ingredient, along with a portion of belladonna and hemlock. They all need to be finely chopped, and the quantity required is a "scruple," which is slightly less than two grams. Edna smiles with delight at the charm of these archaic units of measurement that, over time, have merged into the language and acquired surprising meanings. The resulting potion would induce a two-day "sleep," apparently the minimum duration required to fully participate in a Sabbath. This is also affirmed in another treatise by Renaissance philosopher Giambattista Della Porta. Naturally, if someone like De Cesaris could witness her now, holding a glass of Merlot in one hand and diligently compiling magical recipes with the other while engaged in art research on behalf of the very university where he himself works, he would surely have a stroke. But it's merely due to his lack of perspective.

Because although Hieronymus, a self-taught painter, led a quiet bourgeois life, he achieved a hallucinatory perfection in his work. He often painted imaginary worlds densely populated by monsters, demons, and peculiar hybrids born from the fusion of humans, plants, minerals, furniture, and tools. It was as if he had embarked on what we now refer to as "a trip." In fact, these kinds of journeys were quite popular even during the Middle Ages and the Renaissance. Potions, ointments, smoke, powders, and concoctions were used to induce both monstrous and satanic visions, as well as marvelous and heavenly ones. Visions so vivid that people would swear by them even in the face of persecution and torture, as evidenced in the transcripts of trials conducted by the Inquisition and other documents from that era.

Loud noises from outside briefly draw her attention away from the computer, and Cagliostro, with mild curiosity, leaps off the sofa and bounces towards the window.

"It's probably that new neighbor," Edna sighs as she resumes writing. "Seems he can't do anything without causing a commotion and… what the hell?" She pauses, grimly staring at the frozen screen. It remains unresponsive despite her best efforts which include punching the display and slapping the keyboard.

Outside, the banging continues. "Just what I need," Edna grumbles under her breath, storming through the door and across the garden's gneiss flagstones. "What the hell are you doing?" she hisses, confronting her new neighbor, who is busy meddling with her chicken coop.

"Ah, good evening! Did I disturb you? Were you perhaps watching TV?" he smiles, accidentally delivering a deadly insult and waving a hammer in greeting.

"I never watch TV," she replies curtly. "What are you doing?"

"I was so embarrassed by your first impression of me that I'm trying to create a better second impression."

"How?" she asks, intrigued despite herself.

"By fixing this," he explains, gesturing towards the repairs. "And I must say it's coming along quite nicely. What do you think?"

Edna leans over to inspect the chicken coop, initially without much enthusiasm, but she is forced to reconsider. Despite his pretty-boy appearance, he seems to know what he's doing. "Well… thank you," she concedes. It sounds grudging to anyone not trained in Edna-speak but from her, it's practically a heartfelt apology. "Are you a carpenter?"

"Hardly," he laughs. "No, I'm actually a computer engineer."

"So that means you know a thing or two about computers?" she gazes at him, suddenly very interested.

"You could say that."

"Excellent." she nods, satisfied. "Do you like Merlot?"

***

"These photographs are quite beautiful," he remarks calmly, savoring his glass of Merlot. "They remind me a lot of Doisneau and Cartier-Bresson. Are they yours?"

"Yes," Edna shrugs. "They're from a time when it was still possible to photograph people on the street without being accompanied by your lawyer. Can you imagine Doisneau tapping those two lovers on the shoulder and getting them to sign a release before capturing his famous *Baiser de l'Hotel De Ville*? That's why I changed genres. I checked: In Italy, you can get four to six months in jail for taking pictures without permission. So far, I've never been to jail, although I came close once. Nothing to do with photography, though."

"Too bad," he continues, observing the pictures. "You have a way of observing humanity that reveals a truly passionate curiosity."

"Perhaps." She shrugs again, wearing the expression of someone who is accustomed to having the things she cares about the most snatched away by circumstance and stupidity.

"So here's the computer." she says, getting down to business. "As you can see, it's frozen and there's no way to unfreeze it. I even tried turning it off and on again, which is pretty much the limit of my computer repair skills. It usually works – I wish I could do the same thing with people – but not this time. In fact, I couldn't even turn it off."

36

He glances at the scattered papers next to the keyboard and at the serious face of Hieronymus Bosch peering through the wrinkles of his rather unflattering self-portrait. Then he looks at the reproductions of paintings crowded with strange creatures, monsters, and demons, before finally taking in the recipe for the "ointment to participate in a Witches' Sabbath" dominating the frozen computer screen. He raises a single eyebrow but says nothing and begins fiddling with the keys and the space bar, as if sipping a glass of red wine with a wanna-be daughter of Satan were the most ordinary thing in the world.

"Done," he smiles, turning the screen towards her. "It's working now."

"Thanks! Very impressive." Amazed, she puts on her glasses. "Fantastic, it's working perfectly. Leonardo, if I'm not mistaken, right? *Nomen omen*!" She nods, extending her hand. "Edna, Edna Silvera."

"I know," he smiles again, shaking her hand.

"How is it that you know?"

"Well, let's just say I'm not only good at fixing computers," he winks at her.

"Well, apart from me having an unnatural interest in bat blood, shadows of the night, wolf roots, five-fingered grass, and so on, which, I must clarify, are only fanciful names referring to the natural powers of herbs in medieval times, what else do you happen to know about me? If you don't mind me asking."

"That you're a highly respected restorer and art historian, who has been teaching at both University College London and the School of Cultural Heritage in Genoa for the last twenty years. I've also learned that you take beautiful photographs. Apparently, you are also someone who knows how to party." He chuckles, nodding at the recipe for the ointment still displayed on the screen.

"If you want, I can get you an invitation," she raises an eyebrow, calmly closing the page.

"Delighted, but only if you allow me to accompany you."

She crosses her arms, removes her glasses, and gazes at him.

"Do you sweep all women off their feet like this?"

"What?"

"Handsome, cultured, polite, with a mischievous smile, good observer, attentive to details, saying what they want to hear… and they fall at your feet. I don't believe you're flirting with me, mind you. Your response was just an elegant repartee to my provocation, but I have figured you out and I appreciate the style."

"Touché," he spreads his arms with a slight bow. "Is it working?"

She suppresses a smile. "Well, Leonardo, I would invite you to stay for dinner, but today has been a particularly turbulent day, and my culinary inspirations are limited to defrosting something in the microwave, an experience I do not recommend because a core sampling of my freezer would date back to the last ice age."

"Well, if you don't mind the boxes still to be unpacked and the campsite atmosphere, I can offer you a *pasta carbonara* that I am quite proud of. And, in case you were wondering, no, I'm not trying to make you fall at my feet."

"Uhm… It is not my habit to accept invitations from…"

"From strangers?" he interrupts her, waiving his wine glass.

"Not at all. I'm fine with strangers. It's people that I know that I can't stand. I try to avoid good neighborly relations. They're too intrusive. I believe I've set foot on the property you're now renting just once, and it was only to throw stones at that damned alarm that constantly went off at the slightest breath of wind."

"I'm afraid the good neighborly relations ship has already sailed," he says, waiving the wine glass again. "However, I promise you that this dinner won't have any intrusive implications," he swears, crossing his heart. "And if you like, you can bring this bottle of Merlot with you to seal the deal."

Clever, sneaky, and a bit naughty. Edna has already sized him up. But overall, he's honest enough to be likable. So she grabs the bottle and follows Leonardo. And in any case, between a nice *pasta carbonara* and defrosting mammoth remains, it's not even a competition.

Chapter Eleven

Panting, Kalina makes her way along the state highway leading to Gattorna, dragging her wheeled suitcase with one hand and her *palacinka*, her treasured, cast-iron frying pan, with the other. She didn't leave her home, her life, and her family, she reflects, to come to Italy and be called a nincompoop or to become a punching bag for an elderly lady who babbled about fish and ice cream. No, sir. It was time for her to take the wheel and turn things around.

This U-turn in her fortunes had not gotten off to a great start. In fact, she seemed to have backed herself into a ditch. She had begun by getting off at the wrong bus stop and was now trying to find her way on foot without knowing exactly where she was or where she needed to go. Under such circumstances, she supposed that one direction was as good as another but that was small comfort.

To make matters worse, she found herself unfortunately overdressed for trudging along the road at that time of the evening. She had wanted to make a good impression on her new employer so she had worn the light red flowered dress that suits her so well. A bit too well, perhaps, since three cars – and counting – had passed her slowly and shouted fortunately-unintelligible offers and suggestions.

Kalina shakes her head, angrily brushing away the brown lock of hair that escaped from her hair clip. She's tired, hungry, and even needs to pee. A large tear rolls down her cheek and hits the gray asphalt, a raindrop heralding a coming storm. Kalina just wants to stop for a moment, catch her breath, and set down the frying pan and the suitcase, whose wheels do not roll but scrape roughly through the gravel. If the pan weren't a gift from her good friend Olga from Hungary, she would have already abandoned it.

But now, as she rounds a curve, she sees a light ahead, a low building with a brightly-lit shop window. The sight fills her heart with joy. Surely there must be a restroom there!

She quickens her pace, dragging her suitcase behind her in the knowledge that her bladder is likely to give out before her strength. Triumphantly, she reaches the building and pushes open the door with a shy, yet determined, "Hello? Is anyone here?" She doesn't notice the old, grey Renault Clio with a dented bumper parked across the road that pulls into the parking lot while switching on its headlights.

Chapter Twelve

"Nice of you to join us," Cagliostro says, or at least he would, if he could talk. Cagliostro is remarkably sarcastic, even for a cat, and his narrowed eyes and mortally offended air reveal that he didn't expect to be treated in this manner.

Edna stares at him from the entrance with annoyance, then with a sharp (and intentional) thud, she shuts the door behind her, drops the keys on the shelf, and enters the living room, positioning herself in front of him.

"Well? Do you plan on standing there like a candlestick on a high altar for an eternity?" she says over the tinkling of the cat food pouring into his empty bowl. "I believe you're supposed to be a country cat, aren't you? If you're hungry, go out and get your own snack instead of bristling at me!" Cagliostro just stares at her.

"If you're trying to make me feel guilty, it isn't working." snorts Edna, sinking into her armchair. "You wanted to eat. Now eat!" Edna waves her hand dismissively, then kicks off her beloved sneakers, dropping them on the floor without bothering to untie their laces, and puts her feet up on the table, disregarding his disapproving gaze.

"Are you still standing there? Perhaps I've misjudged you and you are curious to hear what happened rather than simply hungry. Very well. The Dodero house is definitely different from how I remembered it. Wilma Dodero had crammed every nook and cranny with furniture, knick-knacks, and doilies, creating a rather distasteful cacophony. But today, I found myself in a semi-empty house, tastefully arranged."

Cagliostro gazes at her for a moment, now radiating intense boredom. Turning his back on her, he jumps down and saunters over to his bowl. A gentle crunching fills the room.

Edna closes her eyes and begins massaging the back of her neck. Well, yes, Cagliostro is correct. Perhaps she had not led with the more interesting aspects of her evening. She had enjoyed a highly respectable pasta carbonara cooked by Leonardo. She also drank copious amounts of wine, and engaged in extensive conversation. Perhaps she drank more than she talked. Among other things, she discovered that he's not just an IT guy, he's a computer genius.

Originally, she had half-suspected that he was also some sort of wizard who had sold his soul to the devil. First, there was the unhealthy interest in that recipe. Second, he was unnaturally good-looking and charming, a classic symptom in the better class of demonic possession. But most damning was how he had somehow managed to empty the house of all Wilma Dodero's furniture and knickknacks – a prodigious task in itself – while replacing them with his own far more minimalist and tasteful décor. And all without her even realizing anything was happening.

Alas, the truth, at least about the furniture, was far more prosaic. The Doderos had hired a company that, within two days, packed all their trinkets into several containers and freshened up the house. The next day, Leonardo, with the assistance of three friends and a rented van, unloaded his belongings in just a few hours. Since all of this occurred during the week she was in London conducting a seminar on Paolo Uccello, no supernatural intervention had been required. Regardless, after years of blissful solitude, she now has someone in her way, including a motorcycle louder than a fighter-bomber. A genuine ambush! And without even having a chance to express her opinion.

Naturally, she has no intention of planning another retaliation involving cars and chicken poop – for one thing, he had a motorcycle – but she knows that she could have come up with something. He didn't seem easily frightened, however, and besides, having spent an entire evening in his company, she had concluded that he might qualify as an actual human. In short, she rather liked him and reluctantly decided to forego exacting an imaginative revenge for his crime of moving in next door. She sighs. It was a real pity.

Pling! A WhatsApp message interrupts her thoughts. It's Ottavio.

"Where the hell are you?"

Edna rolls her eyes. "At home, where do you think?"

"I called you earlier, and you didn't answer," Ottavio writes.

"I was at dinner with someone and turned my phone off since I didn't want to be rude."

"Really? Since when?"

Edna dials his number to call him because she despises wearing out her fingertips typing messages as long as sonnets.

"Isn't it a little late to call? What if I'd been asleep?" Ottavio whispers.

"You just sent me a message!" she snorts, rubbing her face in frustration. "And besides, why are you whispering? My mother can sleep through an air raid siren."

"So where were you?" he insists.

"Out at the chicken coop," she curtly replies, too tired to explain her whereabouts for the evening.

"You were having dinner with the chickens?"

"Yes. What's it to you?" she snorts.

"Nothing. I'm just wondering what kind of chickens you're raising."

"I enjoy watching them eat. It relaxes me. Do you find it strange?"

"No, what's strange is giving them names, playing pop music for them, and preferring them to humans."

"You're only annoyed because my chickens prefer Abba over Bach. And anyway, they make good company, they're fun and relaxing, not to mention they also lay eggs," she shrugs. "You can't say that about most people."

"About most people, no, at least not the laying eggs part." he concedes.

"You're being pedantic," she yawns, "pedantic and annoying."

"So you keep telling me. You're starting to repeat yourself, you know, and that's not a good sign," Ottavio chuckles, stifling a yawn. "And it's not about being pedantic; it's simply about not losing sight of the details. It's crucial. Don't forget that, my dear."

"Speaking of details, why did you call? Surely it wasn't to talk about chickens."

"Speaking of details, you called me."

"What do you want, Ottavio?" she growls, menacingly.

"Well, after all this fascinating repartee, I seem to have forgotten. But I'm sure it will come back to me. Goodnight!" he says as he hangs up the phone.

Details. Edna snorts, turning off her cell phone. For years, she has been emphasizing the importance of details in her mind. She takes her feet off the table and stands up to turn off the big lamp, the same kind of lamp local fishermen use for catching anchovies. Right now, all she wants is to climb into bed and forget all about this stressful day.

Chapter Thirteen

Marlena has switched off all the lights, and he can hear her snoring two doors away. When she's awake, she sounds like a bulldozer; when she's asleep, she sounds like a chainsaw.

He blinks a little, allowing his eyes to adjust to the darkness, and carefully makes his way to the window. The fig tree is nothing more than a shadow, a black cutout in the darkness.

The fig tree is a traitor. How well he knows! One should never climb its branches. Never! Besides, even if he wanted to, he couldn't – the window is securely closed. Marlena has even put a bike lock on the handle. All he can do is press his face against the glass. But it is enough. He can still see the banana-colored van. Bananas have always disgusted him.

Just a little further on, the gray road emerges from the darkness, illuminated by the milky cone of light cast by the street lamp. The road stretches down to the rectangular patch of light where the "ANTIQUES" sign hangs.

He blinks again and shifts his gaze, but there is nothing more. Nothing remains of the comings and goings that held him captive by the windowpane two hours ago. There is only silence, the van, and the rectangle of light where only darkness should be by now. This matter of the van and the peculiar light crackles in his mind like electricity before a storm. And that's not good. Not good at all.

He sways on his feet, unsure of what to do. Then his eye catches a slow, gray movement in the star-studded black sky. The bird is back. It's the kite, once again. He recognizes it by its tail. Strange. Kites are creatures of the day. Strange.

He presses his ear against the window. But again, there is only silence.

Strange. He straightens up cautiously. Incredibly strange, the silence. Sound is to the night as light is to the day. And the all-encompassing silence is like a darkness at noon.

Chapter Fourteen

"I see someone had a bit of a night out," Ottavio remarks, scrutinizing her with a critical gaze. "If it were anyone else, I'd put your appearance down to a night of wild passion. But it's not anyone else so I'll assume it's just a hangover. At least you weren't drinking alone. Come on in, Flora just brought us hot coffee, and your mother has been up for half an hour already." He turns and shuffles toward the living room, his caterpillar slippers softly scraping the floor. "Today, as you can see, we've gone with a peacock blue theme." Ottavio sidles up to Zara and deftly adjusts her chiffon robe with a flick of his wrist. "There. Isn't she magnificent? She looks as if she's just stepped out of a John William Waterhouse painting."

"Sometimes I wonder if taking care of my mother truly is the enormous favor you claim. Are you really earning that Negri etching that you extorted from me yesterday? Or are you actually enjoying this?" Edna sinks into a chair, massaging her temples. He wasn't wrong about the hangover. "You're supposed to be looking after my mother, not playing Octogenarian Barbie Dress-up."

"And who, exactly, might you be referring to?" her mother inquires, busily adding sugar to her coffee with a tablespoon.

"Well, I'll leave you to guess. There are three of us, one of whom resembles a two-hundred-and-sixty-pound caterpillar, so he's out. And I've been compared to a lot of things but never to Barbie… or a pre-Raphaelite virgin, for that matter. And enough with the sugar, Mom! What are you, a hummingbird?"

Zara drops the spoon, lifts her chin, and crosses her arms, visibly offended.

"You possess all the grace and delicacy of a rutting moose," Ottavio shakes his head, grabbing another cup. Then he approaches her and whispers, "Why do you have to discuss the Negri and our… um, agreement in front of her, as if she were a teapot or a potted plant, for God's sake? Now look, she's doing her impression of Saint Monica praying for patience."

"Good for her. As far as I'm concerned, she can display all the dramatic talent of Marlene Dietrich," Edna says as she rises and heads towards the door. "I'm leaving. I only came to ensure that you had survived the night and were bearing up under the torture of this forced cohabitation." She nods towards Zara, who is still maintaining her dramatic pose and is evidently determined to sustain it. "I also wanted to let you know I'll be out of town all day on university business. And before you start, no, I am not returning to work in the department, and no, Vice-Provost Schiaffino has nothing to do with it. Well, at least he has nothing to do with what you're imagining. He's merely an enthusiastic provider of annoying assignments. So wipe that silly smirk off your face."

"May the heavens forfend!" he raises his hands in surrender. "I'm not imagining anything. May I inquire where you're going and why?"

"Siestri. A charming, crumbling village in the middle of nowhere, nestled in the heart of the Fontanabuona area. Mainly to put some guy in his place. I won't elaborate any further, or I might use words that are not lady-like."

He snorts. "Goodness! We couldn't have that!" He waves his hand casually. "Go on, I wouldn't want your legendary savoir-faire to completely shatter the spirit of camaraderie and good feeling I have managed to establish in this house. In that case, the Negri etching might not be a sufficient compensation."

"Is that a threat?"

"Not at all, just a statement of fact. It's also a reminder not to settle for this temporary solution and to find a new housekeeper as soon as possible. Now, off you go, and… enjoy yourself!" he winks at her as he nudges her outside.

An outside whose prospects are not much more attractive than the house of horrors she's leaving, but at least there will be thirty miles and an entire valley separating her from Zara.

Chapter Fifteen

A circle of Hell, Edna sighs, surveying her surroundings. Which, she supposes, is perfectly fitting for an event dedicated to Dante. But to have agreed to spend the entire day in a social whirlwind blown up from the frozen depths of Hell when she could have stayed home and worked on something useful i.e., her own stuff… It's not only out of character for Edna, but it's also utterly insane for anyone. Anyone, that is, except a committed academic dedicated to climbing the greasy poll of academic politics. This realization causes her to reflect on the political ineptitude, disappointed former students, and poor anger management that she drags along like a chain forged from the deeds, or rather misdeeds, of her university career. Perhaps she should begin calling herself Professor Marley.

Edna snorts and shifts gears to tackle the uphill climb on the narrow dirt road, barely able to pass because of an endless line of cars parked on both sides. This middle-of-nowhere village probably has more visitors today than it has had in the past seven centuries, combined. She rounds the bend and, with a suspicious stroke of luck, spots an available parking space on the left-hand side of the road. Swiftly maneuvering, she squeezes her car between an SUV and a chestnut tree the size of a sequoia, turns off the engine, grabs her bag and cell phone, and opens the door. Then, she has an afterthought and leans over to search under the seat for her camera bag. She decides to bring it along, holding onto the forlorn hope of being able to combine this nightmare with a bit of pleasure. She opens the door, steps out… and finds herself sliding down the side of the Grand Canyon. It's actually only a drainage ditch, but in the heat of the moment, this fine distinction is lost on Edna.

But it could have been worse. It could have been raining. So when she finally arrives at the bottom, there is, fortunately, no water. Clambering out with the help of a protruding root, she reflects that she was right to be suspicious of her good luck and wonders if falling into a ditch is just a taste of things to come. The day, she fears, is going to be even more insufferable than she had imagined. Scanning the sky where the wind is amassing clouds, she prays that it won't rain.

She brushes off her trousers and takes slow, reluctant steps as she begins to make her way into the pit of festival Hell. She can already see there are a great number of self-important people in constant motion, greeting each other, and shaking hands. She wonders what circle of Hell is devoted to perpetual networking.

"Doctor Silvera?"

Edna turns and sees a determined and hurried woman, small and compact like a block of porphyry, but with eyes as lively and sharp as a ferret's, now scrutinizing her with the precision of a laser scanner.

"Good morning," she extends her hand and gives Edna a firm handshake. "Orietta Repetto, Councilor for Tourism and Entertainment for the Municipality of Gattorna. I apologize for the chaos but it's unavoidable when you're preparing for an event like this, so we might as well face it head on. Come along. I'll show you the way," the councilor says as she deftly maneuvers past the barriers.

Edna follows her amidst a Boschian scene of technicians, police officers, bomb-sniffing dogs, and individuals with badges attached to their lapels scurrying through village ruins, cables, scaffolding, and stages still under construction. It's easy for Edna to keep sight of the councilor thanks to her distinctive cherry-red hair, a shining mane that could probably be seen by passing satellites.

"Here we are," Councilor Repetto stops in front of a very large gazebo that serves as the event headquarters. "These are the press agents, and over there is part of the organizing committee," she explains, pointing towards three young men hunched over their laptops, their eyes glued to the screens.

"Few but mighty, I presume," Edna comments, slightly puzzled.

"It may seem so, indeed," the councilor admits. "But the truth is, only the operational team remains here. The bulk of the organization, including your former students, has just moved to Gattorna, to the town hall, where they can work with all the comforts. Professor Pierpaolo Santi Niboni, the head of the national association Amici di Dante, was quite insistent on this point." She shrugs with suspiciously elaborate indifference.

"So, does this mean I came all the way up here when I could have stopped in Gattorna?" Edna blinks, a hint of exasperation in her voice.

"I'm afraid so. If I had known when you were coming, I would have warned you in advance. But if you'd like, we can make your effort worthwhile by giving you a tour of the village in this new atmosphere of pre-event frenzy."

"Do you recommend it?" Edna inquires, contemplating her options.

"Not really, no. Right now, the only person I would truly recommend it to, as a form of poetic justice, is the aforementioned Professor Santi Niboni. However, I can't deny that this mayhem might make for an interesting photo safari." She nods towards the camera bag on Edna's shoulder. "If you'd like, you can wander around for a while, and then we both can head down to Gattorna."

A gust of wind causes the gazebo to shake dangerously, and a rumble of thunder echoes ominously in the distance.

For a moment, Edna remains undecided, torn between accepting the invitation and removing the lens cap from her camera or pulling up the hood of her jacket and running back to her car, perched on the edge of the ditch, to go back to the safety of her home.

"Perhaps it would be best to postpone the safari," the councilor hastily decides, scanning the sky teeming with thick, dark clouds. She turns swiftly and begins elbowing her way towards the exit.

Drops as big as walnuts strike the ground but their hesitant rhythm soon transforms itself into a relentless downpour. The rain drums on rooftops, pummels the ground, and creates small rivulets that meander through the landscape. Thunder booms overhead, shaking the very air and adding an apocalyptic soundtrack to the storm.

Edna dashes down the dirt road, concealing her camera beneath her jacket. She crawls into her car from the passenger side while the councilor retrieves an embarrassingly pink cloak from the trunk of her Panda 4x4. She hastily drapes it over herself and bends down to fiddle near Edna's car bumper.

"Here you go!" she exclaims through Edna's window. "I've placed some pieces of wood under your wheels. Now you can shift into reverse and gently accelerate. You shouldn't get stuck in the mud. That's it, you're doing great!" She gives a thumbs-up in approval.

Once Edna is free, she shakes off the rainwater and disappears into her car, skidding off toward the paved road at the bottom of the hill.

Edna activates the windshield wiper, which gasps and squeaks, struggling to keep up with the torrential downpour which is now a biblical deluge. She mentally berates her own weakness and Edoardo, who manipulated her into accepting this cursed assignment and then abandoned her, leaving her to navigate (literally!) this mess alone.

This is a sign, and not a good one, muses Edna as she attempts to follow the councilor's Panda, now taking the muddy turns at breakneck speed. Yes, it's a sign that no good deed goes unpunished and a warning that she should stop entangling herself in matters that only serve to rob her of her time and patience. This, she swears, will be the last time she finds herself in such a situation. From now on, she will solely focus on her own affairs. Assuming, of course, she does not drown, get struck by lighting, or drive off a cliff on the way down to Gattorna.

Chapter Sixteen

"Congratulations! That's the weirdest thing I've seen all week." exclaims the councilor as she emerges from behind the bumper.

"I would have gladly passed on this distinction, I assure you," sighs Edna, still on her knees and examining the long chestnut branch that protrudes at least five feet from between her front wheels and gives the impression that her car had decided to dress as a sort of steam punk narwhal for Halloween.

"It seems really jammed in there," says the councilor, firmly grasping the obvious. "We might have to get someone to come and give us a hand. We can't even move your car off the road, let alone to the repair shop in the village. Unless you've got something in your trunk we might be able to use?"

"I believe I might have an Allen wrench in there that fell out of my last IKEA purchase. Do you think that will help?" asks Edna dryly. Talk about "signs." The only clearer signs would be a talking bush or being submerged in a river of blood during an invasion of locusts. The only positive note in all this is that at least it has almost stopped raining.

"Let's see…" says the councilor, rummaging in her trunk, "What have I got here? There's a baseball bat… a barbecue spit, make that two… not very useful, I'm afraid."

"Perhaps not." Edna nods, attempting once again to dislodge the branch with her bare hands, and wondering what sort of dodgy activities would prompt a friendly fifty-year-old, who is also the councilor for tourism and entertainment in a small Ligurian town, to keep barbecue spits and baseball bats in her trunk.

"Listen, Doctor Silvera, how about I take you to see your colleagues at Gattorna's town hall? Then I'll go to the repair shop and get someone to come out and fix your car."

"What about the antiques dealer across the street?" Edna points to the low building with the word "ANTIQUES" displayed in the brightly lit window, which is curious as it's eleven in the morning. "If the owner has his workshop there, maybe he's got something we can use. It's worth a try."

"That's Nando Folli's place." the councilor ponders, narrowing her eyes. "Why not? I agree. It won't hurt to try."

***

"Hello? Is anyone here?" Edna pushes open the glass door and is greeted by a familiar scent – a blend of old wood, linseed oil, turpentine, and dust. Lots of dust. Some of her more sentimental colleagues poetically refer to these stubborn layers of grime as "the deposits of time." The only difference from regular dust is that these layers of romanticized crud haven't seen a rag or a feather duster in years and are a paradise for mites.

"Nando?" Councilor Repetto looks around, squinting her ferret-like eyes. "Strange, usually he locks the door even if he steps out for a moment. There's some valuable stuff in here. Where the hell did he go?" She pushes aside a crimson saddle blanket with two fingers, covered in so much "time" that it could almost stand up on its own.

Edna moves leisurely, scanning the meandering labyrinth while making an effort not to be overwhelmed by nostalgia. This elusive Nando had managed to impose a certain order upon the chaos. The arrangement of the individual pieces – furniture, furnishings, silverware, paintings, or artifacts – seems to follow a precise logic. Of course, there's nothing exceptional or unmissable, and there's no shortage of hideous paintings and abominable stuff, causing Edna to shudder as she replaces a pseudo-eighteenth-century landscape with dark and muddy colors. However, taking it all together, she concludes that Nando has a "good eye."

She steps back to examine a chandelier with long, gilded arms, and accidentally backs into a heavy, partially dismantled Chippendale dresser, causing all the wooden boards resting on it to fall loudly like dominos.

"Are you okay?" asks the councilor from somewhere deep inside the shop.

"Yes, apart from the dust," Edna coughs, waving her hands. Then, suddenly, her stomach flutters as she notices the painted corner of one of the fallen boards emerging from beneath a cloth. She bends down, retrieves the wooden panel, and brings it under the uncertain light of a lamp. The wood is undoubtedly very old, she realizes as she examines it

52

from the side, and it depicts two standing figures that appear to be monks, although their dark robes lack any indication of a specific religious order. The robes seem somehow crude and stiff, clashing with the delicately-painted features of their wearers. But what really intrigues her are the colors. Edna looks around furtively, then quickly takes out her cell phone and kneels to capture photographs of the panel from every angle, front and back, cursing herself all the while for leaving her trusty Canon wedged between the seats of her car.

"Doctor Silvera?" the councilor's voice rings out like a gunshot, startling her. Her mobile phone falls on the wooden floorboards with a sharp thud. "I'd say our antiquarian isn't here. So, we can either opt for a self-service solution – I've seen some things here that might help us out – or we can try to… Oh!" she suddenly stops and mutters a barely audible but highly emotional "shit!"

"Councilor?" Edna straightens up, a little worried.

"Um, Doctor Silvera, you'd better come here. Go past that large, dark bookcase with glass panes on the right. Do you have a strong stomach?"

"Did you say stomach? Why?… Oh!" Edna blinks as she emerges from behind the councilor and is left speechless. Shit, indeed.

Because lying on the ground, with a purplish forehead, his pants around his ankles, and his head resting on a large, dark stain of congealed blood, are the remains of the late Nando Folli, antiques dealer.

Chapter Seventeen

"A chestnut branch," the elderly policeman writes diligently in his notebook, displaying the skeptical air of someone accustomed to hearing all sorts of peculiarities. Despite his blasé attitude, discovering a corpse due to a five-foot-long branch stuck in an axle is a new one even for him.

"Listen," Edna sighs, massaging her aching temples, "the councilor and I have been trapped in this damned place for almost three hours, with no food, no water, and no bathroom. And without knowing why you are still keeping us here. It may surprise you but we actually have other things to do today."

The councilor remains silent, contributing to the conversation only with a raised eyebrow that speaks volumes.

The officer lifts his gaze from his notebook and stares at Edna with the warm and friendly look of a sheepdog. This pseudo-amicability does not extend to his thin lips that rarely form a smile.

"Ma'am," he says curtly, "you two have discovered a body. In such cases, the procedure requires us to keep you at the disposal of the investigators as long as is necessary to complete the preliminary investigation." His tone doesn't allow for rebuttal, especially not from civilians who prioritize their own comfort over basic civic responsibility.

"Perhaps if the prosecutor stopped chatting on his cell phone and got on with it, we might get this wrapped up before dinner," offers the councilor. She exudes the calm serenity of a woman accustomed to dealing with even more vexing problems, but this doesn't stop her from putting the boot in when it seems appropriate. But the officer seems more than a match for the councilor. His sheepdog-like gaze remains unaffected and he regards her with quiet indifference.

Edna sighs. If the day weren't taking on the semblance of a Greek tragedy, this might almost be comical. Climbing down off her stool, she begins to pace while observing her surroundings with mild curiosity.

"Excuse me, what do you think you're doing?" asks the officer, blocking her path.

"I'm merely stretching my legs, for Christ's sake! You've had us perched on those stools for over an hour now. The humane treatment of prisoners is guaranteed by the Geneva Convention, in case you were unaware!"

"I remind you that we are at a crime scene," he responds stiffly. "You can't go wandering around as if you were at a market!"

Edna begins to rear back, visions of chicken poop dancing in her head.

"Leave it, Officer Capurro. I'll handle it. Good afternoon, I'm Public Prosecutor Jacopo Bassi," smiles the PP, shaking hands with both Edna and the councilor. "Please, Doctor Silvera, have a seat and forgive us for the delay." He quickly brushes off a dilapidated Thonet chair and takes a seat.

He smiles again.

He smiles too much, Edna notes with annoyance. A subtle movement of the councilor's eyebrow confirms that she shares the same opinion. Moreover, a little of his smile goes a long way as he displays a set of dazzling teeth worthy of a toothpaste commercial.

All of this, along with his preppy jacket and shiny, pointy shoes, gives him a frivolous, mundane air, more suitable for a real estate agent than an administrator of justice. But Edna also knows how often the exterior and interior do not align so she crosses her arms and waits.

"So, both of you came in here, to the workshop/shop of the victim, because your car broke down?" he asks.

"Exactly," Edna confirms. "To be precise, a five-foot-long tree limb got stuck in the axle of my car. We were looking for a tool to remove it and get back on the road without having to call a tow truck."

"Very well," PP Bassi nods. He is not completely clear about the tree branch story, but he doesn't let it show.

"So you entered, and then…?"

"And then nothing," Edna shrugs. "The proprietor, that is, the deceased man, obviously was nowhere to be seen. The councilor here was surprised that he had left the shop with the door open, so we wandered around a bit to look for him, until… Well, you know the rest."

"No, actually, I don't know the rest, that's why I'm here," he smiles, his teeth blindingly white.

"Until I found him on the ground, deader than a mackerel." the councilor concludes with her usual no-nonsense attitude, once again proving how much she dislikes beating around the bush. "So I alerted Doctor Silvera, who was on the other side of the shop, and together we decided it would be best to call 911, rather than make a run for it. So here we are." she concludes dryly, as if she were now regretting her civic-minded impulse.

"And you found him exactly like that, just as the police found him?" Bassi blinks slightly.

"What do you mean by 'exactly like that'?" the councilor leans forward, adopting the attitude of an annoyed mastiff. "What is it you are accusing us of? Do you think Doctor Silvera and I make a habit of pantsing random corpses that we happen to come across? You can't possibly imagine that we pulled down his trousers, surely?"

"I was only asking if you moved or turned him to confirm he was dead," he explains, "and perhaps, in doing so, you grabbed him by the legs, and that's why his trousers could…" He makes a slight gesture with his hand to explain the rest.

"We didn't touch him," Edna intervenes, mostly to contain the councilor's growing indignation, "as you would know perfectly well if you thought about it for five seconds. If we had, the bloodstain would not have maintained such a clean outline, and there would be streaks here and there caused by the victim's hair. Correct?"

PP Bassi nods his head as if to say *touché*, and observes her with renewed interest.

Edna shrugs. Details matter to her. She has built a career in seeing what is there. That, and applying elementary logic to those details. He needn't look like a startled hare simply because she pointed out the obvious.

"May I ask you, Mrs.…." he lowers his eyes to the notepad diligently filled by Officer Capurro, "Mrs. Repetto, my apologies, I should say Councilor Repetto," he smiles brightly, "if you knew the victim?"

"I didn't really *know* him," she raises an eyebrow, "so much as I knew *of* him. I knew who he was, yes, just like everyone in Gattorna, Cicagna, and the surrounding areas knew him. Twenty years ago, Nando Folli took over the family second-hand shop and turned it into an antiques business. As you can see, it was more that just a shop. It's also a workshop. He sold antiques and restored them." She nods towards the two large rooms overflowing with items. "I can't tell you much more than that."

"Was business good for him?"

"How would I know? I just told you, I barely knew him!" snorts the councilor. "Of course, these days, if someone manages to keep a business running for more than twenty years without closing or having everything taken away by the banks, I suppose they aren't doing too badly."

"Unless they rely on 'external' support, perhaps not entirely legitimate," ponders the prosecutor, tapping the notebook with his pen.

The councilor spreads her arms as if to say, "anything is possible," but even if it were true, she wouldn't know.

"Was he married? Did he have a family?" The prosecutor is determined if nothing else. "Come on," he challenges, "people know these things in little villages like this, right?"

The councilor eyes him as if he were a local trout in need of deboning. "No, he wasn't married, and no, he had no family that I know of," she clarifies. "I think that in matters of love, he was what you'd call a free spirit, used to grazing in other people's pastures, if you know what I mean."

"Perfectly," nods the prosecutor, taking notes. "Any potential enemies or feuds that you are aware of?"

"Even if the various betrayed spouses, partners, or lovers were aware of his involvements, people in Gattorna appreciate their privacy and I assure you we never witnessed any shocking public scenes here. It may be different in the big city," she concedes with mock graciousness, "and before you say, 'people know these things in little villages like this,' Nando lived in Cicagna, about ten minutes from here. I suggest you pursue your enquiries there."

Edna chuckles. Her esteem for the councilor is rising at an exponential rate.

"What about you, Doctor Silvera?" asks the prosecutor making a tactical retreat. "What is the famous Edna Silvera," and he pauses, letting her know that he has done his homework, "doing here in Gattorna?"

"Doctor Silvera has been invited by the organizing committee for the commemoration of the seven-hundredth anniversary of Dante's death," the councilor interjects, "as the representative of the Department for Cultural Heritage in Genoa. And three hours ago, we were supposed to join the rest of the committee in the town hall, but instead..." She raises her eyebrows, implying branches stuck in car axles, dead bodies, and above all, endless waiting for the prosecutor busy with other matters.

"So, I presume that you, Doctor Silvera, met Mr. Nando Folli today for the first time? Or perhaps you already knew each other, considering that his work is somewhat related to your former work as a restorer, among other things?" He emphasizes the words "among other things," which makes Edna suspect that this simpering fool of a prosecutor is neither simpering nor a fool. Damn it, perhaps he left them to stew for hours surrounded by old furniture while gathering information on both of them so he could dissect them alive. Those three words, "among other things," dropped far too casually, had the precise purpose of making it clear that he knows – he knows what happened twenty years ago, and he also knows why she gave up her career in art restoration at a certain point.

Edna's eyes become two slits as she leans forward to examine him more carefully. The details, always the details! She should have noticed it before. The Public Prosecutor Jacopo Bassi, once you dismiss his Caribbean tan, dazzling smile, and Happy Hour attitude, has the rapacious gaze of a hawk flying in circles before swooping down on its prey. Edna, of all people, knows that appearances are what people want you to see and are meant to hide as often as reveal.

"No," she replies, "I've never met Mr. Folli before today. If you want to be pedantic, I still have not met him." This draws an approving nod from the councilor. "We ended up here by pure chance, and the rest you know." She, too, emphasizes the words "the rest" to hint that she recognizes he's not the clown he would like to appear to be and that he knows things. Far too many things, for her taste.

Chapter Eighteen

Rita sways slowly, completely enthralled, oblivious to the other hens swirling around her to the rhythm of Abba's "Dancing Queen." Even Garbo, who generally detests these disco sessions, is sitting at the edge of the dance floor today, nodding her head indulgently.

Edna turns up the volume and watches her chickens with a touch of envy. She thought yesterday had been a very difficult day that began at dawn with Kalina's abrupt departure. She certainly didn't imagine that today would be even worse. Her phone pings and she gathers the shards of her attention together to see what fresh hell awaits.

It's a message from Councilor Repetto, asking her if she survived the meeting with the committee or if she ended up sticking her head in the oven. Perhaps meeting the councilor was the only positive thing that had happened in the last eight hours, indeed, probably in the entire week. Edna smiles to herself as she types: "I survived, and right now I'm contemplating drowning my sorrows in a bottle of grappa, but only because I have an electric stove. It's just not the same." She considers adding one of those animated yellow faces but hesitates because she's without her glasses and fears inadvertently propositioning the esteemed councilor by emoji. She taps send and puts the phone in her pocket. The councilor is right. If she were to award the prize for the worst moment of the day, between the discovery of the antiques dealer's corpse and spending time in the town hall with the Dante Committee… well, it had been a pleasure meeting Nando Folli.

"You surprise me. I expected Mahler or Coleman."

Edna jerks her head up and finds her IT neighbor in front of her, holding a helmet in one hand and a bottle of Franciacorta rosé in the other.

"My chickens' musical tastes are their own and strictly limited to the seventies," she shrugs. "Strange, I didn't hear you pull up. Did you put a silencer on your rocket?"

"In a way, yes," he chuckles, "I rode the last stretch with the engine throttled all the way down. But you were so engrossed I needn't have bothered."

Edna raises her eyes to the sky and silences the music which causes general discontent among her hens. One of them swoops in and expresses her disappointment by pecking at Edna's ankles.

"Shoo, Rita, come on, I'm not in the mood!" Edna snorts, pushing her away with her foot.

"Rita?" Leonardo blinks.

"Yes, Rita, as in Hayworth. Do you remember the movie Gilda?"

"More or less," he answers evasively, staring at the red hen who is now giving him a somewhat seductive look.

"Oh, that's right. I forgot that we're separated by two decades of old films." she admits grudgingly. "Well, I hope you at least have a smattering of knowledge about old movies to appreciate the names I've given to my chickens... that one over there, swaying her hips, is Lollobrigida; the busty brunette is Loren; the slightly disheveled and feisty one next to her is Stanwyck." She points them out one by one as they approach him with mild curiosity. "The ditzy blonde is Marilyn, and the little one staring at us with her slightly creepy eyes is Bette Davis... Look, it seems you've managed to pique Garbo's interest," she nods at a rather slender (within poultry limits) hen who gracefully makes her way through the grass. "You should be flattered. Garbo rarely grants anyone her consideration."

"So your movie-star hens listen to the Bee Gees and Abba," Leonardo sums up, quite amused, as he sits on the bench next to Edna.

Edna bends down to remove a dry leaf from Loren's feathers. "I suspect that being hatched in a chicken coop at the back of an old bar, whose jukebox hasn't updated its repertoire since 1980, had something to do with their musical taste."

"And does the music serve a particular purpose, like increasing egg production, for example?"

"Not really. They just enjoy it. And their pleasure is contagious. It relaxes me. And I could do with a little relaxation." she explains calmly.

"Rough day?"

"Well, let's see. I had an argument with my mother, fell into a ditch, waded through a flood, got a five-foot long branch stuck in my car, and found a dead body. And that was all before lunch. You tell me."

"A dead body?" he turns abruptly to stare at her.

"Yes. To think that with a tree branch stuck under my car, I believed I had reached the nadir of bad luck… and instead…"

"And where did this happen?"

"I had business to attend to in Siestri, for the commemoration of the 700th anniversary of Dante's death…"

He looks at her with a vacant expression.

Edna rolls her eyes and sighs. "That famous canto in Dante's *Purgatory*, remember? Ottobono Fieschi (known at that time as pope Adrian V) says:

Between Siestri and Chiaveri there runs down

a lovely stream and with its name

the title of my line has marked its shield.

"You must have studied Italian literature in high school, right? Or were you only interested in circuits and bytes?" she asks with a hint of sarcasm.

"Studied, yes. Committed every word to memory? No." he calmly replies.

"I'm afraid I'm boring you. And it seems you have things to do, or am I mistaken?" She points to the bottle of Franciacorta rosé placed on the ground, which Marilyn has been studying with keen interest for the past ten minutes. "If you need it for tonight, it would be better to put it in the fridge, don't you think?"

"Ah, yes," he nods. "I mean, no, you're not boring me at all, and yes, I should put it in the fridge. Now I know why you went to Siestri, but I'm still a little vague about where the dead body comes in… If I'm not being too forward, that is."

"Not at all. There's not much to say. I went to Siestri because the department assigned me the annoying duty of acting as their representative. The councilor in charge and I got caught in a deluge, and while driving, I hit a chestnut branch that got stuck in my car's axle. So we stopped in front of an antiques dealer's shop, hoping that he might have some tools we could use to remove the branch. However, instead of tools, we found his body. That, of course, unleashed chaos, as you can imagine. Except you can't as it was much worse than that. Now I'm here, the worse for wear, and obliged to remain available to the police until further notice."

"Wow!" he blinks. "But was it an accidental death or…" he mimes a stabbing motion.

"Who knows?" she shrugs. "Anything is possible. Perhaps he had a sudden heart attack. But when you find someone dead in a pool of blood, with their pants around their ankles, it invites questions."

"Wow!" he repeats, even more impressed.

"I don't want to send you away, but if your evening plans involve seduction, a lukewarm Franciacorta isn't going to get you very far."

"Yeah," he chuckles, standing up. He gently nudges Marilyn away and picks up the bottle. "Are you sure you're okay?"

"I'm fine, I'm fine," she dismisses him hastily. "Don't worry, Leonardo, and have fun," she concludes, throwing a meaningful glance at the bottle.

He looks at her for a moment, then gets up and nods goodbye with a slight bow before making his way back to his motorcycle.

Edna, on the other hand, remains there, inhaling the twilight air and the scent of damp earth, trying to swallow the strange lump of melancholy that suddenly forms in her throat, like an avocado pit. Because aging has always seemed to her like a sort of liberation from existential angst and social expectations, but recently, she has felt a sense of disquiet that disrupts her inner balance and her comfortable universe. And that bothers her. Quite a lot, actually. It seems like a silly thing, not at all useful, and very unpleasant.

"Why are you looking at me like that?" she snorts at Bette Davis, who is studying her with her small, protruding eyes. "Okay, perhaps I'm getting old," she concedes. "So what?"

Bette Davis tilts her head, as if to say, "No problem." and settles herself companionably next to Edna's shin.

Chapter Nineteen

Evening came, followed by morning, and then evening once again. The yellow van remains in its place. Likewise, he remains there, stuck to the closed window pane. However, not everything has stayed the same. He shifts his round eyes to gaze beyond the fig tree. Some things have changed now.

On the gray strip of road, the street lamps have turned on, but the illuminated window that shone down on the highway yesterday is now dark, black.

There was plenty of light and many people throughout the day, but not anymore. Everything is empty. Very empty. And black.

So black that the yellow van appears even more vibrant in contrast. This is not good. It's very bad.

He moves his head jerkily, distracted by the enticing aromas wafting up from downstairs.

Marlena is working in the kitchen, and he feels a slight hunger pang, but it could be an opportune moment to attempt something. To attempt to fly away.

To fly away from all this yellow and black.

However, not from the window. The window is still secured by OMG's bike lock on its handle. No, he could try to fly away from the door below, the door that opens onto the garden. He could pass under the fig tree and then… just fly away.

He swiftly walks to the back of the room and casts a final glance at the window. Through its glass, all he can see is the pattern of fig branches against the sky. He stretches his neck, but no, he can't spot the yellow van from here.

He takes the stairs, pushes open the garden door, passes beneath the fig tree, and takes flight. He flies, flies, flies away into the evening. No one can see him, except perhaps the silent kite, which now glides leisurely over the highway and then ascends, disappearing into the darkness of the encroaching night.

Chapter Twenty

"The white egg, in mythical cosmology, symbolizes genesis. However, Bosch's artistic universe is often obscure and multifaceted, offering countless possible interpretations. In fact…" Edna grumbles and erases the last two words. It's horrible; today she feels utterly useless.

With a sigh, she closes the image of *Le Concert dans l'œuf* by Hieronymus Bosch, moves the pile of notes, the large volume of Della Porta, and Cennini's treatise from her desk, and surrenders to the urge that has been tormenting her all morning.

Half-an-hour later, she clicks on yet another link, only to find it completely useless once again. Frustration builds up inside her and she gives her keyboard a slap. It seems that PP Bassi has managed to uncover every little detail about her, while she has only managed to find a few dull lines about him, essentially just his résumé. It's an uneven battle, like David against Goliath, with David forgetting his sling at home.

It's not that she feels the need to prepare a defense. She found herself at the crime scene purely by chance, and she has nothing to worry about. But it bothers her to be at a disadvantage, that's all. She'd like to have something handy that will wipe that hidden smirk off his face, should it ever be necessary.

Edna bites her lip and returns to pounding on the keys. No luck. She gives the keyboard another slap and crosses her arms. It's a dead end. There's no public dirt available on Public Prosecutor Jacopo Bassi. The next step would be recruiting her neighbor with his magical IT skills and hacking into some secret government files somewhere. This seems slightly extreme for settling an imaginary score, even to her.

This is maddening. Not only did Schiaffino's brilliant idea cause her to waste an entire day, but now her mind is filled with so much information about biblical floods, tree branches, and dead bodies that it's ruining her evening, too.

She might as well quit working and find something else to do. But what? Sometimes she regrets refusing her nannies' attempts to teach her embroidery and crochet. An utterly mindless activity might be just the thing for eliminating troublesome and distracting thoughts.

As it is, her brain, like her mouth, never shuts down. Usually, neither of these is a problem – at least not for her. But it's different when obnoxious, unwanted thoughts manage to leap over the defenses and barricades she has built over the years. It's happening now, as PP Bassi and his relentless probing are causing thoughts of her past to break through the barriers. Despite her efforts to bolster them with layers of commitment, passions, studies, work, even hens, memories of too many tears and too few caresses were bubbling to the surface.

She rises from her desk and looks out the windows of the veranda, where the moon reflects on the silvery olive trees with the ethereal vagueness of a landscape by Leonardo. On a night like this, there's only one thing to do. Watch TV.

Edna sinks into her armchair and begins channel surfing. What was it, she muses, that Bruce Springsteen said? Fifty-seven channels and nothing on? She sighs. It's certainly true tonight so she clicks the TV off and drops the remote on the table. Cagliostro, never the most patient of roommates, is annoyed by all this and indignantly jumps off the sofa and heads towards the bedroom.

Edna supposes he's in search of some peace and quiet, so she gets a glass of wine from the kitchen and settles down to have a look at the images of that strange panel she had found at the late Nando Folli's shop. Perhaps she should have told PP Bassi that she had taken them. Yes, she definitely should have. It was her civic duty and her failure might make Public Prosecutor Bassi's job more difficult. Edna smiles contentedly.

After all, she hadn't done it on purpose. In all the commotion following Folli's death, she simply forgot all about them. Next time she discovered a dead body, she'd be sure and do better. She lowers her glasses to the tip of her nose and lazily runs her finger across the display.

Suddenly, she straightens up and mutters, "Impossible!" She attempts to enlarge the photo on the screen but despite her efforts it keeps snapping back to its original size. After several minutes of increasing frustration, she jumps to her feet and starts rummaging through desk drawers, bookshelves, pen holders, sofa cushions, her bag, and the jumbled bundle of her notes. *She must know.*

"It must be somewhere around here, I'm sure," Edna mutters, sweeping her hands across the carpet in search of the cable she uses to download photos from her phone. Nothing. Where could she have put it? She curses her habit of dropping things wherever she happens to be when she is done with them. For the 817th time, she vows to be more organized in the future.

There's only one solution. She hesitates for a moment, as good manners would dictate letting it go for now and postponing everything until tomorrow. But no one would mistake Edna for Emily Post so she slips her phone into her pocket, grabs her sweater, and steps out into the cool, damp evening.

Chapter Twenty-One

"Edna?! Is something wrong?" Leonardo exclaims as he opens the door.

She gives him a quick smile. "Nothing too serious. Sorry for the late hour, but I'm in a dilemma. May I come in?"

"Ahh, yes, of course…" he hesitates for a moment, then steps aside to let her in.

"Thank you. You see, I was at home trying to find that darn cable to download some photos from my phone, and then…" as she steps into the living room, her brain registers the soft lights, the candles, the ice bucket, Miles Davis playing in the background… Like a flashback in a movie, she is suddenly reliving her conversation about Franciacorta rosé, chickens, and seduction. Uh oh.

Confirming her worst fears, a young brunette rises from the sofa – a flute full of bubbles in her hands and a pair of legs that deserve respect. At first, she looks at Edna with a cautious hostility, but once she takes in the whiff of chicken manure, the baggy sweater hanging lopsidedly on her, and the hair resembling uncarded wool, the look fades to mere annoyance. Obviously, Edna has not come at a good time.

"Err," Edna stutters. But she has been in much more embarrassing situations than this and the moment passes. She hands her phone to Leonardo, pointing at the display with her finger. "Hey, I'm sorry, I need to examine these images in detail… I wanted to transfer them to the computer, but as I mentioned, I can't find my cable anymore, and so…" She shrugs to explain the interruption, the late hour, the bad timing, and everything else.

The young brunette gives her an incredulous look, torn between the urge to laugh at her and to take off a shoe and plant a good portion of her stiletto heel in Edna's forehead.

Leonardo, however, is nothing if not a gentleman. "Of course, Edna. Did you bring your laptop with you?" he asks politely.

"Oh, how silly of me. I didn't think about it… Well, if you want, I can quickly go back home and get it if…" Edna trails off in mid-sentence, realizing that this might be a bit much, even for her. By the look of incredulity on her face, the brunette clearly agrees.

"No problem, Edna," he quickly decides, despite the more than eloquent look on his companion's face. "I can download them on my laptop and send them to you by email. It'll be faster. Will that work?" He sits down in front of the screen and connects her cell phone.

"Yes, them." Edna says, leaning over his shoulder and pointing at the crystal-clear twenty-four-inch monitor.

"A painting?" he notes with surprise.

"Yes, an oil painting on wood, to be precise," she explains, putting on the glasses she brought with her. "It was in the antiques dealer's shop."

"*That* antiques dealer?" he turns abruptly to look at her.

"That one, yes," Edna nods impatiently, moving even closer to the monitor. "It's just what I thought. Those dark robes don't match anything else in the painting, you see? The brushstrokes are stiff, careless, and there aren't any iconographic elements indicating a specific monastic order. Not to mention the color itself."

"It seems like a very ordinary dark brown to me. What's so strange about it?"

"Well, in this context, everything!" she spreads her arms. "The so-called umbers – the range of colors from brown to chestnut – were not widely used before the end of the fifteenth century. Vasari himself, in his sixteenth-century treatise, describes their use as relatively new in his time. But this painting on a wood panel is characteristic of the late Gothic period, so it's earlier than that. Moreover, this shade, so deep… could you enhance the contrast a bit more?"

"Is that enough, Edna?"

Leonardo's date has had enough. "I'm going outside for a cigarette," she says. And, from the look on her face, possibly an Uber. She gets up off the couch and somehow manages to stomp her way across the parquet floor and out the door while wearing five-inch heels.

Leonardo watches her go with a sigh but he is hooked. "You were saying something about the color of the robes?"

"Are you sure you really want to know? I mean, having you here to work on this on the computer is a godsend for me, but I wouldn't want to ruin your evening."

"Don't worry about it. You've intrigued me now and she'll be back in a few minutes."

She smiles slightly. She's not sure if this is something that can be unraveled in the time it takes to smoke a cigarette. But on the other hand, if the brunette's bad mood isn't a problem for him, it certainly isn't a problem for her.

"I should verify it on the actual painting," she continues, "but it appears to be a specific brown pigment called Cassel Earth or Cologne Earth." Edna looks around, grabs a chair, and settles in front of the monitor next to him. "It's a pigment from Northern Europe, mainly composed of organic matter such as soil and peat, which later became known as 'Van Dyck brown'… which would be absurd…"

"Why absurd?"

"Because we are talking about a pigment that was created and used from the seventeenth century onwards, while, as I mentioned, this panel was painted at least two centuries earlier. That's why it's absurd. Now, would you please enlarge the lower right corner?" she points towards the bottom of the image. Edna's suspicions have proved correct because the brunette has now reentered the room trailing a cloud of smoke and evening dampness with her while hissing, "Is she still here?!"

Leonardo is too focused to notice, or perhaps he heard her but prefers to pretend he did not because he fulfills Edna's request and enlarges the corner of the image. "Hmm… There's a fragment of dark blue, but it's very limited," he notes.

"Just as I thought," she nods. "And it's not just any blue, but 'ultramarine blue,' a pigment obtained by grinding lapis lazuli imported from what they would have called the Orient, the lands beyond the sea. In fact, the word 'ultramarine' means 'beyond the sea.' And for this reason, it was a very expensive pigment."

"Is that a problem?"

"No, but rather a sort of clue, if we want to put it that way."

"A clue?" Leonardo's eyes widen. He seems to be enjoying himself. The brunette continues her "concert for sighs" and refills her champagne glass while reinstalling herself on the sofa.

"In the past, especially during the Middle Ages, the choice of colors was never a matter of chance or the artist's personal taste." Edna takes off her glasses to clean them with her sweater sleeve. "The artist didn't paint for his own pleasure, but almost exclusively on commission. Let's say we have a client, who can be a prince, a banker, a religious congregation, the pope, or anyone else. What matters is the prestige that the artwork confers upon those who commission it. And how is prestige measured?" she asks, as if she were facing one of her students during an examination.

"Fame?" he guesses, with little conviction.

"Not at all," she shakes her head, "It was how much you spent. In short, art had to showcase talent and genius, of course, but at the same time, it had to clearly show how much it cost. And for this reason, the final decisions about almost everything belonged to the people who paid the bills. Choosing materials was always a key consideration."

"I don't follow," he frowns.

"That's because today, if you go into an art store and buy a tube of ultramarine blue, you pay the same price as you would for any other shade of blue. However, in the fifteenth century, the price difference between azurite blue and ultramarine blue was the same as the difference between wine-in-a-box and a magnum of Dom Pérignon. And back then, people could tell which one you had used just by looking. Do you get the idea?"

"Quite well, indeed," he nods.

"Good. Then you'll also see that the choice of one color over another, at that time, conferred a big leap in social status. Take Brunelleschi, for example, the artist who designed the dome of Santa Maria del Fiore in Florence. Nowadays, we regard him as a great and inspired architect, but his relationship with the Medici was akin to our relationship with the plumber who renovates our bathroom: We hire him to do the work, but we want to choose the tiling and fixtures ourselves."

"I must admit, I had never considered art in these terms," Leonardo rubs his chin, clearly amused. "So, coming back to this small fragment of blue? Obviously, this has real significance, at least to you. As for me, well, it merely reminds me of the color of the sky on certain spectacular September days… and the t-shirt I wear to the gym."

"Exactly," she nods appreciatively. Her young friend seems to have a keen eye. "Or the color of the sky depicted on the ceilings of churches. In fact, the most influential patrons of the fourteenth and fifteenth centuries were merchants and bankers, and their prosperity, as you can imagine, primarily came from usury, or in more colloquial terms, loan sharking. These people made money through interest accumulated over time. But, since the control of time is God's prerogative, utilizing time to earn money was considered a grave sin… And in the fourteenth and fifteenth century, eternal damnation was something people took very seriously, even bankers. Do you remember Savonarola?"

"Oh yes, 'remember, brother, that you must die!'" he chuckles. "So, what were you saying about eternal damnation?"

"Well, for example, Dante punishes Reginaldo Scrovegni in his *Inferno* in the circle of usurers. His son, who was also a banker, commissioned Giotto to decorate the family chapel which included twenty-six-hundred square feet of ultramarine blue on the ceiling. Clearly, he thought he and his family had a lot to atone for! Nobles, merchants, and bankers were always trying to save their souls by dedicating part of their wealth to charity or to the glorification of God through art. And the more they spent, the smoother their path to Paradise became. Or at least, that's what the Church told them."

"This means that the blue triangle in the lower right…"

"…was probably a piece of clothing, likely a robe. And a robe painted with extravagantly-expensive ultramarine blue was typically reserved for just one person." Edna removes her glasses once again and crosses her arms. "A young woman who emerged from obscurity, seemingly without a past, yet is widely known in every corner of the world. Someone who has inspired artists of all kinds, in every culture and country. Arguably, the most beloved and popular figure in history. Someone who has influenced the behavior and choices of people around the world."

"Taylor Swift?"

"Close, Mary, God's influencer," she chuckles.

He stares at her, squinting his eyes, not entirely sure if he understands. "Do you mean Mary, as in the Virgin Mary?"

"Exactly, but the term 'God's Influencer' is not mine; I borrowed it from Pope Bergoglio. However, it is a perfect definition from a historical, sociological, and artistic standpoint," she says, leaning back and stretching her legs. "Starting from the late Middle Ages, the ultramarine blue robe becomes her exclusive privilege. And this suggests another hypothesis."

A slight noise catches their attention, and they both turn towards the sofa where Leonardo's brunette friend has given up and is now snoring softly with her face against the cushions.

"Um, sorry about that…" Edna says, leaning forward to look at her, almost tenderly. "It's a shame that all that good Franciacorta has gone to waste."

Leonardo shakes his head, torn between regret and resignation. "Well, the night is still young. At least she didn't just leave. I'll make it up to her once I get rid of you. But you're right about the Franciacorta." He gets up, grabs the bottle, and places it on the desk. "What did you say about another hypothesis?"

"It's evident that the two individuals in dark robes are in the company of someone else, presumably the Madonna. However, she's not visible. And now we come to my hypothesis… Do you mind opening the other image, the one of the back of the panel, and enlarging it as much as you can? Yes, just as I thought." She points her finger at two round holes. "The panels were often fastened together on the back with wooden pegs to create a smooth surface."

"But the pegs are no longer there."

"Indeed. The peculiar thing, though, is that it wouldn't have made sense to use them on a panel of this size. They were meant for much larger installations. Unless we're dealing with something different…" Edna continues, pouring herself a generous glass of Franciacorta. "Because these holes, along with the presence of a piece of the missing Madonna's robe, suggest that this panel was part of a polyptych – a series of individual panels joined together to form a single artwork inserted into a frame. A polyptych that has been disassembled. Not to mention that someone, more recently, has added brown robes to these figures."

"But why would someone go to such lengths?"

"I imagine it was done to make sure it wouldn't be recognized and to make it pass as the work of a mediocre painter. It would also ensure that no one would connect it with the other missing pieces and, consequently, prevent any potential attribution. As you can imagine, it's one thing to sell or auction off a portion of something that, although very old, you don't know what is exactly. It's an entirely different matter to know that you have a portion of a Beato Angelico or a Simone Martini in your possession. Can you fathom the value of such a work, if it's authentic?"

"It would be too many zeros to even think about… If you're right, people would die to have this painting. Or kill for it, wouldn't you say?"

"Yes," sighs Edna, feeling a little sick to her stomach. It looked like she would be doing her civic duty after all.

Chapter Twenty-Two

PP Jacopo Bassi shuts down his laptop and moves it to the small table nearby, massaging the bridge of his nose with his fingertips. It's very late, and his investigation hasn't made any progress since the afternoon. The body of Nando Folli, a fifty-one-year-old single man residing in Cicagna and owner of an antiques warehouse and workshop on Gattorna's state highway 225, was discovered this morning in the aforementioned premises. He had a severe head contusion, a large wound on his temple, and his trousers were dropped down to his ankles. That, of course, is the detail that most puzzles Bassi.

How should he interpret it? A sex crime? Perhaps a killer's signature? He snorts. It seems unlikely. That sort of thing usually involved severed tongues and gouged eyes. What sort of self-respecting killer would want to be knows as the "moon murderer?"

On top of that, the victim dealt in "antiques." But from what Bassi can gather, he seems to have been just a half-step above a junk dealer. Trading in the sort of tat Folli dealt with did not draw the attention of the mafia and the kind of people who could have you killed. Unless he had stumbled upon something out of his league and had gotten too big for his britches. PP Bassi snorts again.

He sighs and sinks back into his chair. Dr. Edna Silvera, the art historian and restorer, respected, if not exactly famous, throughout Europe. Was her involvement, if you could call it that, really the odd coincidence that it seemed? And, if it wasn't, why show up at Folli's shop with a local politician?

PP Bassi had a thing about art and his mind always went into overdrive whenever the slightest connection reared its head. And in this case, it wasn't just Silvera. Folli appeared to be little more than a dealer in second-hand furniture but who knew what was hiding in that mess he called a shop? Folli did, of course, but he was no longer in a position to tell anyone.

Bassi's obsession with the world of stolen artwork went back to a case he had handled earlier in his career. And for a while, it consumed him. He hadn't eaten. He hadn't slept. Not properly, anyway. He had

had no social life. And then the case hit a dead end. And it was closed, just like that. A file of evidence – a file he had painstakingly compiled – as thick as a dictionary, sent off to the archives, never to be seen again. And Bassi, of course, was supposed to be a good little investigator and just move on to the next case. To forget about it as if it had never happened.

He couldn't do that. Once he got his teeth into something like that, he hated leaving loose ends, things unfinished. It was just the way he was.

The case involved a network of seemingly innocent professionals. They were entrepreneurs, bankers, art restorers, shipping brokers – even government officials – all involved in the illicit trading of Italian artworks. It was a massive enterprise. And all his work had come to nothing.

Or maybe not. Bassi could never take good advice when it came to leaving well enough alone so he had arranged to get the file into the hands of someone he knew at Tutela Patrimonio Culturale – the office for the Protection of Cultural Heritage. That was something, at least.

Bassi wrenches his thoughts back to his current case. There was no official autopsy report yet, but the coroner was pretty confident that the time of death was between seven and eleven the previous evening. The sign on the door said the shop closes at 5:30pm and the locals he had interviewed had said Folli was far more likely to close the shop early than stay late. So what was Nando Folli doing in his workshop at that time of night?

That suggests that whoever killed him knew he would be there and had gone to meet him. Was it a specific appointment? They had Folli's mobile phone and he was confident that the tech team would be able to unlock it. Maybe, despite its odd features, this case would be easy to crack after all.

PP Bassi stands up from his chair and stretches his back. He knows – how he knows! – that it's not healthy to bring his work home. But sometimes, he can't help himself.

Because he really, *really* dislikes leaving things unfinished.

Chapter Twenty-Three

It's not yet dawn, and the road, houses, hills, and sky blend into shades of pinkish gray.

Edna steps out of her car and inhales the air filled with scents of earth, wet asphalt, and dew. She closes the car door and walks purposefully toward the agreed meeting place.

"Ah, here you are. Did you have a hard time finding me?" Councilor Repetto rises from the ground, brushing off the dirt from her trousers.

"None," Edna replies. How could she? Orietta Repetto's hair is a shining beacon amidst this gray monochrome, making her impossible to miss.

"Good. If you're ready, we can start." she says with her usual no-nonsense attitude while heading toward the dark building.

"Are you sure you want to do this, Orietta?" Edna asks, catching up to her. She would prefer not to involve the councilor in this. "I know this was your idea, but please don't feel obligated to…"

"Are you kidding, Edna? Deprive myself of this? Why do you think I suggested it?" Orietta unlocks the metal door, which creaks ominously, yielding as it turns on its hinges. "Here we go, I'll lead the way," says the councilor, stepping inside and switching on the flashlight she brought with her.

They walk along a narrow, mold-dampened hallway and emerge in a storage room filled with worn-out boxes and folders, likely untouched by human hands for decades.

"Fifty years ago, the Land Registry office rented this place to serve as a warehouse for archived files destined for destruction. As administrations came and went, the original plan was shelved and forgotten." explains Orietta, scanning the dismal monument to bureaucratic inertia with her flashlight. "Don't ask me how I know about this place. Let's just say that before becoming a councilor, I was involved in extermination. Anyway, here we are. Could you hold the flashlight for a moment? This is going to be the hard part." The councilor removes a sturdy screwdriver from her pocket and examines the padlocked door in front of her. "Hmm. I was going to take apart the latch, but perhaps there's an easier way." She inserts her screwdriver into the hasp and wrenches it away from the door with a dry splintering sound. "After you!"

Edna is enveloped by the familiar scent of old wood, linseed oil, turpentine, and dust. As she enters the workshop-laboratory of the late Nando Folli, she tries to push aside thoughts of the various crimes she's committing, breaking and entering, trespassing, tampering with a crime scene… There may be others, but these are enough to land her in prison for quite a while, not to mention what it would do to her career. Well, she straightens her back while inhaling deeply, it seems like I'm already on the bike, so I might as well pedal.

"So, we're looking for a painting on wood, right?" the councilor asks.

"That's correct. However, while I've expressed my disappointment to you for not being able to get my hands on it to analyse it properly, it's another thing to know that by doing so, I'm exposing you to the risk of getting into trouble. I'm truly grateful, Orietta, but from this point on, I can manage on my own, really! Why don't you get out of here?"

"Ha! No chance! Anyway, I doubt very much we'll get caught. There's hardly a soul for miles, much less anyone awake at this time. We've left the seals on the door untouched, and as I mentioned earlier, this passage at the back of the shop is known only to me, a few old rats, and possibly Folli. Folli is dead, my lips are sealed, and I'll take my chances with the rats." The councilor spreads her arms wide. "Relax, Edna. Enjoy the adventure."

"Very well," Edna sighs, advancing cautiously. The panel we're looking for was next to a Chippendale chest of drawers. It's where I was standing when you found Folli's body."

"So, if we retrace our steps…" says the councilor, bouncing through the aisles with the agility of a pinball, "could this be the chest of drawers you're referring to?" she asks, pointing the torch.

Edna cranes her neck to follow the beam of light. "It looks like it to me, yes." She bends down to move some boards and there, exactly where she had hastily hidden it the morning before, she finds the panel. She delicately unwraps it.

"So, this is it," the councilor observes the painting, intrigued. "You'll need some sort of table to work on." She puts the flashlight under her arm and lifts one of the wider planks (and she does it as if it were a sheet of Styrofoam and not a three-finger-thick piece of wood, Edna notes) placing it across the chest of drawers and a nearby shelf.

"Here's your workbench," she says, leaning on it with both hands to test its stability. It's a bit dusty," she admits, wiping her palms on her thighs, "but you don't seem to mind things like that. I'll hold the flashlight so you can see what you're doing."

"Thank you very much, Orietta." Edna squints her eyes and very gently runs her fingertips over the surface of the panel, detecting reliefs, protrusions, and irregularities. "Just as I thought," she nods, moving her fingers as if she were reading in Braille. "The brushstrokes on the robes are materially different from the rest of the painting. Would you like to feel it too?"

"Can I?"

"Close your eyes." Edna takes her hand to guide her. "Focus on the sensations: smooth, silky, polished, porous, rugged, rough… can you feel it?"

"Uh, yes, it's different here. I would say more rippled, almost rough," says the councilor, getting excited.

"Exactly," Edna confirms, pulling out a pair of glasses from her purse and placing them on the tip of her nose. "And now, while I wouldn't do this in a properly-equipped laboratory, let's try the 'manual' method." She takes her thumbnail and gently touches the upper corner of the background. She nods and repeats the process on the suspicious robes.

"Isn't that really more of a rule of thumb?" chuckles the councilor.

Edna smiles. "It's a little imprecise, but with some experience, it can provide a good indication. It's a quick test used to determine the resistance of the paint layer to penetration. Listen carefully." Edna taps her fingernail here and there on the panel. "The sound is different because the paint solidifies over time and becomes stiffer. The older it is, the harder it gets, and the sharper the sound. So a fingernail will encounter more difficulty penetrating an older layer than a newer one. Keep in mind that we're talking about distinguishing modifications that took place centuries apart, not weeks."

"And what do you conclude from all this?"

"That my initial hypothesis was correct. Sometimes, in the middle of painting, an artist will change his or her mind and paint over something they've already done. Most often, it's a design change rather than a mistake. That's called a *pentimento*, which translates as something like 'a repentance.' But that's not what this is. These robes were definitely added a long time after the painting was originally done."

"How much time is a long time after?"

"Well, in terms of style and the hardness of the paint layer, this panel could easily date back to the mid-fifteenth century, in the middle of the late Gothic period. Whereas the robes… If I had to guess based on my experience…" Edna tests the two different areas of the panel again with her fingernail. "I would say… Taking into account the type of pigment used… There could be no less than five centuries between them."

"Which would mean they were probably added sometime in the first half of the twentieth century," the councilor observes, narrowing her eyes. "Now who would do a thing like that in the midst of war and depression?" asks the councilor, already knowing the answer.

Edna sighs. "You know very well, who. The rise of Hitler and the Third Reich saw a massive art exodus. The Nazis were looting important art works from across Europe with the help of collaborating dealers, officials, and scholars."

"So, do you think painting over the robes could have been a German ploy to take the panel out of Italy?"

"It seems hardly necessary. Göring, Hitler's art-looting henchman, had no need to resort to subterfuge. He simply took what he wanted. Who was going to stop him? No, I'm more inclined to think this is related to the period after the 1947 Treaty of Paris," Edna caresses the panel, lost in thought. "The period when Rodolfo Siviero tracked down hundreds of looted masterpieces and was able to return them to Italy, often from high-ranking Nazi officials who had fraudulently 'purchased' them before the end of the war."

"So you think it was an attempt to hide the panel to avoid having to return it?"

"Yes. Or perhaps an attempt to smuggle it out of the country by disguising it as something pedestrian and of little value. That it's part of a larger artwork that's been dismembered makes me think there's a complicated story here." Edna puts on her glasses again, turns the painting over, and runs her hand over the back. Then she lifts it up to examine it from the side. "It looks like poplar wood. If so, it's likely that our artist is Italian. Generally, artists used different kinds of wood depending on the region: oak or fir for Flanders and Northern Europe, walnut for France, pine for Spain… All these little details help us build up a complete picture — no pun intended — and to identify fakes and forgeries."

"Wow, I had no idea this was all so complicated. It almost makes you want to root for the forgers!" responds the councilor, leaning over to examine the panel more closely.

"Well, yes, a good forger is a true art expert. But forgeries are like lies and gossip — they always find someone ready to believe them and spread them. It's also true, however, that masterpieces are difficult to forge. And I assure you, the artist who painted this panel was not untalented."

Edna turns the panel over once again and observes the painting: the delicate realism of the two faces, the refined details of the leaves against the golden background and…

"If you say so. It seems a little random to me. For example, what is that whitish thing peeking out from under the robe of the man on the far right?" the councilor points with her finger.

Edna grabs her hand which is holding the flashlight and steadies the beam on the spot in question. She stares and mutters something unintelligible and very rude under her breath. "If that's what I think it is," she says bleakly, "then I was wrong. This isn't a painting of a Madonna in Majesty."

The councilor looks at her with a puzzled expression but, for once, keeps her comments to herself as Edna rummages in her jacket pocket and retrieves a small dark glass bottle along with a cotton swab.

"I would have preferred to avoid this, but…" She dips the swab into the liquid and quickly passes it over the brown corner of the robe.

"What the…" the councilor exclaims, peeking from under Edna's elbow. Her surprise is so great that she can no longer contain herself. "But that's…"

"Yes," sighs Edna, taking off her glasses and leaning back against the shelf behind her, suddenly feeling immensely tired. "That's exactly what it is. An egg. A white egg."

Chapter Twenty-Four

"Now you'll explain to me," Public Prosecutor Bassi interlaces his hands under his chin, "why you, Dr. Silvera, having found yourself by pure chance in a shop you claimed never to have visited before and having discovered the owner's corpse in a pool of blood just two shelves away from you, decided to browse the merchandise… and take pictures of your favorite items. Please enlighten me; I'm all ears."

Edna stares at him with irritation. But if she's honest with herself, she admits that most of it is directed at herself. She's been blundering from one idiotic decision to the next lately. And the most mind-numbingly stupid she's made in a very long time is listening to her conscience and coming clean to PP Bassi rather than shutting up and minding her own business.

"I wasn't aware that Folli was a corpse, at the time," she scoffs finally. "You've seen the place, haven't you? Yes, it's a junk shop crammed with all sorts of stuff, but it piqued my curiosity. In all that mess, I sensed a good 'eye.' While admiring a chandelier with gilded arms, I accidentally backed into a partially-dismantled chest of drawers, causing all the wooden boards leaning against it to topple over. And as I was picking them up, I came across this painted panel. For God's sake, I've been studying art for over thirty years. You should be suspicious if I didn't instantly notice this painting. And those faces, so delicate and refined, that didn't match those cursed robes. And then there were the colors. So I took out my phone and snapped a picture so I could study it later. Right at that moment Councilor Repetto discovered Folli's body. After that, an old painting, no matter how intriguing, fell off the radar. I completely forgot about it until I got home and had a glass of wine. Look, Mr. Bassi, don't you think that if I were being anything but honest with you I would have just kept everything to myself? Why on earth would I have come here to tell you?"

"I have no idea. You tell me," the prosecutor responds, cracking his sinister, gleaming smile.

"Perhaps you are not quite as intelligent as I had assumed," says Edna, as if she were addressing an intentionally-obtuse student. "I have just informed you that Nando Folli had been keeping, hidden beside an old piece of furniture, a painting that likely belongs to a 15th-century polyptych. That is quite remarkable enough. But I have reasons to believe that this isn't an ordinary 15th-century polyptych. Rather, it is a very specific work of art by an old master. If my suspicions are correct, Folli had something in his shop so valuable that it could easily have gotten him killed. And you, too, if it comes to that. Do I make myself clear?"

"Perfectly," nods the public prosecutor. "However, if I am not mistaken, Folli is dead, yet the painting in question is still there. How do you explain this?"

"I don't. That would be your job. Perhaps the killers couldn't find it. After all, there's a lot of junk in the shop. I only discovered it by accident. It was concealed but in a conspicuous place, hiding in plain sight, if you will. If you were searching his shop for a hidden masterpiece worth a fortune, you'd be there a long time before you looked under a stack of old boards leaning against a broken dresser," she shrugs.

"Hmm. It does appear plausible. However, the fact remains that you not only discovered it, but also made the effort to photograph it from all angles. In essence, Dr. Silvera, it could be a random coincidence that you happened to be in Fontanabuona; another coincidence that you ended up at Folli's workshop shortly after someone had killed him; yet another coincidence that you found the painting, and yet another that you felt compelled to photograph it… That's a lot of coincidences." says Bassi, shaking his head as he leans back in his elegant and very comfortable leather office chair.

Edna crosses her arms and leans back as well, but her chair, undoubtedly a designer piece made of a peculiar Plexiglass material, is unquestionably the most uncomfortable seat in Bassi's entire office. Nonetheless, she gazes at him placidly, the image of a righteous soul at rest that cares nothing for the opinion of the world – or PP Bassi.

"And you deduced all of this – the period, attribution, and authenticity of the painting – just from a few photos taken with a phone in a dimly lit warehouse? I knew you were excellent at your job, but this is almost miraculous," he remarks, smoothing his already flawless hair and resting his chin on his hands while staring at her intently.

"Consider it merely a well-founded hypothesis," she says, meeting his gaze. "My conclusions were drawn from chromatic comparisons, pictorial elements, and a certain eye developed through a lifetime of experience… But that's a preliminary analysis subject to further examination of the actual physical painting." She damned well won't be mentioning conniving councilors, land registry office oversights, secret passages, and early morning break-ins.

"I'm not sure if you're presenting me with a motive, a lead, or offering your assistance, Dr. Silvera."

"That's entirely up to you, Mr. Bassi," Edna shrugs once more. "None of this is really any of my concern. I simply felt it my civic duty to bring my theory to your attention and suggest that if what I believe is true, it would be appropriate to remove the panel from Folli's shop and transfer it to a secure location. And with that, I bid you farewell and good day." Edna rises from the most uncomfortable chair on the planet, and makes her way toward the door of PP Jacopo Bassi's modern (albeit slightly pretentious) office, hoping never to set foot – or buttocks – there again.

"What's the rush, Dr. Silvera?" he says, rising from his chair. "I have a lot of questions about this enigmatic painted panel and even more about the elusive polyptych it originates from. And yes, I am well acquainted with both polyptychs and the late Gothic art of the 15th century. So, if you would kindly make yourself comfortable…" His smile is unnervingly bright and dangerous as he gestures toward the diabolical Plexiglass chair.

Edna glances at him, then at the chair, and finally at the door, wearing an exasperated expression. This is all grossly unfair. She had heard it said that no good deed goes unpunished but this is ridiculous.

"You know what?" he continues, "I will take you directly to the actual location so that you can assess the panel 'in person' and provide me with your expert opinion."

"When you say 'the actual location,' do you mean…" Edna stammers, caught off guard.

"Indeed, Folli's shop, where the painting still resides. Where else? You did offer your assistance. And if you're correct, we shouldn't delay. I'm sure you'll be pleased to have the opportunity to confirm your theory in person."

Ecstatic, Edna mutters to herself, trailing behind Prosecutor Bassi, engulfed in the scent of expensive aftershave and leather. Oh, she's simply ecstatic to drag herself back to Fontanabuona for the sixth time in the past twenty-four hours, serving as a tour guide for someone who, just ten minutes ago, labeled her a potential thief and murderer.

And what fun it will be explaining to Prosecutor Bassi how a square centimeter of one of the brown robes on the panel has mysteriously vanished overnight, making way for a white egg that certainly wasn't present in the photos she took at the crime scene!

Ecstatic, indeed.

Chapter Twenty-Five

"Have you heard of Locard?" PP Bassi asks, standing in Folli's shop next to the painting like an elegant Corinthian column.

"No, I don't think so," Edna replies laconically.

"He was a French criminologist, as well as the father of forensic medicine, and known for the famous Locard's Exchange Principle. No bells?"

"Nope," she repeats even more laconically.

"A pity," he smiles, caressing his chin pensively while showing off his perfect profile. "Locard says that every criminal leaves a trace at the crime scene and takes a trace away, in a sort of inevitable exchange."

"Mmh mmh," Edna says distractedly, recalling that yes, perhaps she had heard the name before. Right now, however, her attention is focused on devising a way to delete the photos she took the day the body was found and cursing herself for not doing it before since they are proof that damn egg was not visible on the panel. She had hoped to do it during the drive there, but she was forced to ride in the official police car, together with Bassi and an annoyed officer Capurro, who kept frowning at her from the rearview mirror the whole way. She did manage to speed dial her partner in crime, Orietta Repetto, hoping she would listen in on the conversation during the fifteen-mile drive back to Folli's warehouse. The most galling thing, even worse than the prospect of prison, was that Edna Silvera (two B.A.s, a degree from a school of specialization, a PhD, as well as more than thirty years of experience in the art field and a master schemer, especially at revenge) was foolish enough to rush to the prosecutor's office and blurt out the whole story of late-Gothic paintings, dismembered polyptychs, photos taken with a cell phone, and so on, without thinking that Bassi would, quite naturally, want to see her evidence. She bets that Locard's "Exchange Principle" didn't include criminals carrying around crime scene souvenirs in their pockets. She was an idiot!

She sighs.

"You seem distracted. Is something worrying you, Dr. Silvera?" Bassi inquires unctuously.

Edna shakes her head slightly, trying to appear bored and unconcerned. She's saved from further questioning by the insistent ringing of her phone. It's the cavalry coming to her rescue in the form of the resourceful Councilor Repetto.

"Edna, what's wrong? Why are you in a police car? Can you talk?"

"Very well, thank you, Councilor. What can I do for you?" responds Edna, irrelevantly.

"Do for me? I assumed you were in some sort of trouble and needed my help."

"Yes, I do have that list of names we talked about. Do you need it right away? I'm a little busy just now."

"List of names? What are you... Oh shit, you left those damn photos on you phone, didn't you?" There is a suspicious gurgle of barely-controlled laughter in the councilor's voice.

"Oh. In that case, I might have them on my phone. It might take me a few minutes to find them but if I have them, I'll send them to you right away.

"Yes, please do," the councilor responds, finally playing along. "We can't really proceed without them."

Edna steps away implying the need for a little privacy while trying not to arouse suspicion. "Oh dear. Was Dr. Santi Niboni very upset?"

"Horribly. He was completely beside himself. We thought he might have a stroke." The councilor is now playing along a little too enthusiastically.

"No, it's no trouble. I'm sorry for the confusion. Yes, I'll get them to you as soon as I hang up."

"Thank you. Dr. Santi Niboni will be so pleased. Best to PP Bassi!" replies the councilor, hanging up.

"I'm sorry, Mr. Bassi. Academic crisis. This won't take a minute. If you'll excuse me?" bluffs Edna.

"Certainly," PP Bassi says, distractedly, without taking his eyes off the painted panel.

"Thank you," Edna nods, as she unloads fifteen weighty images from her phone. Her self-respect is still burdened by the weight of her mistakes. She knows that she will only really get away with this if Bassi is an idiot with the memory of a tree squirrel – something she strongly doubts – but at least there is no longer any tangible evidence against her.

"We were discussing Locard's Exchange Principle," he continues nonchalantly, bending down to sniff the panel in several places. He finally focuses his full attention on the lower right corner where the white egg, to Edna's eyes, shines like a searchlight.

"Well, you were discussing it. I believe you said it was the inevitable exchange between two things that come into contact?" replies Edna, crossing her arms. Seeing him sniffing around the spot where she worked earlier this morning does not bode well.

"Exactly," he smiles with his pearly whites, looking at her with his ominously benevolent gaze, "and as I was saying, perhaps it would have been useful for you to remember it when… last night? Or perhaps early this morning? Yes, I would think early this morning."

"Excuse me?" Edna says, narrowing her eyes.

"May I?" he leans in, disregarding her question, gently grabbing her wrist to turn her hand to the side. "You see this?" he points to a streaked brown stain on her little finger. "I noticed it this morning when you were in my office, but I attributed it to a bit of carelessness, assuming it was a residue from breakfast, like chocolate or coffee."

Edna waits in silence.

"Then I started examining this peculiar painting, and almost unconsciously, I noticed how much these robes, which seem to trouble you so much, have the exact same color as the stain on your hand. Not to mention," he brings his nose close to her hand and sniffs. "Just as I suspected," he smiles lethally, releasing her wrist. "So if I'm not mistaken, we have here," the prosecutor concludes, folding his hands under his chin, "a color that has transferred from the painting onto you, and a scent of solvent that has transferred from you to the painting. Do you now see the relevance of Locard's Exchange Principle?" he asks, professorially.

Once again, Edna shakes her head, somewhere between a maybe and a perhaps, with the polished nonchalance of someone who had hoped to actually get away with it but deep down knew she would be caught. It had been a good try with the photos, though.

"I must admit that without that revealing stain, I probably wouldn't have noticed anything," Bassi crosses his arms, leaning against the shelf next to Edna. "With your well-known expertise, you removed that small portion of the robe with surgical precision, to the extent that the painting appears to have been created like this, with that incongruous white egg placed at the feet of that slender figure. And now, the most important question arises: what motivated you, Dr. Silvera, to come here early this morning, secretly work on that painting, and reveal what the robe was concealing? And this leads to the second, even more intriguing question: unless your undoubted skills include walking through walls, how did you manage to sneak in here without breaking the police seals? Please, I'm all agog. You have my undivided attention."

Edna's phone begins ringing again but she doesn't even glance at it. Nothing can save her now except for an asteroid striking the earth, and, with any luck, PP Bassi. Edna unconsciously shifts slightly to her left, just in case.

But no sweet meteor of death is going to save her. And Bassi is patiently staring at her, waiting for an explanation.

Chapter Twenty-Six

Edna says nothing because there is nothing she can say without throwing her partner in crime, Councilor Repetto, under the bus. PP Bassi finally breaks the now-intolerable silence. "How about this, Dr. Silvera," he says, with the ghost of a smile. "You tell me every detail about this painting and its surrounding context," he continues, "so that I can assess whether it can be somehow linked to Mr. Folli's passing. Naturally, I require your full and enthusiastic cooperation. In return for that cooperation, I will refrain from asking how you gained access to this place and who assisted you." Bassi already has his suspicions in this regard but he is only one man and tangling with both Edna and the councilor would be a full-time job. He does not really suspect Edna's involvement in this case and overlooking her "enthusiasm" is a small price to pay for solving Folli's murder, if murder it was. "Do we have a deal, Doctor?" he asks, extending his hand.

Edna hesitates, taking her time to ponder the offer, her expression suggesting a strong desire to be anywhere else. Finally, with some reluctance, she shakes his hand and sighs.

"Excellent!" he nods, pleased. "Shall we start with the reason that compelled you to return here to examine the painting? I assume it was something you noticed in the photographs you took yesterday…"

Edna shrugs and approaches the painted panel. "Yes, you're correct. When I looked at the photographs, I noticed some details that I thought deserved closer examination. I had no answers at that point, only questions. That is, in fact, the reason I came back here without asking you first. Had I come into your office and demanded the opportunity to experiment on the painting because the monks were wearing brown robes, you would have thought I was a lunatic. Because that is where my suspicions began, the color of the robes – the brown hue that you observed as a stain on my hand."

He nods and smiles encouragingly at her.

"It's a color that originated in Northern Europe," she continues, caressing the panel with her fingertips. "It is primarily composed of organic matter, and later became known as 'Van Dyck brown.' This pigment only began to appear on artists' palettes long after the execution of this painting. I needed to determine whether these figures were 'dressed' in their robes, let's say, in the seventeenth century, a time when this brown color started to gain widespread usage, or in a later period. The only way to find out was by directly examining the panel."

"And what did you discover?"

"That these robes were painted at least five centuries later, probably between the two World Wars, give or take a year."

"From your tone, I assume this is an important fact?"

"Perhaps," Edna shrugs again. "It depends on the perspective you take."

He stares at her, waiting.

"As you can probably imagine, it's too early to say. More detailed and in-depth examinations are necessary. I have a lot of experience, but I'm not a psychic, by God!" She rolls her eyes. "However, the period between the two wars was a terrible time for the artistic heritage of Europe as a whole. Starting with Hitler and his desire to create the world's largest Museum of Fine Arts in Linz, as well as his own personal collection. His mania for collecting was shared by both Göring and Himmler. Göring, in fact, was so obsessed with symbols and myths that he would organize parties in his castle on the outskirts of Berlin, dressed as an ancient Roman."

"That's… eccentric."

"Indeed. You don't know the half of it. Göring was mentally disturbed, even by Nazi standards, a man whose relationship with works of art almost became a sexual obsession. As for his sexual activities, he engaged in them with his second wife, yes, but also and above all with other 'priestesses' of the Reich, all under the indifferent gaze of Titian's *Danaë*, a voluptuous naked woman languidly lying on the bed, ready to welcome Zeus' golden rain between her thighs. Göring had stolen this painting from the Neapolitan museum of Capodimonte to hang it in his bedroom. Do you get the idea?"

"Quite, yes," he admits, both curious and amused. "But how does all of this relate to our painting, in your opinion?"

"At first, I thought it was a post-World War II subterfuge. During that time, numerous initiatives arose to systematically recover artworks confiscated by high-ranking Nazis before the end of the war. I thought this was probably one of the many Enthroned Madonnas stolen from various Italian churches. Perhaps a polyptych that had been dismembered during the Nazi era and subsequently disguised to be sold piece by piece, or to hide the identity of the original work. It's easier to smuggle – and sell – an unknown or mediocre work of art than it is a famous one."

"But instead…? From your tone, it seems like you changed your mind."

"It's because of this," she points to the white egg glowing in the lower right corner of the panel. "In fact, I specifically cleaned that corner of the robe to verify what was there."

"And why would the presence of an egg, as incongruous as it is, be so important?"

Edna yawns and leans back on the shelf, confirming the prosecutor's suspicion that she did indeed wake up early that morning.

"It's a rather long story," she warns him, without much enthusiasm. "So I'll try to keep it short. In Greek mythology, from the egg of Leda, fertilized by Zeus who had transformed into a swan for the occasion, two sets of twins of different sexes were born: the famous Castor and Pollux, and Helen and Clytemnestra. For the Greeks, they represented the two poles of creation. Christianity, as it often did, adopted pagan traditions, appropriating the egg as a symbol of resurrection. In fact, do you know where the entire Easter egg tradition comes from?"

"Aah, I see!" Bassi exhales, fascinated. He had never thought about eggs in quite this way.

"In the Middle Ages, it was customary to distribute blessed boiled eggs in church as a symbol of the risen Christ, for example. But along with Christian doctrines, there were more esoteric traditions around the egg as well. In alchemy, for example, the symbol of the egg is very significant. First and foremost, it is the archetype capable of restoring every element to its original purity. That's why the famous philosopher's stone, sought after by alchemists, was…"

"Egg-shaped," he supplies, proud of himself.

"Exactly," she nods, unimpressed. She had practically handed him the answer on a silver platter. "This is partly because the shell, the egg white, and the yolk – the three elements of the egg – reflect the three alchemical stages of Nigredo, Albedo, and Rubedo. These stages culminate in the *Magnum Opus*, the great work of creating the philosopher's stone. But it's also because of the cosmological meaning symbolized by the egg: the vessel and the ancestral origin of life, the snake biting its tail, or even the cyclic resurrection of the phoenix from its ashes. Even the *Major Arcanum* in the Tarot deck, 'The World,' depicts a woman in the center of an egg-shaped wreath... So, as you can see..." she yawns again.

"Okay, I agree that the presence of the egg holds significant meaning. But I still don't understand why its presence led you to change your assumptions about the painting."

"Well, the presence of the egg indicates that these two figures in the painting are not in front of an Enthroned Madonna, as I initially assumed. Instead, they are in front of a *Pietas* – a dead Christ awaiting resurrection – enveloped, in fact, in an egg. But that's not all. Do you see this object in the hand of the figure on the left?"

Bassi approaches to take a closer look. "You mean the greenish stick?"

"Not a stick. A stem, to be precise, and with thorns, suggesting it's a rose stem. And if we imagine that the stem continues upward here," Edna traces the painting with the nail of her little finger, "what would appear over his shoulder is the top of a flower. White. So it's a white rose."

"I don't want to sound repetitive, Dr. Silvera, but once again, your tone implies this has significance."

"Well, do you recall Dante's 'White Rose of Paradise,' Mr. Bassi? The rose within whose petals the blessed reside? On its own, it may be unimportant, if it weren't for the presence of that cursed egg. Because the *Divine Comedy* was also considered a kind of metaphorical journey that led to the rose and the knowledge of God, through... Let's see if you've been paying attention."

"I bow to your superior wisdom." he says, opening his arms. She can sense his frustration.

"...through the three stages of alchemical transformation, the aforementioned Nigredo, which corresponds to Hell, Albedo – Purgatory – and Rubedo, Paradise. However, the rose also symbolizes the Grail."

"The Grail? As in 'Holy Grail'?" Bassi stares at her. This conversation was taking a lot of unanticipated twists and turns.

"Yes, the cup that collected the blood of Christ and carries the power of immortality. There are other symbolisms as well, such as the

Madonna being seen as a Grail since she carries the Son of God in her womb, and so on… But let's focus on the main point," Edna crosses her arms, suppressing another yawn.

"Yes. Let's." he presses, slightly annoyed because when it comes to being reticent, Dr. Silvera could give lessons to a mafia boss.

"Well, these are just my speculations, I repeat," she shrugs. "But in my opinion, this panel is one of what we call 'lost works of art.' Works of art for which we may have some drawings, descriptions, or images, but whose actual whereabouts are lost to history.

"And this is where I should circle back to Heinrich Himmler, Hitler's right-hand henchman. He was a small man with round glasses and the benign expression of a peaceful country train conductor. He served as the 'Reichsführer' of a school for the ideological education of SS officers. To fulfill this purpose, he chose the castle of Wewelsburg, near two significant places in ancient German mythology. He had it renovated by top architects of the Reich and an esotericism expert – yes, you heard correctly – to resemble the legendary castle of King Arthur, Camelot. It became one of the symbolic power centers of the Reich, with the specific goal of creating a racially pure German elite.

"Don't make that face, Mr. Bassi," she raises an eyebrow, "at least not yet, because you haven't heard the best part. Our dear Himmler, besides having his personal art museum, attempted to prove the Aryan lineage of Jesus and committed atrocious crimes to acquire anything he deemed useful for this purpose. Including works of art. As part of that, he searched tirelessly, gathering hypothetical traces left here and there over the centuries, to create a kind of 'map' that would lead him to what he believed was the greatest artifact of all time. Yes, it's true. Himmler was on a quest to find the Holy Grail." Edna nods, with the gravity of someone who knows they have just dropped a bombshell.

Bassi blinks, dumbfounded. All this talk of artwork, eggs, dead Christs, and roses was bad enough. But now he seems to have stumbled into a Monty Python film.

Chapter Twenty-Seven

The bright midday sky hits Edna in the face like a cannon shot. She squints as she pushes open the glass door of the ex-antiques dealer Folli's shop and finds herself entangled in police tape, lazily fluttering in the tepid September air.

"Oh, for the love of…" she mutters through her teeth, trying to free herself from the plastic tape but impeded by the cosmic weariness that engulfs her. Eventually, she struggles free, sighs, and leans against the wall. The nearly sleepless night and her early morning adventure are catching up with her. Once, a little thing like breaking-and-entering would not have phased her in the slightest. She sighs again. Perhaps she isn't as young as she used to be, she reflects. To make matters worse, in the excitement of the last couple of days, she has not even called to check if Ottavio is still alive or whether he has been beaten to death with a plastic bottle. Nor has she contacted the agency to find a new housekeeper to replace Kalina, as she had promised to do. That is going to be an adventure in itself as she suspects that Zara's reputation in the caretaker world far precedes her. Hopefully there is some far corner of the earth where Zara's fame as an absolute pain in the ass has not yet spread. Are there caretakers in Antarctica? she wonders.

She scans her surroundings, hoping to catch sight of the councilor's cherry-colored head off in the distance, but the only thing worth noting is the blue police car parked in the scarce shade of a hazelnut tree. She absently watches Agent Capurro diligently cleaning gnats from the windshield wipers, careful not to dirty his uniform. Eventually her gaze drifts across the street, where she can see a vaguely familiar thin woman walking briskly along the narrow sidewalk, head down. As the woman approaches, she suddenly stops and lifts her head.

Edna blinks and blinks again, attempting to focus on what her eyes have registered but her brain is refusing to process. Because the person now walking slowly toward Edna and Folli's shop is perhaps the last person on earth Edna had expected to see, here or anywhere.

"Kalina?!" Edna's voice echoes along the empty state highway like a pistol shot.

Kalina freezes.

From this point on, everything moves in slow motion: Kalina stops dead and stares at Edna. Then she turns and stares in the direction of a perplexed Officer Capurro, who is adjusting his uniform cuffs and staring at her in return. She then brings both hands to her face, freezing in a Munch-like silent scream, turns around, and begins to run.

Edna's eyes follow Kalina as she disappears around the bend. She turns to Officer Capurro, seeking confirmation that he, too, witnessed this apparition or if it was just her imagination. The policeman spreads his arms and taps his temple with his index finger. It may not be a favorable assessment of Kalina's sanity, but it does confirm that Edna's own sanity is thankfully intact.

"Forgive me, Dr. Silvera."

Edna jumps half out of her skin. She was so intent on the sudden appearance of Kalina that she had not realized that Bassi was now standing next to her.

"Ahh! I'm sorry. I thought you were still inside the shop!" she gasps.

"No. I'm sorry. I didn't mean to frighten you."

"I was preoccupied with something else and didn't expect to see you, that's all," Edna mutters, stealing one last glance at the curve where Kalina has disappeared.

"There is one question that I do need to ask you," he says, smiling, albeit with less flamboyance than usual. "I kindly request that you respond with equal precision and absolutely truthfully."

Edna imperceptibly raises an eyebrow. In the span of a single morning, this dandy had already insinuated she might be a potential thief, a potential murderer, and now a potential liar. "What question?" she retorts curtly.

"Can someone confirm that you were at your house between seven in the evening and midnight the day before yesterday? Perhaps a phone call, or…"

"No," she interrupts bluntly.

"Not even someone who might…" he suggests deferentially.

"I said no, Mr. Bassi," she yawns nonchalantly. Bassi is getting agitated so she decides to take pity on him. "No one can confirm I was at home because I was not at home."

"Ah," he gazes at her with narrowed eyes. "May I inquire where you were, if you don't mind?"

"You may."

Bassi sighs. He had asked for precision and absolute truth. "And where were you?"

"I was having dinner at my new neighbor's house, where I remained the entire evening before returning home… I can't pinpoint the exact time, but it was after midnight, I suppose."

Bassi looks at her, caught between astonishment and embarrassment. "And your neighbor is…"

"Sacco, Leonardo Sacco. He's an engineer," she provides helpfully.

"Thank you. Capurro, please make a note of this and forward it to Inspector Guerci for verification. Excellent," he smiles kindly, "and could Engineer Sacco confirm that you, Dr. Silvera, were indeed in his company?"

"I believe so."

"And what about last night?"

Edna looks at him quizzically. "What about last night?"

"Apparently, someone sneaked into Folli's yellow van – which we had sealed, though it was still parked in front of Folli's shop – and pushed it down the hill, where it crashed into a chestnut tree."

"Do you have any idea why?" Edna asks, still puzzled.

"Perhaps it was an unrelated attempted theft. Or maybe the intruder was searching for something important he thought was left inside, another piece of the famous polyptych…?" he stares directly at her. "And perhaps they attempted to make it appear as some sort of prank. So I need to know if anyone can confirm that you were at your house last night, let's say between 10 pm and midnight."

"No."

He looks at her with some annoyance. "I thought you spent the evening examining the photos of the painting you took."

"Yes, I did."

"And you were examining them by yourself?"

"No."

Bassi sighs. "Let me guess. You were not at home."

"Correct."

Bassi knows when he's beaten. "Dr. Silvera, perhaps a little less precision and a little more accuracy?"

"Very well. Shortly after 10 pm, I left my house and went to my neighbor's where I examined the photos using his computer. Then returned to my house well after midnight."

"I see." Bassi mutters, increasingly embarrassed.

"I doubt it. As you have guessed, I was visiting my neighbor, Leonardo Sacco."

"And, again, he will confirm this, I suppose."

"You suppose correctly, both he and his guest: a beautiful dark-haired girl whom, alas, I can't tell you much about except that she had a low tolerance for Franciacorta rosé."

PP Bassi slightly tilts his head and observes her, trying to assess whether she's jesting or not. Then his natural curiosity takes over. "And the three of you spent…" he calculates quickly, "more than two hours looking at images of a late Gothic painted panel with two men in brown robes and little else?" he asks, trying – and failing – to disguise his skepticism.

"Not exactly. The girl collapsed on the sofa after barely half an hour, perhaps succumbing more to boredom than the rosé, which she nevertheless drank with great enthusiasm. Leonardo and I, however, did delve into the matter a bit, it's true. The panel intrigued him, and you know how it goes… one thing leads to another," she shrugs, breezing past the rest with candid indifference.

"I can imagine," PP Bassi sighs, staring at his fingernails, not quite sure what to think.

"Is there anything else you need to know?" Edna asks brusquely. Councilor Repetto's Panda is pulling up and she prefers to wrap up this meeting before the prosecutor decides to grill her as well.

"Yes, there is one more thing," Bassi rests his chin on his clasped hands, a gesture Edna has now recognized as his affected habit, "Dr. Silvera, what comes to mind when you think of a blunt instrument with a broad, flat base capable of delivering a fairly uniform blow? Something that could possibly be found there, among Folli's belongings…"

"Nothing," Edna shrugs, eager to return to her house and leave Bassi to untangle this mess on his own. "There must be about five thousand cubic feet of stuff in there. I imagine there are any number of things that fit that description. Maybe it was a frying pan!" she laughs.

"A frying pan. Yes. Thank you." Bassi can't resist a smile in return. For all her faults, Dr. Silvera has a well-developed sense of the absurd.

"If you don't require my presence any longer, Mr. Bassi," Edna interrupts his musings, "I have a prior engagement."

"Certainly, my apologies, Dr. Silvera. Capurro will provide you with a ride to wherever you need to go."

"That won't be necessary," Edna interrupts, "I still have a few things to attend to here regarding the Dante event I mentioned earlier. I'll figure out a way to make my way back home. I'm sure I'll find a ride."

"As you wish. Please give my regards to Councilor Repetto," the PP says, nodding towards the Panda where Orietta is waiting patiently.

Edna forces a smile. She must remember that Bassi does not miss much.

Chapter Twenty-Eight

"So?" Orietta reaches out to open the car door for Edna.

"Boy, that Bassi is relentless, let me tell you!" Edna snorts as she fastens her seatbelt. "We could have spared ourselves the charade of that phone call. He'd already figured out that I had been there this morning."

"And?" Orietta prompts.

"And nothing," Edna sighs. "He offered me a deal: he won't ask how or *with whom*," she looks at Orietta meaningfully, "and in return, I agree to tell him everything I already know and will discover about the panel. I didn't really have the chance to think this through. It may completely blow up on me. But it's done now."

"Well, worst-case scenario, we'll enjoy a three to six-month vacation at the state's expense. It'll be like attending a particularly Spartan weight-loss spa! I don't know about you, but I could stand to lose a few pounds." opines the councilor, making such an enthusiastic U-turn that Edna momentarily regrets declining a ride with the grumpy Capurro. "Your buddy Bassi would almost be doing me a favor. Perhaps I'll go and turn myself in."

"If you put it like that, it doesn't sound so bad," Edna chuckles, stretching against the backrest. "So anyway, he took note of what we discovered about the panel, including the egg. Then he casually asked if I had an alibi for the evening Folli died and also for last night when someone apparently sent the yellow van belonging to the antiques dealer down the ravine."

"Yes, that's true. I saw the tow truck taking it away this morning after you left. And what about your alibi? Do you have one?" Orietta inquires.

"Are you asking because you're suspicious too?" Edna glances at her sideways, amused.

"Not at all. Although, I must admit, driving on a state highway with a serial killer sitting next to you could be one of those stories to tell your grandchildren." Orietta laughs while maneuvering the curves of the road as if it were a Formula One track. "I'm just curious as to whether you managed to satisfy him or whether you are now his prime suspect."

"I do have an alibi, Orietta, for both evenings in question. An alibi who stands six feet five inches tall and has a shoulder span of five feet."

"You go, girl!" The councilor leans towards Edna, gazing at her with genuine admiration while coming within a hairsbreadth of leaving a layer of her car spread over the guardrail.

Edna snorts. "It's not like that. Don't get any strange ideas, Orietta. He's just a neighbor. Just pleasant conversation and good wine, that's all. I have different tastes in men."

"Well I don't. If you happen to have any similar neighbors to spare, I'm more than happy to volunteer," the councilor swerves, narrowly avoiding a pedestrian innocently standing by the side of the road. "Any updates on Folli's death?"

"Not much. The prosecutor mentioned something about a blunt instrument as being the murder weapon. He wanted to know what I thought it might be, as if I would have any idea."

"What did you say?"

"A frying pan!"

The councilor laughs. "Considering that you have a solid alibi and managed to escape being charged with burglary and destruction of evidence, you still seem remarkably tense. What gives?"

"Nothing really. Well, there was one thing." Edna admits. "I'm not sure if I mentioned my mother's Romanian housekeeper, the woman who unexpectedly quit the day before yesterday."

"Not that I recall." says Orietta.

"Well, in short, I saw her, Kalina, walking on the sidewalk in front of Folli's shop just a little while ago."

"Really? That's an odd coincidence."

"Yes, but it wasn't just the oddity of running into her. It was what happened just *after* I saw her. Kalina stared at me, looked at Capurro, turned and took off running. It was like she was... Oh shit." Edna freezes, her eyes widening and her face displaying a mix of shock and realization.

"Edna?" the councilor leans closer. "What's wrong? Should I be worried?"

"The frying pan, Orietta, the frying pan!"

"I'm afraid I don't follow, Edna. Do you want us to stop for a moment? I might have some brandy in the trunk and..."

"Kalina wasn't staring at me. She was staring at Folli's shop that had been sealed off by police tape. And she wasn't looking at Capurro, she was looking at the police car. That's why I thought of a frying pan! Damn!"

"Sorry. Still not following." the councilor looks at Edna, growing increasingly confused. "What does your mother's ex-housekeeper have to do with..."

"It's the frying pan, Orietta! Kalina left my mother's house the day before yesterday with a suitcase and a ten-pound cast-iron frying pan. And now I find her, of all places, in front of Folli's shop in Gattorna, running for the hills from a murder scene that involved," Edna thought for a moment, "*a blunt instrument with a broad, flat base capable of delivering a fairly uniform blow. Now do you see?"*

"Well, when you put it that way, I can see the problem. Are you going to tell Bassi?"

Edna shakes her head in despair. It really is darkest before it's totally black.

Chapter Twenty-Nine

Marlena's baleful wrath hangs heavy like dark clouds before a storm. He is aware of it, despite not having seen her since he hastily fled through the back door, the one that leads to the lawn beneath the fig tree. Marlena only locks that door before going to bed, as she knows he never ventures near it. As everyone knows, it's a treacherous tree, and he knows it, too. He learned about it, just like he learned many other things, such as the Pythagorean theorem stating that in any right triangle, the square of the hypotenuse equals the sum of the squares of the legs, and that $E=mc^2$, and that on July 14, 1789, the French people stormed the Bastille, chanting *liberté égalité fraternité*, and that π equals 3.14159265358979. Now, he is returning from the hazel wood, feeling a little weary. Despite his awareness of the fig tree's treachery, he still ventured out through that door last night. Even though he feared the fig tree greatly – and Marlena even more – he had to fly away, and so he did.

He passes beneath the low wall that slopes down toward the stream, hidden from the road running just above it. He swivels his head quickly and cautiously because, as OMG always says, "A moment's distraction, a lifetime's destruction." He hasn't fully grasped the meaning of this yet, but he understands the significance of avoiding distractions. Always.

With two swift hops, he distances himself from the low wall, seeking refuge in the shade of the chestnut tree. However, the yellow van is no longer there. His round eyes survey the flattened grass and the tire tracks. They took it away this morning, he witnessed it. And he feels joy, yes, immense joy. Now he can finally return home; he is tired and famished. Marlena will scold him with her bulldozer voice. As he contemplates this, his fear of her surges back, surpassing his fear of the treacherous fig tree.

So, he chooses to linger here a while longer, finding solace in its perceived safety. There is a delightful fragrance in the air. The crickets and birds sing harmoniously, and the temperature is just right. The chestnut leaves display a pleasing shade of green, with not too much yellow. In essence, everything is finally proceeding smoothly, as if the troubles he witnessed on the road and beyond had vanished along with the yellow van.

He raises his head, scanning the pale blue sky that feels just right.

To an extent.

Because now, in the glaring midday brightness, the gray silhouette of a kite emerges, gliding in slow, silent circles. Then, with a gentle jolt, it makes a sharp u-turn, momentarily suspending itself in the white sky before swiftly diving and disappearing amidst the beech trees of Monte Caucaso.

Perhaps not everything vanished with the yellow van.

There he stands, as upright as a lamppost, gazing at the mountain without knowing what to do or, more importantly, what to think.

OMG's voice echoes again in his mind, "A moment's distraction, a lifetime's destruction." And he is well and truly distracted now, immensely distracted!

Marlena's baleful wrath, which unleashed countless misfortunes upon the Achaeans, has found him now. Her anger reverberates across the plains of Gattorna, a hundred, a thousand bulldozers.

Chapter Thirty

A yellow van and a frying pan. One is an important element in the case. The other, nothing more than a joke. And yet, they are both popping up in his thoughts at odd moments.

Bassi leans back, resting his shoulders against the chair and clasping his hands under his chin.

This bothers him. It bothers him that the damn van only really drew his attention after it inexplicably plummeted into a ravine and collided with a tree. At first, he had largely disregarded it, thinking it only notable as a product of poor aesthetic judgment. But it hadn't been pushed into a ravine because it was an eyesore, had it? What was so important inside that van?

And now, the frying pan. His intuition told him there was something there, even though a frying pan as a murder weapon was something out of a comic strip. Nonetheless, Dr. Silvera's quip, as ridiculous as it was, could not be ruled out.

He opens the folder containing the partial autopsy report, meticulously prepared by Inspector Guerci. Bassi appreciates Guerci; they share the same tenacious approach to investigations. And that's why, despite probably wondering why a prosecutor – who could delegate all the fuss of interrogations and inspections to others – wants to personally and meticulously examine the details of this case, Guerci refrains from asking questions and simply provides him the material he asks for.

Bassi carefully reads through the report, learning that Nando Folli, fifty-one years old, died between 8 and 10 pm two nights prior, on September 15, due to a head injury. Although, if he had continued with his normal lifestyle, he might well have died from a bleeding ulcer. Bassi wonders why Folli had not sought proper treatment and instead consumed heartburn tablets as if they were candy, as shown by the empty and half-empty Maalox blister packs found among his personal belongings.

He sighs and returns to reading about Folli's cause of death. From the initial examination, it appears that there were two traumas. One larger and more widespread to the forehead, significant but probably not fatal according to the pathologist. The other blow, however, was delivered to the temple. It was small but had fractured the skull. It would have been fatal.

He arranges the photographs on his desk.

Two blows to distinctly different areas of the head. This was puzzling enough. But then there was the question of Folli's pants having been pulled down without apparent reason. The coroner had confirmed that Folli had not engaged in any sexual activity around the time of his death. So despite appearances this crime probably did not involve sex.

Jealousy, perhaps, as suggested by Councilor Repetto? Or the more intriguing "artistic" angle proposed by Dr. Silvera?

Hm.

He returns to browsing through the folder, searching for what he had been waiting for. There it is, he nods as he retrieves the stapled pages. The inspector has also included the backup of Folli's phone records. Immediately preceding his death, the antiques dealer had received fifty-two messages from a certain "Franka." These messages ranged from endearing to intimidating. Besides Franka displaying a certain degree of bipolarity, there is enough evidence to accuse her of stalking. Fifty-two messages! Reading through his rare and cautious responses, Bassi develops some insight into Folli's ulcer. All considered, it seems a small price to pay for his involvement with this particular partner. Bassi only hopes that Folli never owned a rabbit. If Councilor Repetto can be believed, he had a habit of dating women who were already romantically involved. If this was an attempt to avoid excessive entanglement, it had failed spectacularly in Franka's case.

At first glance, you wouldn't have thought Folli was a ladies' man, but evidently, he had hidden charms. Otherwise, it is difficult to explain the extensive list of female names that appear on Folli's call list. However, Franka's persistence sets her apart from the rest of the contenders, and Bassi underlines her name and corresponding phone number, intending to further investigate her.

He flips through the pages again and, amidst the myriad of calls and messages from Franka, three items catch his eye. Two of them fall just before the time frame in which Folli's death is estimated to have occurred. The third has the number saved in the address book under the label "Pole," and he recalls Silvera suggesting a potential connection between the painted panel and Nazi raids. Apparently, Folli had difficulty remembering people by their actual names and often associated phone numbers with his personal menagerie of nick names, comprised of places, animals, birds of prey, food, and comic book characters. Bassi is intrigued by this mysterious "Pole" contact.

The other two phone calls came from a landline, apparently in Genoa. It's saved under the name "Filipponi," and appears frequently in Folli's call history. They spoke at 7:02 pm and again at 7:44 — these were the last two calls Folli made. There are other texts but they are all from the infamous Franka who appeared to have been on a sort of emotional bender. Her texts stopped at 7:14 except for one final one at 8:48, "You're a shitty asshole, don't ever call me again." In this, at least, Franka seems to have gotten her wish.

Bassi stretches and rises from his swivel chair. The sky burns with an epochal sunset, which he glimpses only as purple fragments between rooftops and tree branches from his office window. Silvera comes to mind again with her tales of painted eggs, old and new hues, dismembered polyptychs, presumed Madonnas, and her resolute determination to get to the bottom of it all. He wonders why someone like her, who appeared so unflappable, would become so involved in this, especially considering what happened twenty years ago, that ugly incident for which she was even sued. And yet, she jumped in with both feet, indifferent to the potential risk. Silvera was more lucky than smart. By all rights, her stunt should have landed her in a jail cell. Perhaps she had hoped he wouldn't notice. She must have a pretty dim view of his intelligence... Or perhaps not. Had she not discovered something so important that she felt compelled to come forward, she would, indeed, have gotten away with it. Neither the mystery panel or her free-lance investigation would have come to his notice at all. When you put it that way, you could say that she was more principled than smart.

That panel...

He steps away from the window and returns to the photographs.

What if they had been searching the van for the panel? If Silvera was right, the whole thing was way out of Folli's league. Perhaps he let something slip to the wrong people or tried to arrange a deal himself. Suppose someone set up a meeting with him at his shop (Filipponi, perhaps?) but the deal goes badly wrong and Folli gets killed. The murderer searches for the panel and doesn't find it – how could he, in that mess? – so he tries looking in the van.

But that doesn't explain why Folli wasn't wearing pants and it doesn't explain why the murderer waited twenty-four hours to search the van, especially when it had already been sealed by the police. But, OK, let's start with this as a working hypothesis.

How long had the panel been there? He closes his eyes and tries to concentrate, but no matter how hard he tries, he can't recall any detail that might suggest whether the panel had been in Folli's shop for a few hours or a few years. It's also true that Silvera had handled it extensively so even if there had been dust… He freezes.

"Of course!" he exclaims, rolling his eyes. Silvera! She had a keen eye and was very observant, at least when it came to art. Perhaps she could answer his questions about the condition of the panel when she had first seen it.

He picks up his cell phone and hesitates, weighing the pros and cons of calling her. Ultimately, his enthusiasm prevails. He dials her number and she answers.

His enthusiasm is not reciprocated.

Chapter Thirty-One

"Yes?" Edna growls into her phone, immediately on the defensive. What is it with Bassi today? She's had less-persistent – and more enjoyable – head colds.

"What can I tell you?" she snorts after Bassi explains his latest question. "The lighting was horrible, and there was dust everywhere. The panel was wrapped in a cloth, as you saw, a filthy scrap of cloth so dirty that it could stand on its own. Not to mention that Folli had wedged it in among a bunch of other wooden planks that had been there for who knows how long. In short, even if it had been there for only a matter of hours, considering what fell on it and rubbed against it, I really don't see how I could be of any help." Edna sighs and gazes at the carpet, trying hard not to be distracted by the two-hundred and sixty-five pounds wrapped in burgundy velvet sitting in front of her, making incomprehensible gestures and signs that she has no interest in trying to decode.

"Yes, Mr. Bassi, if anything comes to mind, I'll let you know. And yes, I remember our agreement from this morning," she rolls her eyes as the two-hundred-and-sixty-five pounds wrapped in burgundy velvet invades her field of vision, making questioning gestures under her nose. "I'm unlikely to forget it if you are going to remind me of it every time we talk. Very well, good evening to you too." She ends the call, throws her cell phone on the table, and crosses her arms in fury.

Ottavio smiles at her, smoothing his burgundy collar. "Now that I know who your interlocutor was, I'm curious to know more about what you meant by 'our agreement from this morning'." He presses tobacco inside his pipe with his thumb and plants his eyes in her face. "One doesn't start negotiating with a public prosecutor unless they're in some sort of trouble, am I right?"

"I didn't come here to discuss that," she snaps resentfully.

"And you didn't come here to discuss your mother either, obviously, because you've been here for fifteen minutes and you haven't even asked how she's doing."

"Actually, given the nature of this arrangement, I'm more concerned about *you* than her. Aside from that burgundy velvet mumu that seems to have come straight out of Pavarotti's wardrobe, you look pretty good and I can hear the old lady chattering on the phone in the next room. So unless it's a recording because you've murdered her and stuffed her in the freezer I'm confident she's doing just fine."

"Stuffed in the freezer, for heaven's sake, what a dreadful image!" Ottavio shakes his head, blowing out the match. "If you're quite finished, I'd like you to tell me the real reason you're here, so we can deal with that first, and then we can focus on the matter of the agreement with the PP, which intrigues me quite a bit."

"You have absolutely no concept of 'minding your own business,' do you?"

"You should know that by now, my dear," he smiles over his pipe, waving his hand to encourage her to continue.

"Fine. You'll never guess who I ran into this morning on a sidewalk in Gattorna."

"Since you already know that I wouldn't be able to guess," Ottavio looks at her, blowing smoke rings, "just tell me. Let's skip the beating around the bush. In fact, be good and start from the beginning: first," he raises his finger, "what were you doing in Fontanabuona this morning in the company of a magistrate? Second, why is a public prosecutor calling you at a time more suitable for cocktails than official business? For that matter, why does he have your phone number at all? And third," he continues, waving three of his thick pink fingers in front of her nose, "what have you done that required you to come to an 'agreement' with a criminal prosecutor? Once we have cleared all that up, you can tell me who you met on the sidewalk in Gattorna." He leans back in his chair, crosses his legs, and waits comfortably.

"I thought you wanted to hear about the reason I came here first?"

"I did. I changed my mind. So sue me."

Edna sighs. "Didn't you read the local newspaper this morning? It was on the front page."

"Not really. I only read gossip and obituary notices in the newspapers. The former for work and the latter for pleasure. There is nothing that exemplifies human nature more than obituaries. So the short answer is no."

"To answer your questions in chronological order," Edna adjusts the pillow behind her back, "I was already in Gattorna at dawn. I was in Gattorna because of what had happened the day before," she begins to explain, covering everything from biblical storms to tenacious chestnut branches, including deceased antiques dealers, secret photographs, tech-savvy neighbors, alleged late-Gothic wood panels, and conniving councilors aiding in illegal break-ins.

"So, if I understood correctly," Ottavio scrutinizes her calmly amidst the soft curls of smoke, "you and the councilor entered a crime scene to rummage through the belongings of a dead man, with the intention of obsessing over a fifteenth-century panel. Do you realize that this alone could be enough to land both of you in jail with the key thrown away? Just so I understand."

"Oh my goodness! That never occurred to me!" Edna gives Ottavio an exasperated look. "Stop being so melodramatic. You talk as if I had killed the antiques dealer myself." she rolls her eyes. "And anyway, everything is fine now."

"Everything is fine, you say?" Ottavio leans forward, pinning her in place with his gaze. "Does that have something to do with this mysterious 'agreement' you're so tight-lipped about? Let me take a guess: The prosecutor caught you, then decided to sweep the matter under the rug in exchange for something." Ottavio ponders, nibbling on the stem of his pipe. "So, I'm curious to know what you traded for him turning a blind eye," he narrows his eyes, deep in thought. "Does it have something to do with this fifteenth-century panel and you being a renowned art historian?"

. "More or less," Edna concedes.

"A laconic and far from exhaustive answer, my dear. Don't think you can get away with that."

"You've already apparently worked everything out for yourself. What do you need my help for?" she snorts, frustrated. For the past twelve hours, she has wanted nothing more than to be at home with her books and chickens. Instead, she has spent the entire day having to explain herself to everyone.

"I suppose the prosecutor made sure to ascertain that it wasn't you who killed the antiques dealer. It would be rather risky to recruit a potential murderer as an expert witness, don't you agree? All I know is that the morning after the murder, you arrived here, ready to leave for

Siestri and talking in passing about an evening of drinks with friends…
Is that your alibi then?”

“You are remarkably persistent and observant for a musicologist-collector. Perhaps you’re really a spy and I should have PP Bassi look into you. Yes, my neighbor is also my alibi, as long as he confirms it. Are you done interrogating me now?”

“Even if I were a spy, what interest would a foreign power have in your love life?”

“Very funny. I know you just enjoy grilling me and testing my patience to make me miserable!”

“Now who’s being melodramatic?” Ottavio spreads his arms. “I guess the apple doesn’t fall far from the tree. Do you want a stage and a curtain too? And let me tell you, my dear, testing your patience is no challenge. You’re the first to admit that your patience is like a meringue, it shatters to dust at the first touch. Test your patience! A chirping sparrow tests your patience. But, for the moment, let’s move on. Now you may tell me who you met on the sidewalk in Gattorna this morning.”

“Kalina,” Edna blurts out, cutting to the chase without any further delay.

“Well,” Ottavio shrugs, somewhat disappointed, “that’s a funny coincidence, I suppose, but it hardly seems worth the trip here to tell me about it, especially after the day you’ve had.”

“Prosecutor Bassi told me that the antiques dealer had been struck with a blunt object that, from his description, made me think of a frying pan. And just a few minutes earlier, I saw Kalina on the sidewalk in Gattorna. When she left, Kalina was openly carrying just such a pan. But it’s not just that. When I saw Kalina, she saw me as well. She looked at me, pointed towards the antiques dealer’s building and then at the uniformed officer in front of the building. At the end of all this pointing, she turned around and started running as if she had Attila and all the Huns chasing her, which I suppose is even a more frightening thing in Romania than it is here. Now do I have your attention?”

“Yes, I see…” Ottavio nods, his usual composure starting to crumble. “And you believe that this, let’s be generous and call it a ‘train of thought,’ merits branding Kalina as a murderer? Don’t you think you might be missing a few of the traditional pieces, like motive? Why would she beat a poor antiques dealer from Gattorna to death with a frying pan? I mean, she resisted that temptation with Zara for weeks. Why would she start with a random antiques dealer who, so far as we know, she'd never even met? Your whole theory seems a bit forced to me. Perhaps Kalina was simply running away from you, Edna Silvera, terrified by the idea that you had hunted her all the way to Gattorna to force her to return as the housekeeper for your mother. If I were in her shoes, I would have run away too. This seems a lot more plausible to me than your theory."

"Mmmh," Edna nods, considering his point. "Actually, that does seem plausible, although…" Her words are interrupted by a short, hesitant ringing of the doorbell. "Are you expecting someone?" Edna furrows her brow.

"Me? Here at Zara's?" Ottavio raises an eyebrow. "Flora has the keys, and who else would know I'm here? I don't brag that I take care of my friends' mothers out of the kindness of my heart, otherwise there would be a line outside."

"Out of the kindness of your heart! Does this mean you no longer want the seventeenth-century tenebroso etching you were demanding? And would you mind going to open the door before they break it down?" Edna demands in frustration, as the doorbell continues to ring in short bursts.

"When I said your patience is as strong as a meringue, I wasn't mistaken," Ottavio sighs, getting up. "And just so you know, my overtime work as a doorman is not covered by the etching you promised."

Edna shakes her head, then she leans forward and stares at Ottavio, who strangely, after opening the door, remains there, hand on the handle, blocking the entrance with his bulk.

"Have you fallen asleep or have you had a stroke?" she asks, her patience now at an all-time low.

Ottavio slowly moves aside, revealing half a doorway and a frail figure peeking inside, wide-eyed, wringing her hands.

Edna's eyes widen too, and, for the second time today, utters a surprised "Kalina?"

Chapter Thirty-Two

"I don't know, Signora Edna, I just don't know…" Kalina shakes her head, tears streaming down her face.

"Now, let's calm down for a moment, Kalina, and figure this out," Edna tries to soothe her, taking the cup of chamomile tea prepared by Ottavio from her hands and offering her a fresh tissue.

"Well, I don't see what there is still to figure out," Zara shrugs, crossing her arms in annoyance. "This woman here bashed that poor man's head with a frying pan, end of story. And she's the one who made a big fuss over a couple of taps I gave her with an empty plastic bottle," she concludes, visibly irritated.

"Mom!" Edna exclaims angrily. She had desperately wanted to keep her mother out of this situation, but trying to keep Zara's nose out of some things is like trying to chase ants away from a picnic. No matter how much effort you put in, you know from the beginning that it's going to be futile.

Now Kalina starts crying again, wailing like a wounded animal, while Ottavio stands there, shifting awkwardly and embarrassed in his burgundy robe that makes him resemble a hot air balloon filled with Merlot. And here she is, Edna, contemplating how she has angered the Gods and what sort of bizarre curse they have put on her. For the past three days, Dadaesque disasters have been seeking her out with the unerring precision of guided missiles.

"So, Kalina, let's recap," Edna sighs, rubbing her temples wearily. "The day before yesterday, you were supposed to meet the owner of a pizzeria in Gattorna, where you were planning to start working as a waitress, correct?"

"Yes, Signora," Kalina nods, blowing her nose. "I had had enough, I decided no more working for old ladies," she wipes her eyes, studiously ignoring Zara who placed her hands on her hips at the mention of the word "old."

"Okay," Edna nods, ignoring Zara as well. "And you accidentally got off at the wrong bus stop. So far, so good. You were walking along the highway that leads to Gattorna. What happened next?"

"I was tired, it was the day I left here, I was tired and scared that I no longer had a job. I wasn't even sure where I was going to sleep… So I had put on my best dress – the one with the flowers – so I would make a good impression. But people in cars were whistling at me, and it started getting dark, and I was praying to the Madonna… I didn't know what to do, I wanted to sit down, but I wasn't going to sit down on the side of the road! What would the people whistling think then? And then it started raining, and I needed to pee," she explains in a rush, her voice getting higher with each subsequent catastrophic event in her story. "And then, I saw a light in a shop window. 'Finally!' I said to myself, thinking I had made it to the village. But it was just one shop. But it *was* raining and I *really* needed to pee so I went inside anyway, calling out 'Hello? Hello? Anybody here? Can I come in?' but there was nothing, just silence. So I started looking around and then… Oh, ametit, ametit, ametit… matusaaa!" she burst out crying again.

"And who is this Ametit?" Ottavio whispers.

"Nobody," Zara interjects, waving her hand dismissively. "It's just the equivalent of 'Holy Shit!' in Romanian."

Edna blinks in surprise. "Since when do you speak Romanian?" she asks.

"How long have you been inflicting these runaway Romanians or Russians or whatever on me? Since then." Zara snorts resentfully, crossing her arms.

"Ametit, matusa, yes, it means holy shit," confirms Kalina through her tears.

Edna reaches for the cup of chamomile tea on the table to offer it to Kalina again but catches a whiff of something and turns abruptly to Ottavio. "What did you put in there?" she hisses in his ear. "She's already in shock, do you want to get her drunk too?"

"It's nothing," he defends himself in a low voice. "I barely added a finger of vodka to cheer her up a bit, poor girl. Can't you see the state she's in?"

"Great," Edna shakes her head. "When you say 'a finger' do you mean one of your fingers? I'm surprised she's not under the table already." she snorts, firmly placing the cup out of Kalina's reach.

"And what happened once you were inside the shop?" Edna asks, turning back to Kalina, her patience now wearing thin.

"The shop was full of stuff." she mutters, still clutching her tissue. "And there I was with my suitcase and my frying pan. I was upset at being whistled at and I was frightened because I was lost and because that shop was so creepy, like an abandoned warehouse, you saw it." Edna nods and Kalina continues. "But it was raining outside and, like I said, I really needed to pee. So I made my way further into the shop. Eventually, I turned a corner and there he was.

"The antiques dealer, you mean?"

Kalina nods.

"And then?"

"I screamed." she recounts, her lips trembling. "His pants were down around his ankles and he turned and lunged at me. I just reacted…"

"Reacted how?" asks Edna, already knowing the answer.

"I, I swung my frying pan and… Oh, Holy Madonna!" she wails, bursting into tears.

"There, what did I say?" Zara waves her arms, her bracelets tinkling, with the annoyed air of a misunderstood Cassandra. "My former housekeeper killed someone with a frying pan."

"Mom!" Edna snaps. Dragging this out of Kalina is hard enough already. Next, her mother would be talking about bringing back the death penalty. "In any case, it could have been self-defense. And Kalina is telling the truth. We *did* find the antiques dealer with his pants down."

"Pah!" Zara rolls her eyes and chuckles. "If I had to kill all the exhibitionist perverts I've encountered in my life, I'd never have had time for anything else."

Edna shakes her head. This is beginning to get out control. Not, she admits, that between Zara, Ottavio, and Kalina she had ever had any control in the first place.

"So what happens next?" Kalina squeaks, her face emerging wet and swollen from behind the now-useless tissue.

"Next we…" Edna pauses. It's a very good question indeed.

Chapter Thirty-Three

Bette Davis stares up at her with a clear look of reproach, ignoring the extra handful of the savory mix of corn, beans, bran, alfalfa, and sugarcane molasses, the new organic feed that costs, pound-for-pound, more than foie gras.

"Listen," Edna snorts, leaning over to clean the troughs, "you may be annoyed because I'm only arriving now, but if you consider it a tragedy that you had to spend the whole day in a chicken coop with more comforts than a suite at the Savoy, then I'll gladly recount the details of my day to you and then we'll see who wins the 'dreadful day' award. Believe me, there's no competition!"

The chickens peer at her with a condescending air, pecking languorously. Edna rolls her eyes. Today, she really can't deal with the whims of these seven spoiled and stubborn hens. Then she notices a square piece of paper pinned to the coop. She unpins it, but she can't make out a single word of the handwritten note. Between the uncertain light, the fact that she left her glasses somewhere, and that the person writing used a pencil, the note is nearly illegible. She can only guess that there's something scrawled on it, perhaps a phone number, but that's about it. She shrugs and puts it in her pocket, deciding to deal with it later. It's probably time to head back in anyway, she thinks, pulling down the sleeves of her sweater. Yesterday's storm has brought an early taste of autumn, and she can already feel the damp cold sneaking into her bones. She turns off the music, earning offended looks from her chickens, and follows the gneiss slabs back to the house.

All she wants now is a hot shower, a plate of steaming pasta, and a grappa. And not necessarily in that order.

In the bathroom, she rubs her hair with a towel after pouring a second round of grappa into a cup of hot apple juice. Then she goes to the stove, and while trying to decide what pasta sauce to whip up, she notices the crumpled piece of paper she pulled out of the pocket of her trousers before tossing them into the washing machine.

She smoothes out the paper under the light, dons her glasses, and reads the thin, now-distinguishable handwriting.

HELLO EDNA, I DISCOVERED SOMETHING ABOUT THAT PAINTED PANEL. WHEN YOU CAN, CALL ME. LEONARDO

And beneath it, his cell number.

So, the note was from her neighbor. She should have known. Edna drums her fingers on the table, torn between the curiosity to know more about the painting and the visceral desire to remain at home with her overalls, woolen socks and grappa bottle. Her day has been filled with more than enough unexpected twists and turns. She could do without another one. Though, she admitted, whatever Leonardo had discovered would hardly qualify as a "twist" after the pantomime with Kalina and her lethal frying pan.

Zara would have gladly offered the "murderer" her old room, but Kalina said she'd rather spend the night curled up on the doormat on the landing. So at the moment she is sleeping in Ottavio's apartment. Once again, Ottavio proved to be the Only Salvation, this time providing his help free of charge. At least for the moment…

The dilemma between finding out about Leonardo's news and turning off her brain while sprawled on the warm sofa weighs heavily on Edna's mind. What could Leonardo have discovered? Can it wait until tomorrow? As she obsesses about the choice before her, she realizes she has chosen the worst of all possible worlds.

Cagliostro rubs against her ankles with the lazy indolence of someone who would have no doubts about what to do.

"Well, I don't have to go out, right?" she muses, giving the cat a distracted caress. Leonardo has provided his cell number so she can satisfy both her curiosity and her desire to remain at home in her sanctuary until the next leap year.

She picks up the phone and dials Leonardo's number but a stampede of hamsters with extremely cold feet runs up her spine and she thinks better of it, hanging up the phone on the third ring. It's better not to tempt fate, she decides, especially not today. But it is too late. Her phone comes to life and trills for attention, causing it to slip from her now-nerveless fingers.

"Hello?" she gasps, retrieving it from a bowl full of fruit.

"Edna? Did you call just now? You hung up as I was about to answer. Is everything alright?"

"Yes, I found your note with the number, but I realized it was dinner time, and I didn't want to disturb you. We can talk tomorrow."

"No trouble at all, Edna, really. I've been looking forward to hearing from you. First of all, I wanted to let you know that – I'm not sure if you're aware – I was contacted by the police today." He pauses momentarily, searching for the right words. "It was about you, I believe… Yes, well, they wanted to know who I've spent these last two evenings with, and…"

"And?" Edna prompts.

"And I told them the truth. I mentioned that we had dinner together on the first evening and that you joined me and my date the following evening, staying until after midnight. I hope I haven't caused any trouble."

"Absolutely not, Leonardo, on the contrary!"

"It seemed like something from one of those old movies. You know, 'Where were you on the night of December 3rd?'" he chuckles, "but what I really wanted to let you know is that while enlarging the photographs you brought me yesterday, I discovered something that I think you should absolutely see."

"Of course, Leonardo, tell me when," she blurts out, preoccupied with rubbing her cheek because her phone must have come into close contact with the only kiwi in the fruit bowl, leaving those pesky little brown hairs stuck all over her face.

"How about now?"

Oh shit. The nightmare is coming true. "Well, actually…"

"Have you already had dinner? Because I just finished cooking a fabulous goulash."

Edna holds her breath and looks at Cagliostro, who is crouching next to her still cold and unlit stove. She looks at her feet, clad in thick wool socks, and gazes into the oven glass reflecting her still damp hair, clinging to her skull like Gollum's.

Finally, she exhales. She knows when she is beaten. "Okay, I'm coming. Give me five minutes." She wraps the towel around her head and heads towards the door. She might be getting dragged from her sanctuary but, by God, it would be on her own terms, overalls, wool socks and all. She gives one last glance at Cagliostro – who has just curled up on the sofa and stares at her with the imperturbable perplexity of someone who can't quite understand the choices of others but hey, the world is beautiful because of its variety – and with a sigh she closes the door behind her.

Chapter Thirty-Four

"Undoubtedly a bird," confirms Edna as she leans towards the computer screen where the stylized drawing with spread wings looms over the entire field.

"It's on the back of the panel, in the lower right corner," explains Leonardo, opening a smaller icon displaying the whole panel and marking the area with the mouse. "It appears to be some sort of stamp, but it's very faded and was practically invisible. However, with a little image processing, I was able to sharpen it up as you can see."

"Ah, something like that Costner movie, *No Way Out*," nods Edna vigorously, "with the incriminating, partially developed photograph that through painstaking computer work slowly takes shape, more and more and…" Then she stops, noticing Leonardo's perplexed expression. She had forgotten that there were five decades and tons of cinematic films that separated them, not to mention in the late eighties this young man had just emerged from the comforting maternal womb, with years of Teletubbies, cartoons, and TV series ahead of him. She quickly waves her hand to dismiss the reference and refocuses on the image. "Odd that it has faded so much. Red pigment is typically one of the most stable and it would make sense to use it for a stamp… unless someone deliberately tried to erase it."

"Indeed, that's why I wanted to show it to you." Leonardo gets up, disappears briefly and returns with two glasses and a bottle of Scotch. "Do you think it's a Reich stamp?"

Edna swirls the amber liquid in her glass and continues to stare at the image. "No, I don't think so," she finally declares after taking a generous sip, the symphony of peat and sea resonating all the way to her toenails. "It doesn't resemble an eagle."

"But from the beak, it still looks like a bird of prey…"

"That's true, but in classical iconography, eagles and hawks have recurring and easily recognizable traits: a fan-shaped tail, for example, which is not visible here, and very distinct claws, a square head with a crested profile, and a slim body. Here, instead, you can see that the bird is more pot-bellied," she points at the oval belly with her finger, "and the claws are only hinted at and hidden under the body. Even the wings appear softer, and the head is round and smooth…"

"Yes, now that you mention it, apart from the beak, it almost looks like a pigeon," agrees Leonardo. "But who on earth would want to use a flying rat as a symbol of anything? What could it represent?"

"I'm not sure."

"Do you have any idea what it is?"

"No," Edna admits, "but I know someone who might."

***

"So, you must be the much talked-about neighbor," Ottavio says, with his nose almost touching the screen. "Pleased to finally meet you, and let me tell you, my dear, that… Um, Edna? Where are you, please?" he asks, trying to peer sideways through the screen. Ottavio is an accomplished expert on many things but technology is not one of them.

"I'm right here. Where do you imagine I could be, Ottavio? Come on!" she rolls her eyes, approaching Leonardo's shoulder to be better framed by the camera. "Did you see the image we sent you?"

"Yes, I have it on my phone. Wait, I'll get it." The screen suddenly becomes a large burgundy blur. "Here it is. Oh, wait, Zara is muttering something about your outfit. Should I ask for clarification or would you rather ignore her?"

"Ignoring her would be ideal," Edna snorts. "Zara is my mother," she clarifies, addressing Leonardo in a low voice. Seeing his hesitant, slightly embarrassed look, she continues, "And to avoid misunderstandings: no, Ottavio is not my mother's toy boy, although Zara, to be honest, in the last twenty years has often and willingly entertained amorous liaisons with young men who could easily have been her grandsons. But in this case, Ottavio temporarily moved in with her to try and prevent yet another housekeeper from fleeing. That's all."

"Are you interested in what I have to say about this drawing, or would you like to continue gossiping about Zara?" Ottavio leans forward, invading the screen with half an eye and his bushy blonde eyebrow.

"No, no, God forbid, Mr. Battiston. Please, tell us," Leonardo apologizes.

121

"Don't apologize, you'll only encourage him. Ottavio just loves melodrama," Edna snorts.

"You're neither amusing nor pleasant." Ottavio retorts, straightening up haughtily. "If we could return to the question at hand," he grabs his cell phone and taps it with his thick fingertips to adjust the image, "it's definitely a bird of prey, yes, and definitely not an eagle or a falcon – or a pigeon. I would venture to say that it's a kite."

"A kite?" Edna squints.

"Yes, a kite. It strongly reminds me of the kite of the Order of the Golden Kite: the highest decoration for Japanese Military Valor after the Order of the Chrysanthemum. It was founded by Emperor Meiji at the end of the 19th century."

"So, it's a relatively recent symbol," Leonardo muses, fiddling with his phone, in turn, to bring up a series of images of honorary objects in silver, enamel, and gold featuring the bird, which indeed resembles the one on the stamp, perched with spread wings on coats of arms and samurai swords.

"Yes," Ottavio nods, "and it also had a rather short life; it was abolished in 1947. And to complete the circle: our bird is not placed there by chance, but it's linked to an ancient Japanese legend. According to the legend, a shining kite appeared in the sky to the first emperor of Japan, Jinmu, in 660 BC, to herald his victory in battle. And there you have it."

"Ah," Leonardo says, rather impressed.

"But what would a Japanese military order have to do with a late-Gothic European panel? Given the context, it's really a stretch. There are all sorts of kites," Edna raises her glass and takes another sip of Scotch. "For example, the Egyptian one: Isis and her sister Nephthys are often depicted like this. Or the 'Great Kite,' the flying wooden machine conceived by Leonardo da Vinci and named as such by Zanon. It even appears in literature. In *The Betrothed*, the right-hand man of The Unnamed is called Nibbio, which means kite in Italian. Kites are a common symbol and can mean all sorts of things." She spreads her arms wide. "So, how do we proceed?"

"How about you contribute your vast knowledge, and I contribute the 600-horsepower motorboat of technology for surfing the net," Leonardo smiles slyly. "And if there's something similar out there, rest assured we'll find it."

"But my dear boy, you only have a stamp, a kite, and a ton of variables on the subject," Ottavio leans forward, showing a merciless close-up of his left ear. "Not that I doubt your abilities, but it doesn't seem very much to go on."

"It's a lot more than I'm used to working with, believe me," Leonardo chuckles. "Just so you know, the last time my only clue was a simple extra 'j,' so…"

"And what exactly do you do, young man, if I may ask?" Ottavio gets even closer to the screen, as if to lend an ear for who knows what secrets or confessions.

"I'm a blockchain developer."

"Ah, yes…" Ottavio nods his big head, unable to hide the enormous "?" that is stamped on his features in 100 point font.

"It's a new technology," explains Leonardo with the calm resignation of someone accustomed to constantly having to give explanations on the subject. "Let's say it's like a master book that collects all the transactions related to an asset, where the database is structured in interconnected blocks, running through a network of computers that must approve each change."

"Computers. So you're a computer engineer." nods Ottavio, grabbing onto the one word he understands as if it were a life-preserver in a stormy sea of techno babble.

"Exactly, and with a solid foundation in encryption," confirms Leonardo, his fingers still moving on the keyboard.

"Excellent. Let's say no more about it." pleads Ottavio, retreating like a hermit crab into the carapace of his armchair.

"Out of curiosity," says Edna, mercifully changing the subject, "can you replicate this process of enlarging, refining, and enhancing on the front of the panel as well?"

"Certainly!" Leonardo nods, quickly tapping the keys as if playing a piece by Rachmaninoff. "Where would you like me to start?"

"Let's say from the edges of those infamous robes that were added later."

Leonardo complies, and the blurry and indistinct brown spot begins to emerge more and more clearly.

"Uh, wait a minute, could you widen this area, please?" Edna indicates, squinting.

And right in that spot, between the greenish shadow of the jaw and the clumsy brushstroke of the hood, a thin strip appears that is most likely the real color of the garment hidden beneath the brown paint.

"Oh, crap!" Edna gasps, taking off her glasses and leaning back in her seat.

"What is it?" exclaims Ottavio, reduced to an icon slightly larger than a postage stamp. "What did she see?"

"I don't know," Leonardo blinks, "all I can see is a jaw floating over a robe. Are you alright, Edna?"

"I'm fine, yes," she nods thoughtfully, "except that we now know what our guy is actually wearing under his robe."

"So what is it? Boxers or briefs? You say it as if it were something shocking," says Leonardo looking at her with a mix of astonishment and amusement.

"They didn't have boxers or briefs in the 14th century," says Edna distractedly, "but that would have made more sense," she opines, nibbling on the arms of her glasses, "because our friend seems to be dressed in the one color that he should not be wearing."

"You're joking. It isn't yellow, is it?" gasps Ottavio, vainly trying to peer sideways through the screen again to see for himself.

"It's the color yellow, yes," Edna nods.

This discovery may have nothing to do with Folli's death, but it's shocking enough anyway.

Chapter Thirty-Five

"Yellow seems to be a motif in this case, don't you think, Dr. Silvera?" PP Bassi smiles unctuously, resting his chin on his clasped hands. "Yesterday, they found the victim's yellow van crushed against a chestnut tree, and now you come here with this story about the guy painted on the panel, who apparently wears yellow clothes when he shouldn't. Quite peculiar."

Edna remains silent. Under normal circumstances, she'd have no problem coming up with a crushing retort but it's not even nine in the morning, and she has endured two almost sleepless nights. The last night, in particular, was spent arguing about pigments and colors while downing an entire bottle of sixteen-year-old Scotch. So her patience is a bit thin, even for her. All considered, she prefers to refrain from commenting and avoid any further unnecessary complications. The panel wouldn't actually fit in there, anyway.

"Therefore, in virtue of the fact that you're bringing this matter to my attention," continues Bassi, undeterred and unaffected by her silence, "am I to infer that the chromatic choice made by a painter over six hundred years ago can somehow be useful to us today, particularly at this juncture?" He gazes at her with narrowed eyes, his chin still resting on his clasped hands. "Because apart from the artist's perverse decision to depict that man, immortalized for eternity, in yellow attire like a medieval Tweety Bird, I honestly fail to see any relevance to our murder case, Dr. Silvera. Unless you happen to know that our elusive painter was actually murdered at the time he painted the panel. In that case, I could speculate about our yellow-clad man as a potential culprit."

"I suppose that's a possibility," Edna chuckles in spite of herself. She hadn't expected anything resembling humor from Bassi, at least not at this time of the morning. "But the reason I'm telling you all this is that I want you to give me access to that panel and let me remove those added robes. That's all."

Now it is Bassi who appreciates Edna's sense of humor. "Oh, is that all? And in your opinion, during a murder investigation, allowing the person who discovered the body to handle one of the key pieces of evidence, which happens to be a priceless fifteenth-century work of art, is a trivial request?" Prosecutor Bassi furrows his brow, trying to decide whether to lose his temper or start laughing at this ridiculous request.

"Well, if I'm not mistaken, my alibi for the night of the murder has been confirmed… Otherwise, I wouldn't be here having a pleasant chat with you, would I?"

The prosecutor nods to confirm that, indeed, her alibi checked out, but his expression says that hardly justifies her request.

"Perhaps I should explain," sighs Edna. She'd rather avoid it, but she can now see that she has no choice.

"Perhaps you should. I'm all ears." he says, crossing his arms and leaning back against his leather chair.

"You must understand that each color has its own life and history," Edna rubs the bridge of her nose, attempting to gather the thoughts that lazily float in her weary gray matter, still frayed from lack of sleep and alcohol. "Sometimes, that history leave traces even in our idiomatic expressions, like 'being green with envy,' or 'having the blues,' and so on. As usual, superstition and science have played a significant role in shaping the history of colors. Nowadays, we're accustomed to Pantone swatch books, where we can choose shades like dove gray or sage green and have them mixed up immediately to order. But it wasn't always like this. Color choices were based not only on aesthetics, but also on their meanings. I understand it may seem complicated," she admits, thinking that she would give her kingdom at this moment, not for a horse, but for a cup of coffee. "Just to give you an example, we know that once a color was prepared, it had to rest for three days or nine months. Does that remind you of anything?"

"Well, nine months seems obvious to me," comments Bassi.

"Exactly," she nods, "the nine months of a pregnancy or the three days needed for a biblical resurrection, like with Lazarus and Jesus Christ. In reality, these are allegorical durations symbolizing a 'transformation.' In fact, alchemy held great importance during that time. That's why it was strictly forbidden to mix colors together. If I were to ask you something you learned in middle school – how to obtain purple if you don't have the color already prepared – what would you answer?"

"Well, it may surprise you, but I still remember it quite well: you just need to mix two primary colors, blue and red," he replies, feeling rather proud. "And if you'd like, I'm also prepared on orange and green."

"Wrong," she corrects him.

"I don't think so! I clearly remember…" Bassi flounders, taken aback. It's clear that he takes defeat quite poorly.

"Okay, nowadays, when you can squeeze the colors out of a tube, your answer is correct." she concedes. "However, for a medieval person, it was not only incorrect but sacrilegious. Mixing the red of the cochineal, which is an insect, with the blue of the lapis lazuli meant tinkering with the essence of an animal and the dust of a stone and would have been alchemically unacceptable. It also wouldn't have been practical to work with. In fact, dye makers worked in separate groups according to color, each having their own dedicated street to prevent any contamination. In Nuremberg, for instance, when a blue dyer was caught dipping his fabrics into hidden yellow tubs under the counter to obtain a beautiful and fashionable green… Good heavens, he faced an actual *trial*. Not for using yellow without a license, mind you, but simply for mixing the colors. Ironically, his idea was ingenious because green has always been one of the most unstable colors, and the shade obtained from copper oxidation using urine is even poisonous, in fact…"

"Excuse me, did you say *urine?*" Bassi looks at her, disgusted.

"Why do you think the dyers' and tanners' streets were located so far from the heart of the city?" Edna rolls her eyes. "For tanning and fixing colors, you need an acidic reagent, which could be vinegar, a costly ingredient, or urine, which was freely available in abundance. The emperor Vespasian even had the brilliant idea of taxing the collection of urine. It certainly filled the empire's coffers, and, even today, public urinals in Italy are called *vespasiani*. Quite a remarkable legacy, don't you think?"

The prosecutor concedes that it is, but she can see from his expression that, in his mind, the scent of the public urinal still lingers in those velvets, silks, and brocades.

"Where were we? Ah, yes, the instability of the color green, which is also associated with gaming tables where chance and fate play a huge role. For the same reason, it is also considered the color of madness…

And have you ever noticed what color is used for evil spirits, demons, poisonous potions, ogres, and malevolent creatures?"

"Greenish, now that you mention it."

"Indeed. Even the classic 'little green men' from Mars carry the medieval association of green with them."

"I never thought about it," he admits, listening intently.

"Of course, things have taken a slightly different turn in modern times. Green is now synonymous with ecology. Companies use the color green for branding when they want to suggest that their product is good, healthy and organic. Nonetheless, certain traditional associations have endured. I apologize, Mr. Bassi, for expanding at length about this topic, but I wanted to provide you with a general understanding of the significance of 'color' during the era we are discussing, where colors possessed a precise coded language."

"Actually, it's very interesting," he admits, "and perhaps I'm starting to grasp the importance of what you are suggesting. But as this is clearly going to take a while, with your permission, I'll have someone bring us some coffee. In the meantime, please continue."

"Coffee would be perfect," Edna exhales gratefully. "As I mentioned earlier, colors in the past were almost always metaphors or symbols of something else, and light ruled over everything. It was always associated with the divine – a ray descending from the sky, the halo surrounding saints and Madonnas, Caravaggio's swords of light piercing through darkness, cathedral windows, and even alabaster windows that allowed the sun to shine through, just as the Holy Spirit did with Mary during the Immaculate Conception. Metaphors upon metaphors. And this brings us to the color yellow. Now, let me ask you, Mr. Bassi, when you were a child with your box of crayons, what color did you choose to make the sun?"

"I would undoubtedly say yellow, but given the way this conversation is going, I'm going to say I was wrong."

"That's correct, on both counts." Edna smiles. "The color yellow evokes the sun, heat, energy, and, by extension, life. However, in the Middle Ages, gold started to be used. You can immediately understand the unfair competition our poor yellow faced. Gold shines with divine radiance, while yellow appears, by contrast, dull, opaque, and sad – a color associated with dead leaves, dry grass, and disease. As we've seen with the instability of green, it's easy for a color to come to reflect moral qualities as well. In fact, we find that the wardrobe of all the despicable characters undergoes a transformation. First and foremost, that of the greatest traitor in history, Judas. Suddenly, artists from Italy to Germany, England, and throughout Western Europe dress Judas in yellow. From that moment on, anyone who visits churches and passes by canvases and frescoes, whether literate or illiterate, knows: if someone's dressed in yellow, he's Judas.

"Then, through indirect association, yellow becomes the color of liars, swindlers, and cheaters. The houses of counterfeiters are marked with yellow, and yellow becomes the color affixed to those who must be condemned or excluded."

"You mean like the yellow star worn by Jews during deportations?"

"Yes," Edna nods. She has started to wonder if this promised coffee is being flown in from Brazil rather than brought up from the police canteen. "And it all starts with that yellow robe worn by Judas. The Nazis were simply picking up an old tradition. Not only were yellow badges for Jews traditional, they also stood out prominently against the dark clothing of the 1930s – all in all, a triumph of German design," she concludes bitterly.

"So you believe that Judas is depicted in that panel?" Bassi elegantly brings the conversation back to the matter at hand.

"No." Edna responds.

"Then what, exactly, was the point of the history lesson? I assume it had one?" He had started to follow her reasoning, and now she's reshuffling the deck. He doesn't like it.

"Yes, by which I mean, no, it is not Judas. As I mentioned yesterday in relation to the presence of the egg, this panel most likely depicts a *Pietà* – the dead Christ in the arms of the Madonna – or the Deposition, the removal of Jesus from the cross."

"And?" Bassi blinks, failing to grasp the connection.

"For goodness' sake, Mr. Bassi! Maybe you didn't attend Bible school but surely you can apply a little logic. Why would Judas, of all people, be at either of those events? Not to mention that, according to the Bible, Judas hanged himself on a fig tree the night before Jesus died. So he was already dead *before* Jesus died. Therefore, it can't be him. And don't for a second think that this could be an artistic license taken by the painter, because at that time, religion was a matter taken damn seriously. For doing something like that, an artist would be burned at the stake as a heretic, and their family would be banned from working for at least three generations."

"Then who is it?" he asks, slightly miffed.

"Give me ten minutes with that panel, and I'll be able to give you an answer," she says, crossing her arms over her chest, exuding the serene confidence of someone who finally feels they have the upper hand.

Chapter Thirty-Six

Marlena's yellow hair sways like the tresses of Medusa, filled with snakes, as she moves about the room. The room is small, and Marlena's strides are long, a sign of her anger, which causes him to stay with his face turned towards the wall. Each time she turns and passes by his bed, he presses himself closer against the wall, wishing he could slip under the bed, but he cannot. He cannot because all of Marlena's anger, swirling around her like a swarm of hornets, is directed at him, who flew away from his room the previous night.

He had been cautious, but then a kite had fallen from the sky like a Blohm und Voss BV 141 Luftwaffe reconnaissance aircraft, causing him to become distracted. That's how Marlena discovered him, and now he feels helpless, unable even to pull the bedspread over his face to shield himself from the sight of those wriggling yellow snakes. He can't do it because, if he does, Marlena will start shouting things at him in her bulldozer voice.

He ducks his head between his shoulders, squeezing his eyes tightly shut, hoping that perhaps when he opens them again, Marlena will be gone.

And maybe it's worked this time, because he hears heavy footsteps descending the stairs.

However, he doesn't have time to relish in the relief before the footsteps return – doubled. Doubled, as if two people were coming up the stairs.

He moves his head in slight jerks and cautiously opens one eye just a little bit, only one.

And he sees him.

"Hello, Omero."

"Hello, Mr. Doctor," he immediately replies, opening both eyes because Mr. Doctor is kind. Mr. Doctor has a pleasant scent of syrup and tobacco, and he always warms the stethoscope on the sleeve of his sweater before placing it on his back and chest to listen to the sounds within. He muses briefly on how the word "stethoscope" comes from the Greek words "stéthos," meaning "chest," and "skòpion," meaning "to observe."

"So, Omero, you took a little stroll the day before yesterday," says Mr. Doctor, but he says it in a tone that implies he already knows, rather than as a question. He then sets the bag down at the foot of the bed, because he is considerate and remembers that Omero doesn't like it when he places it on the bed.

He nods his head in response and looks up at Marlena, who stands in the middle of the room with her legs apart, fists on her hips, and her chin jutting out.

"And where were you all night?" asks Mr. Doctor, showing how he wants him to take deep breaths while he listens to his chest. "You know it gets cold after dark, Omero, and you might end up getting sick. And when you get sick, you know you have to take your medicine. You don't really want to have to take medicine, do you?"

Omero breathes with his mouth open and shakes his head, even though some medicines taste quite good, and he would gladly drink a lot of them. But Marlena says, "Just one spoonful, that's it!" and she sticks the spoon in his mouth in a hurried, rude manner, which always hurts his gums because Marlena can't be nice, even when she tries. But it's not her fault; it's just as OMG says, Marlena must have been out sick the day the good Lord was distributing kindness.

But Mr. Doctor is kind. He tells him that no, he hasn't been out in the cold during the dark of the night.

"Oh, no?" Mr. Doctor tilts his gray head with the air of astonishment, resembling a barn owl.

No, Omero explains. He didn't fly away impulsively, no sir, but he had something important to do, something very important.

"And what would that be, Omero? Tell me," Mr. Doctor gently palpates his throat under his ears, "because I'd really like to know that you haven't been out in the cold all night, you know."

It was because of that yellow van, Omero explains, the one that almost ran over Berta the hen, and all that yellow around here, which is not good because yellow is bad, very bad. That's why he flew away. Because of all that yellow.

"Of course," Mr. Doctor nods encouragingly.

Yes, Omero continues calmly, and that's why he moved it from where it was, yes sir, then he climbed inside it, just to keep an eye on it.

And in the end, he slept all night, yes, all night inside there, not outside! he concludes, satisfied he has made Mr. Doctor happy.

"But inside where, Omero?" asks Mr. Doctor, who seems to have lost track of the explanation.

Inside the yellow van, Omero explains, the one that the police had wrapped with tape like a present! He had put it in neutral and pushed it down the hill, and…

That's all he manages to say because Marlena's scream, a scream that resonates like an army of bulldozers, tears through the air, causing him to narrow his eyes and fold his wings over his ears.

Chapter Thirty-Seven

"Newton's Third Law, does this ring a bell, Dr. Silvera?"

Edna takes a sip of coffee. The coffee. She has the look of someone who, until a second ago, was crawling on her elbows through fiery desert dunes and now finds herself faced not with an oasis of three stunted palm trees, but with a five-star resort, and she's certain it's not a mirage. She shakes her head no.

"You remember. 'For every action, there is an equal and opposite reaction.'"

"Ah," she comments monosyllabically, showing no particular interest.

"This means that we could compare my potential permission to give you that painted panel to an action of a certain weight directed towards you, which must, therefore, elicit a reaction of equal magnitude in the opposite direction. In short, a simple quid pro quo." As usual, he rests his chin on his clasped hands and tilts his head to assess the impact of his proposal. "I will take the liberty of emphasizing how weighty my action is, Dr. Silvera. Do you have anything to offer me that can adequately counterbalance it?"

Edna places her cup on the desk and gazes at him with the exquisitely blank face of a veteran poker player, evaluating what she holds and the face of the person in front of her.

"If I'm not mistaken, Mr. Bassi, it is *I* who am offering you, for the second time, my assistance... And I also 'take the liberty of emphasizing' this fact," her voice vibrating around the inverted commas. "I believed that deciphering the panel could be beneficial for your investigation but, apparently, I *was* mistaken. My apologies." she concludes smoothly.

"So, you're saying that you're not interested in knowing what is truly concealed beneath those robes?" he leans forward, utterly convinced of the opposite, just as he is certain that Silvera is a tough nut to crack.

"Of course, I'm interested. However, my interest is purely a matter of personal curiosity, whereas yours is a matter of professional necessity. Or perhaps not... that's up to you to say." she crosses her arms and looks at him, waiting.

He exhales and leans back in his chair. This hand is taking a slightly different turn than he had anticipated. And now, he is the one who needs to assess whether he's bluffing or whether she is.

He taps the back of his pencil on the folder in front of him, the one containing the investigation's details – full of plausible theories, doubts, and confusion.

First, there's the question of the "Pole," whose phone number apparently belongs to a certain Carlo Kowalski, with whom Folli had been exchanging calls the week before he was killed. For now, he is nowhere to be found, just like the infamous Franka, whose number is registered to a certain Santina Sanguineti, who passed away seven years ago. Therefore, apart from Signor Filipponi, in Genoa, with whom they have an appointment at noon, they are out of fresh leads and hitting a wall.

"As you wish," Edna gets up with a sigh, interpreting his indecision as a refusal. "I'll leave you to your investigation and say goodbye," she concludes as she makes her way towards the door.

"Ah, perhaps you'll be pleased to know that maybe you were right about the frying pan," he blurts out, hoping he won't regret it.

Edna stops with her hand still suspended above the handle.

"I have the coroner's report on the cause of death here," he says, slapping his palm on the folder.

"So it really was a frying pan..." she exhales, her voice cracking slightly as if the news had caught her by surprise.

"You're not happy about it?" he asks. He had thrown her this bone in an attempt to appease her, but he senses that it has had the opposite effect. "Your lucky guess seems to have been correct."

"Let me make sure I understand. Did the coroner determine that Folli was sent to meet his Creator with a single blow from a frying pan?" Her voice is unsteady as she turns slowly to face Bassi.

Bassi is surprised by this unexpected reaction. He thought she would laugh but she is clearly upset by the news.

"Well, the report doesn't exactly say it was a 'frying pan,' but it suggests that Folli was struck on the forehead by a blunt object with a large, flat shape that could 'resemble,' among other things, a frying pan." Bassi stares at her attentively, trying to gauge the extent to which this piece of news has unsettled her, who remains motionless between the door and the desk, unable to decide what to do.

"I see…" she nods, her expression becoming, if possible, even more inscrutable.

"An unusual weapon, but it is what you guessed." Bassi is alert now. Something is going on, though he has no idea what. He watches her closely but there is nothing. Her face might be chiseled from marble.

"Well, I say a lot of things…" she shrugs, as if she didn't remember mentioning a frying pan.

"I was quite surprised when you mentioned a frying pan," he persists. "I wondered at the time where you had gotten the idea, especially considering that Folli's laboratory contains all sorts of items, true, but kitchen utensils would have been at the bottom of the list. If someone did hit him with a frying pan, they would almost certainly have had to bring it with them. Quite amusing, isn't it? I mean, it's not something you can fit in your pocket, and between us, anyone with a shred of common sense would opt for a more practical and efficient weapon, especially if the intention was *truly* to kill, and with premeditation. Don't you think, Dr. Silvera?"

"What do you mean by 'truly kill'?" she replies dryly.

"I mean that Folli didn't die from being struck by our frying pan," he calmly explains, resting his chin on his clasped hands with a sigh, aware that he has just revealed some extremely sensitive information and hoping he won't regret it later. "Yes, the fatal blow occurred *after* our hypothetical strike with a frying pan. But now I have a more important question. This new information is making your face light up as if you had just won the lottery. Why is that?"

"Does that Newton's Third Law analogy still apply?" she inquires. "Because if it does you're about to be in orbit."

"Very well, Dr. Silvera, let's lay our cards on the table then." he smiles. It seems that the game is far from over.

Chapter Thirty-Eight

"Help me understand," Prosecutor Bassi stares at her with narrowed eyes, his folded hands firmly pressed against his chin. "You've known since yesterday that your mother's former housekeeper, who may be the last person to have seen the victim alive, is also responsible for delivering the infamous blow with a frying pan. And not only are you telling me about it just now, after twenty-four hours, but if I hadn't brought up the subject, you would have left my office without mentioning it?" The last sentence is uttered in a thundering crescendo that causes the glass on the oak bookcase behind him to vibrate.

"Actually, to be precise, I have only known since last night, when Kalina burst into my mother's house in tears," Edna points out. "Before that, it was merely a horrible suspicion with no actual facts to back it up. I could hardly come here to inform you that I had an obsessive thought about my mother's former housekeeper based on nothing, could I?"

"Excuse me, what do you mean by 'only since last night'?" Bassi leans forward. His expression clearly communicates that, if he had a frying pan at hand – to remain on topic – he wouldn't hesitate to use it. "What were you waiting for, exactly, before telling me? Or perhaps you don't understand the meaning of such concepts as 'obstruction of justice' and 'concealment of evidence'?"

"Oh, please! I also understand the meaning of 'wasting police time.' And you're speaking as if I had let months go by!" Edna rolls her eyes. "I found out last night. It's now nine o'clock in the morning, and here I am, telling you about it, am I not? What was I supposed to do, show up under your window at midnight and serenade you with this information?"

"Nonsense. You didn't come here to inform me that your mother's housekeeper had 'frying-panned' Folli," Bassi retorts dryly. "You came to request permission to tamper with that panel. And when I asked if you had something to offer in return, you remained silent. In fact, you were about to leave. You only spilled the beans when you found out that Nando Folli *didn't* die from the blow of the frying pan and that this woman wasn't actually a murderer. Otherwise, you would have said nothing. Am I mistaken?"

Edna bobbles her head in a gesture that could have meant either yes or no.

"We had an agreement," the prosecutor concludes gravely, crossing his arms.

"Indeed we did." Edna nods. "The agreement was that I would act as your art expert and tell you everything I know about the panel, and I did just that. Last night, I discovered some yellow paint, and here I am reporting it to you. Our agreement did not cover frying pans, housekeepers, and fatal blows with delayed effects. The topics never even came up."

"Can you hear yourself?" Bassi exclaims sharply. "This woman was present at the crime scene and struck a man who subsequently died, for God's sake! This goes beyond any agreement we had; it's purely a matter of you ignoring basic civic responsibility. And that's only if I choose not to treat your obstruction as a crime!"

"You brought up the matter of our agreement," Edna shrugs, "not me. In any case, that I didn't inform you about Kalina the minute I got in the door doesn't mean I intended to keep it to myself. And these are delicate matters. I was just contemplating what to do."

"What were you contemplating, may I ask?"

"You have to understand," says Edna, as she tries to explain. "She showed up in tears, rambling about pretty dresses, catcalls from passing cars, needing to pee, and antique dealers attacking her with their pants down… Look, I'm not suggesting that a woman should go around assaulting anyone who dares to express unsolicited admiration, but what was she supposed to do when confronted by a man leaping on her naked from the waist down?"

"If you take that view, then what purpose do I serve?" Bassi stands up, forcefully pushing his chair against the bookcase. "Let's all behave as if we're in the Wild West where we can all be our own sheriffs and dispense our own justice."

"As I told you, I was contemplating the right moment to inform you," Edna snorts. "I'm not suggesting that Kalina ought to be celebrated as the Calamity Jane of the Fontanabuona Valley."

"And where is she now?" Bassi exhales, leaning against the window.

"She's at my mother's neighbor's house. And stop thinking what you are thinking." Edna responds. "As I mentioned, she is the sixth housekeeper my mother has managed to scare away in a matter of months. Kalina would rather sleep in the morgue alongside Folli than share a roof with her. She is now under the watchful eye of my neighbor's maid, who is tougher than a KGB agent. Rest assured, she won't escape."

"Right now I have to go to Genoa with Inspector Guerci," Bassi rubs his tired face. This meeting had been more exhausting than a wrestling match. "However, this afternoon, I will be speaking to this…" he gestures with his fingers, as if trying to pluck the name from the air.

"Kalina," Edna comes to his aid, "Kalina Dumitrescu. I'm happy to introduce you. But what about the panel?" Perhaps this isn't the most opportune moment to follow up on this request, but Edna knows that she has provided him with a very respectable new lead – and possibly two – that he could have never obtained on his own. If they were talking quid pro quo, she would be entitled to go to the beach and use that panel as a surfboard.

"I don't think now is the right time to discuss it," he retorts dryly.

"Yes. But fortunately, there isn't anything to discuss. And we're both busy. Just sign the authorization for me to retrieve the panel, and I'll take care of the rest." Edna doesn't give up. Negotiating and bartering have been her daily bread for years, dealing with Zara and that pain in the ass Schiaffino.

"You can forget about that," Bassi begins to gather the papers on his desk to place them in his soft and buttery leather briefcase. "Any further meddling with that panel will have to be done in my presence."

"Certainly. If you can spare the time." Edna smiles calmly.

"Good," he nods. "Where shall we meet this afternoon?"

"Oh, forgive me, Mr. Bassi, but I've just remembered that today I have a commitment that I can't cancel. You understand. I'm sorry, it seems we'll have to postpone," she says in a melodic voice, adjusting her hair.

The prosecutor lets out a sigh that would have done credit to a surfacing sperm whale and rests his fists on the desk. "You've gone from obstruction of justice to blackmail in less than an hour, do you realize that?" He stares at her again with narrowed eyes, as if attempting to incinerate her with his thoughts. "So I will ask you again: Where shall we meet this afternoon?"

Edna begins to object but he holds up his hand. "If the meeting proves satisfactory, then, and only then, will you get your hands on that cursed panel. With me present, of course."

"Fine. Here you go," she scribbles an address on a piece of paper and hands it to him. "And take the panel with you. That will spare you the hassle of driving from Chiavari to Gattorna in the late afternoon traffic. Oh, and do dress comfortably. Cleaning those robes will take quite some time and might be a little messy." With that, she stands up, waves goodbye, and walks out the door.

Chapter Thirty-Nine

Mr. Filipponi proved to be a dodgy character, both in nature and appearance. He was a diminutive man with greasy and thinly combed-over hair on a disproportionately large skull. He had sharp, fish-like teeth, and his complexion had a yellowish tinge that Silvera would certainly have commented on.

After meeting with him, Public Prosecutor Bassi is about to merge onto the E80 on his way back to Chiavari and he slows down to activate the toll sensor that raises the automatic gate. He had decided to take his own car – and spend his own money on the tolls – rather than ride in the official police car with Guerci and Capurro. He had always suffered from motion sickness and the state highways around Genoa brought back horrible childhood memories. Now that he has the choice, unless the state highway to his destination is as straight as a plumb line, he always opts for the toll road.

His trip to see Filipponi turned out to be a waste of gas. All he managed to extract was an admission, if you could call it that, that the two men had arranged a meeting in Genoa on the evening Folli died, but in the end, the antiques dealer hadn't shown up. That was it. According to what he claims, Filipponi has no idea what prompted Nando Folli to organize the meeting. Bassi strongly doubts this claim. Filipponi introduced himself as a restorer of old paintings, but Bassi's instincts detected the scent of a fence a mile away. Thus, the first thought that crosses Bassi's mind is that Folli had gotten a hold of something he should not have had, perhaps the panel unearthed by Silvera. Thinking he hit the jackpot, but lacking both the expertise to be certain of it and the contacts to get rid of it, he had decided to show it to Filipponi.

Here, a web of hypotheses unfolds, all plausible and all ending up in the same place. After ending the phone call with Folli, Filipponi could have gone straight to Gattorna and killed him. Perhaps he hadn't managed to locate the panel and had searched the yellow van, which somehow ended up crushed against a tree.

Alternatively, Filipponi might have sent someone to carry out his dirty work. Or perhaps Filipponi is merely a pawn in a larger scheme. If Silvera was right, this panel would attract a lot of attention from a lot of very shady people.

And what about the sudden appearance of the former housekeeper, coincidentally the ex-housekeeper of Silvera's mother, who struck Folli on the head on the same evening he was killed?

Bassi sighs, because from whichever angle he looks at it, he can only see three focal points in this whole affair at which all the various ramifications intersect: the mysterious panel, Filipponi, and Silvera. That assumes that someone other than Folli was actually aware of the existence of this panel.

But then, someone must have been, though they might not have known what it was. Folli must have bought – or stolen – it from someone. From whom? And when?

Or perhaps the panel had nothing at all to do with anything and Folli was killed for an entirely different reason. Perhaps the previously hypothesized crime of passion? There's no question that Folli had a colorful love life. Or maybe it was a matter of theft, but unrelated to the panel, which might have just been stuck there next to the chest of drawers, for who knows how long, without Folli or anyone else realizing its true value.

In short, everything could be true. Bassi sighs. If everything is true, nothing is certain and he has no idea where to begin to solve this mystery.

His cell phone rings.

Bassi listlessly accepts the call. He puts Inspector Guerci on the speakerphone, although he can't imagine what could have happened considering he left him in the official police car less than fifteen minutes ago, along with Officer Capurro.

"Sir, we have found the Pole," Guerci begins. Bassi perks up. Apparently he does have something important to report.

"Excellent! I need some good news today." Bassi replies.

"I'm sorry to disappoint you, sir, but it's not actually good news," Guerci says without trying to soften the blow. Indeed, Guerci didn't excel in tact, but on the other hand, *savoir-faire* is not a requirement for advancement in the Italian police force. "Our Pole, Carlo Kowalski by birth, was found dead a few hours ago in his home on via Bonghi in

Milan. Apparently, it was due to cardiac arrest, or at least that's what the emergency physician said. The police were notified by the building's porter. It was she who discovered Kowalski; she cleans his house once a week. When he didn't answer the door, she entered with her keys."

"Dead?!" Bassi exclaims, slapping the steering wheel. "And in Milan, you say…" he continues, taken aback. "Well, thanks, Guerci. See what else you can find out and update me as soon as possible." He ends the call with a swipe and lets the news sink in. Things just got better and better. First, Silvera's fireworks, and now this. And the day was barely half over.

However, he ponders that this piece of news, albeit unpleasant, may not be entirely useless. Bassi taps his fingertips on the steering wheel. While a deadly heart attack might be an unfortunate accident, it might also be a cover for murder. With a less-than-rigorous post-mortem, "natural causes" might actually be most unnatural indeed. Inducing a heart attack didn't take much and all it required was a little knowledge of pharmacology that could easily be obtained on-line. Of course, that Folli and the Pole had spoken a few times on the phone the week before Folli's demise, and then had both died two days apart from each other, might be simply a coincidence. Bassi hated coincidences, especially in murder investigations.

Then, there is the matter of Milan. Somehow, Bassi needs to determine whether Folli had gone there, and, if so, the purpose of his visit, and when it took place.

He must remember that there are other possible lines of investigation that don't involve murderous art traffickers. He had not ruled out that this might be a crime of passion involving the infamous Franka. How could he, since he had not been able to track her down much less interview her? But that must wait. He must focus on his current task. He sighs as he parks his car next to Folli's shop, suddenly struck by the enormity of what he is doing. It is bad enough that he is letting Silvera tamper with what might be an incredibly valuable work of art — possibly, if Silvera is to be believed, a national treasure. But it is also a piece of evidence in a murder investigation. To make matters worse, he is concealing all this from Inspector Guerci and the entire investigative team working on the case with him. Of course, Bassi tells himself he is only doing this to avoid a huge amount of pointless red tape. If Silvera's ideas turn out to be baseless and the panel has no connection with the murder, no one ever need hear of it.

But there is no denying that things might go wrong and that he is committing what some might say – his superiors, for example – is a lengthy list of offenses with "bad judgment" topping the list.

He places the panel in the back seat, starts the car and heads off for his meeting with Silvera. He hopes he won't come to regret it.

Chapter Forty

"You simply must do better, my dear! You're not going to get very far the way you're going," Garbo seems to be saying, staring disapprovingly at Edna from the center of the patio.

"Look, I thought I had already made it clear to you and your buddies that today is not the day," Edna sighs, rising from the wooden swing. "So unless you have something useful to suggest, please bugger off. Standing there like a feathered Cassandra only makes things worse." She brushes off dirt and blades of grass from the hem of her wide trousers, then enters the house, as usual, leaving the French windows open wide to let in the scents of her garden.

Garbo tilts her head, seemingly pondering the matter. Then, with sudden decision, she struts through the French windows and goes to perch haughtily on top of a stack of books.

Rolling her eyes, Edna swiftly grabs some things from her desk, haphazardly tossing them into her bag. "Don't just sit there. Explain to me what I'm missing! It's nothing but a tangled mess, as far as I can see. First, there's Kalina's improbable tale of smacking frying pans on the heads of men caught with their pants down. Then, there's the late-Gothic panel on which, five centuries later, someone took the trouble to turn innocent bystanders into monks by giving them brown robes. Not to mention the stamped kite on the back of that panel that, if Ottavio is to be believed, was put there by Emperor Hirohito." She snorts. "And, of course, the hint of yellow clothing that, hopefully, I'll bring to light tonight if Kalina cooperates and the prosecutor keeps his promises."

Garbo continues to gaze at her, with the resigned expression of someone forced to cast pearls before swine. Then, with a dramatic gesture, she fans her tail over the blue cover of a thick catalog on Dresden and the paintings of the Gemäldegalerie, casts Edna one last meaningful glance, and flutters down to the veranda where she haughtily walks away.

Edna smiles but then her gaze falls upon the blue volume that Garbo just vacated.

Dresden.

And bam! It hits her. The Nightmare, her grumpy and tyrannical university art history professor, who used to accuse his students of thinking like all those people who, for centuries, had walked the halls of the Gemäldegalerie in Dresden. Those people who would pause in front of the *Sleeping Venus*, convinced it was merely a copy of Titian by Sassoferraio, and not a masterpiece by Giorgione. Countless eyes, all gazing upon the *Venus* without truly *seeing* her. And yet, it was right there, clear and unequivocal, in the oval of her face, in the unique shape of her thumb, in the intricate folds of the fabric – only Giorgione could have painted her. "It. Was. Written. In. The. Details!" he would emphasize, tapping his heel on the wooden platform under his desk. "It was written in those small, seemingly insignificant details discovered by Morelli!" he would thunder, raising his index finger and slicing the air.

Edna and her fellow students had heard this story so many times that even the tiles in the departmental bathrooms could have sung it in verse. It became a mantra she repeated to herself throughout her academic journey.

And how to apply that here? She had been focusing on the big picture. Frying pans. Panels. Dead bodies. And none of that made sense. But it had to make sense. It had happened. That could only mean the answer was in the details, details she had been overlooking in favor of the sensational. She must concentrate on the details and let the big picture take care of itself.

Her cell phone rudely interrupts her thoughts with its customary annoying ring, capable of inducing a heart attack. She really should get around to changing that, she thinks as she picks up the phone and grumbles a defensive "What?!" even before Schiaffino has a chance to utter a word.

"Good morning to you, Edna. I can tell that you're in an extraordinarily good mood, as usual," he says with intentionally annoying perkiness.

"A phone call from you is like a day without sunshine. At best it's the prelude to a royal pain in the ass. So forgive me if I don't jump for joy when I see it's you calling."

"Couldn't I being calling just for the pleasure of talking to you or to see how you're doing"?

"No. And I'm fine. Any other questions?"

"I know this is all new to you but non-optional social convention requires you to add, 'How are you?' at the end."

"Listen, Edoardo," she exhales, annoyed. "If you called to comment on my *savoir-faire* and my lack of empathy, let's just hang up now. It's not the day."

"You caught me. I am calling about business. How are you intending to handle things in Siestri? Because, as far as I know, you went AWOL, and Santi Niboni just called me to ask…"

"And there it is." Edna growls sharply. "Every phone call you make is always the goddamn overture to a royal pain in the ass. Goodbye, Schiaffino." She swipes her finger across the display and throws the phone on her desk. Good riddance!

She snorts and lifts her shoulders from the bookcase, then turns to grab the ceramic frame from the shelf – the frame that encloses the periwinkle blue of the sea, the taut corner of a sail, and herself: a young Edna, smiling in the wind between fluttering locks of hair, made very blond by the sun and salt. She stares at the camera with a look full of surprise, unexpected passion, and trust. She was looking at him and that summer was a million years ago. Him: Edoardo Schiaffino.

She sets down the frame, more annoyed by this inopportune nostalgic intrusion than by the memory of the affair itself. It was so long ago that she's surprised she still remembers it so vividly.

Bah, she shakes her head, annoyed. She must be getting old. She's developing holes in her defenses. Once, they were solid walls.

The phone rings again.

"Hello, Mr. Bassi." she says, approaching the window to get a better signal. "All right, give me ten minutes, and I'll be at my mother's house. See you there.

"I have to go; the PP is already there. Shoo, you girls, back to the chicken coop!" Edna waves her arms and slips her cell phone into the pocket of her sweater, rounding up the chickens to direct them along the gneiss slabs and into the coop.

Which is never as easy a feat as getting them out, she snorts as she picks up Marilyn and slips her under her arm while flushing out Lollobrigida from under the hydrangea bush. She closes the door of the chicken coop, runs down the gneiss slabs, locks the French windows, glances in the mirror to make sure she doesn't have straw and twigs in her hair, brushes her hand over her comfortable and tested attire (sweater, shirt, and wide trousers, in Katharine Hepburn's style), then grabs her bag and the house keys. With a thud, she shuts both the door and her thoughts.

Chapter Forty-One

As Kalina perches nervously on the edge of a chair, PP Bassi cautiously enters Ottavio's eclectic, sprawling eighteen-hundred-square-foot apartment. He moves with the circumspection of a speleologist, fascinated by his surroundings but keenly aware that even the slightest misstep could cause the ancient (and quite valuable) objects to come crashing down. That's why he now finds himself seated in a delicate Liberty armchair where he appears to be about as comfortable as a caterpillar on a cactus.

Edna lets out a sigh and glances at Ottavio, who, having exhausted the customary pleasantries, has no choice but to vacate the room and return to Zara. She can tell from his expression that he would be ready to give up his newly acquired fortepiano if he could remain for this interview.

And indeed, Ottavio lingers indecisively. "Um, I was thinking that perhaps I should remain here in case you need anything, perhaps in the adjacent room, if you prefer privacy. Zara is fully occupied. Her friends are over for their weekly canasta game..." he says, swaying on his slippers resembling those of the caterpillar in *Alice in Wonderland* and from which the prosecutor Bassi seems unable to divert his gaze. Edna knows he will eavesdrop shamelessly.

"It's your call, Mr. Bassi. Professor Battiston was present last night when Kalina shared everything with us, so..." Edna offers, deciding to throw Ottavio a bone. And anyway, forcing him to attend a canasta sabbath with four elderly ladies might break their agreement.

"I suppose that would be alright. I don't see any reason why he shouldn't stay," concedes Bassi. "As long as Mrs. Dumitrescu is fine with it."

Kalina gratefully fixes her wide eyes on Ottavio's two-hundred-and-sixty-five-pound frame, now draped in soft green lizard chenille, and nods in agreement.

"Excellent," concludes the prosecutor, mustering one of his smiles that, however, appears rather lackluster, its usual sparkle now only a faint memory. The case must be wearing him down as well, Edna muses with a touch of sympathy. But the impulse fades quickly, as Bassi interlaces his fingers under his chin, adopting his customary Torquemada-esque demeanor. Her irritation snuffs out any remnants of kindness, but she knows she cannot show it. She's here for a quid pro quo governed by strict rules she must adhere to. So she swallows her annoyance and disappointment, making room for Ottavio, who, now emboldened by Bassi's *nihil obstat*, plans on enjoying the spectacle from the front row.

"Please, Mrs. Dumitrescu," Bassi nods encouragingly, "don't worry. We don't think you were responsible for the death of Mr. Folli, so just be truthful about what did happen. Dr. Silvera has already explained the situation you were in and I want to help you if I can. So please, go ahead."

Kalina swallows, bewildered. She has heard many times, in various ways, that she shouldn't worry and that she didn't kill Mr. Folli, but knows full well just how hard she hit him and the man is dead now. Not to mention that, where she is from, the police are not as friendly and helpful as Prosecutor Bassi is pretending to be. So she is afraid, afraid that one misstep, one wrong word, and she'll be in it up to her neck. She begins fidgeting with the handkerchief she keeps crumpled up her sleeve, torn between crying and fleeing, wishing to do both.

"I'll prepare some chamomile tea with a splash of 'little helper,'" winks Ottavio, vanishing into the kitchen, eager to demonstrate that allowing him to remain for the interview was a good decision after all.

Edna rolls her eyes. Ottavio's chamomile concoctions – and especially his "little helper" – are not to be trusted. Drunken Kalina would be even less useful than Terrified Kalina.

In any case, the situation in the room appears to have reached an impasse: Kalina continues sniffling, the prosecutor grows increasingly annoyed, as he had hoped for more cooperation, and Edna... well, Edna begins to be afraid that the possibility of laying her hands on Folli's panel might be disappearing over the horizon.

However, sometimes even the worst situations can turn on a random twist of fate. In this case, the God of Pratfalls chooses to intervene by momentarily nailing one of Ottavio's slippers to the carpet and causing him to go down in a swirl of green chenille accompanied by a torrent of crashing cups, teapots, saucers, and sugar bowls.

There is a moment of stunned silence and then the miracle happens: Bassi laughs. Not a snicker, or a chortle, but a full throated belly laugh that goes on for several seconds. Soon Edna, Kalina, and even Ottavio are laughing too and the tension is broken. Policemen in Romania never laugh like this, thinks Kalina. Perhaps it will be alright after all. Kalina is still tearful, but now she is also talking.

"So, Mr. Folli appeared before you like that, out of nowhere, with his trousers already down?" Bassi asks her once again, seeking confirmation.

"Yes, yes," Kalina confirms emphatically, "suddenly, out of nowhere. I wasn't expecting it."

"And did he speak to you? Or did he not utter a word?"

Edna glances at Ottavio, who reciprocates with an embarrassed look, realizing that neither of them thought to ask her something so obvious and fundamental the night before.

"Well… not exactly. But he did open his mouth. He said only one word."

"Only one word, you say. Do you happen to remember it?" Bassi inquires cautiously and patiently.

"It's not that I don't remember. I couldn't really hear," she shakes her head. "Like I said, he appeared suddenly, and I started screaming… I think I heard something like 'sunoovabeach,' but I can's say for sure… he didn't say anything else because…" her words trail off as her lips begin to tremble, tears streaming down her chin.

Prosecutor Bassi brings his hands together, placing them against his lips, and closes his eyes, pondering the information. He lets out a sigh and continues, "I think I understand. Mrs. Dumitrescu, would you mind reenacting the entire scene for us?" He stands up and gestures for her to follow.

Kalina blinks in confusion, then blows her nose, tucking the handkerchief back into her sleeve, and complies, positioning herself in the center of the room.

"Please, go ahead," the prosecutor nods, urging her to begin.

Kalina launches into her performance: she breathes heavily, moving between armchairs and the sofa, mimicking the effort of dragging the suitcase and the frying pan behind her. She pushes the hypothetical door of the antiques dealer's shop while shouting, "Is anyone here?" and, displaying surprising dramatic talents, she performs a series of jerks, dismay, and horror, leading up to the climax with the blow from the frying pan. So much so that Ottavio bursts into applause, exclaiming, "Bravissima!" in a thunderous voice, causing Kalina to blush and offer a shy giggle, along with a small bow.

"Very well, Mrs. Dumitrescu," smiles Bassi, joining in the applause, "since you are so talented, would you be so kind as to demonstrate Mr. Folli's arrival on the scene and his reaction to you?"

Taking a moment to gather her thoughts, as if she were practicing the Stanislavski method, and under Ottavio's amazed gaze, who now sees her as a contender for an Oscar, she moves to the other side to accurately portray the co-star. Taking two crooked steps, she renders her line – "sunoovabeach" with a suitably excited delivery and falls to the ground.

"I walked that way," Kalina explains, pulling herself up and dusting off her sweater, "because this man who died…"

"Mr. Folli," Bassi interjects with a touch of pedantry.

"Yes, Mr. Folli," Kalina diligently repeats, "he came up to me… slightly turned to the side, as if someone was pulling him from behind."

Edna and Ottavio exchange glances, as this detail hadn't been mentioned the night before. Kalina's words trigger something within the synapses of Edna's mind, but it vanishes as quickly as a soap bubble in the wind.

"Someone pulling him back? Was someone there with him?" Bassi asks intently.

"I don't think so. I didn't see anyone," Kalina shakes her head vigorously, "I only saw Mr. Folli. That's it. And when I hit him with the frying pan, I ran. I ran through the shop and out the door. No looking back. But I didn't think I had killed him. Who has ever heard of someone dying from a blow with a frying pan? It never happens in the cartoons!" she says defensively, wringing her hands, suddenly uncertain if she did the right thing by being so honest and giving her little theatrical performance.

"And how big is this pan?" Bassi asks calmly.

"This big!" Kalina says, indicating with her hands that the pan was about 12 inches across. "A *palacinka* pan has a specific size. Not more, not less. Otherwise, it's not a *palacinka* pan. It's just a frying pan."

Edna's eyes widen, her breath caught in her throat.

Suddenly, she understands.

She understands that Morelli was right.

The details. The cursed details. And she always had them right there. Right under her nose, damn it.

Chapter Forty-Two

The patience of Job, of God, of the Carthusians... All of them were endowed with unparalleled patience, of course. However, today Edna feels she can rightfully include herself among such paragons of patience. She snorts as she finishes arranging the necessary items on the large wooden counter of her home laboratory, determined to ignore the dapper and prim vulture perched on a stool, attentively tracking her every move as if she might make Folli's panel disappear *à la* David Copperfield. PP Bassi is one of the reasons why she had to equip herself with patience, yes, but not the only one. After the epiphany she experienced in Ottavio's living room, she had hoped to work out the implications of her sudden insight. However, Bassi had taken her at her word and brought the renowned panel with him. So all that would have to wait. She would have to take full advantage of this moment before Bassi came to his senses.

"Were you considering completely removing the robes or just partially?" he leans over her, observing her closely as she delicately brushes the surface of the panel.

"If the robes were an addition that had some sort of historical value, I would handle the situation differently," explains Edna, setting her brush aside to unscrew a small dark glass bottle filled with liquid, "but I believe they were painted solely to muddy the waters and pass the panel off as something it's not, and very recently at that. It's akin to someone adding a mustache and beard to the Mona Lisa so they could get it through customs without having to pay any duty. Wouldn't you remove them? So yes, I will be removing them entirely. Is that a problem?"

"Not for me. You're the expert," Bassi sways on the stool.

Edna dons her glasses, dips a cotton swab into the bottle, and begins cleaning the panel's surface.

"What are your thoughts on Signora Dumitrescu's account?"

Edna pauses and raises her head. "I must admit, Mr. Bassi, you were truly adept at extracting a considerably more comprehensive and structured testimony than what Ottavio and I managed to obtain last night," she concedes, placing the swab on the edge of the bottle.

"However, everyone has their own profession, and since I am here to work on the fifteenth-century panel that belonged to the victim, I gather that you found Dumitrescu's testimony satisfactory. So, in response to your question, I think it was great. If you're happy, I'm happy," she concludes, resuming her work with the swab.

"Sure. But I noticed towards the end that you let out a little gasp like you had suddenly realized something. Am I mistaken?" he persists, his tenacity worse than a tar stain on a bathing suit.

Edna rolls her eyes and once again sets the swab down. "Some details came to mind." she explains, her patience stretched tighter than a violin string. "Details that had escaped me because I was distracted by everything else that was going on, that's all," she adds, grabbing her swab again.

"Yes, I understand the importance of details. But you know you are going to have to be more specific than that. We have a deal." He's becoming heated now, causing his stool to creak and squeak.

Edna drops the swab yet again, which is a good thing as she had seriously contemplated planting it in Bassi's left ear and pulling it out the other side. She folds her arms. "Look, Mr. Bassi, as you correctly point out. I am the expert. And I have a job to do here."

"Of course, I didn't mean to distract you. Please, continue working as if I weren't here," he replies, trying to be accommodating.

"But how on earth can I 'continue working as if you weren't here' when you *are* here and you keep asking questions?" she sighs, removing her glasses. "Look, I'm about to handle a painting from six centuries ago that might be a masterpiece. I'm not pulling weeds from my garden. I need to concentrate and that means I need silence. I think I warned you that you might find this tedious. So, if you have any burning questions, ask them quickly; otherwise, keep your mouth shut. It's hard enough working with someone perched on a stool, watching me like a bird of prey. If I also have to engage in conversation…"

"My apologies." Bassi straightens, offended. "I imagined that it was a meticulous procedure, yes, but also a fairly simple one that would allow for conversation. I will be silent now."

Edna refrains from commenting because Bassi isn't entirely wrong. She could indeed work and talk if necessary but she dislikes working with someone in the room. She usually listens to Bach, Pink Floyd, Mozart, Miles Davis… None of that is anything like a prosecutor firing questions like a machine gun, testing her endurance and patience. So she puts her glasses back on, picks up the cotton swab once again, and begins working on the cursed robes.

And in the meantime, she thinks. She thinks about the details that have always been right in front of her eyes, details that even an imbecile would have noticed, yet she needed the help of a hen who decided to perch her haughty bum on a museum monograph and of a Romanian housekeeper. However, there is one thing that eludes her, like a word on the tip of her tongue. She knows it's there but no matter how hard she tries, she can't quite bring it to the surface.

Well, there would be no forcing it. It would come to her eventually. So she tries to forget about it and focuses on cleaning the panel.

Out of the corner of her eye, she notices that Bassi has left his stool and started wandering around the room, peering here and there, before stopping in front of the wall where she has been hanging up images of all kinds: photographs, drawings, clippings… She selects, adds, changes, and rearranges them based on her whims, mood, and thoughts. In essence, it is her most intimate "mental room," which is why she displayed them here in the privacy of her home laboratory. God! This is worse than having Bassi perched on her shoulder asking stupid questions. She feels as if she's standing in front of Bassi in her underwear.

It's not a pleasant feeling. Especially because he seems to have taken root in front of her wall and is now examining it in great detail.

"If you want to take a look, something interesting is coming up," she announces, more to divert his attention than out of any real need to show him anything.

"Uh, you were right, our friend is dressed in yellow," he observes, his face betraying the multitude of questions swelling in his head but that he knows better than to ask at the moment.

"Exactly, he's dressed entirely in yellow," Edna tries to satisfy him to some extent, fearing that his head might explode like popcorn in a microwave. "And I would say he's truly our Judas," she adds, pointing to the little head emerging from the partially erased hood, which bears some writing.

"They look like Greek letters," Bassi furrows his brow, perhaps attempting to recall his classical studies.

"It is Greek, yes. It means Iskariotes: Judas Iscariot, specifically. It's the epithet that sets him apart from the other Judas in the Bible, as well as from Judas Thaddeus, who nobody ever paid much attention to."

"And what does that mean…?"

"No one knows exactly," Edna shrugs, continuing to gently rub the cotton swab on the panel to reveal the slender figure beneath the cloak. "The epithet appears in all the Gospel texts. Some have suggested a connection with the Aramaic term isˇqarya, meaning 'the liar,' referring to what has always distinguished him: falsehood. But there are many other theories, some of which, I must say, are quite imaginative and fascinating."

She dips a fresh swab into the glass bottle and falls silent.

"Sometimes I think you enjoy tormenting people, stopping right at the crucial moment," Bassi looks at her with slight annoyance. "I bet you do the same with your students."

"Quite often, yes," Edna admits, without a trace of remorse.

"So?"

"So nothing. Usually, when I'm with my students, I pause to pique their curiosity, to make them want to delve deeper and perhaps pay more attention in class and not miss my next lecture. But I have no intention of making you come back for more, so I'll just get to the point."

"Good. I was afraid I would have to trade confidential details from the investigation to get the second installment of your explanation," he chuckles, relieved.

"Darn, I should have played my cards better!" she glances at him over her glasses. "Oh well, I'll try to keep it brief. During the Jewish–Roman wars, a series of large-scale revolts by the Jews against the Roman Empire between the years 66 and 135, a group of revolutionaries tried to throw out the Romans and declare independence. One of their trademarks was concealing daggers under their clothing with which they could kill without being noticed. These weapons were similar to small scimitars and had a curved blade like the Roman dagger called the 'sica.' That's where the term 'sicarius,' meaning 'hit man' – Cicero uses the word to mean murderers in general – comes from.

"Anyway, some historians claim that Judas was actually one of these Jewish rabble-rousers, someone who would have followed Jesus in hopes of instigating a popular uprising. So the epithet 'Iscariot' could derive from the Latin 'sicarius.'" Edna pauses suddenly, rests the swab on the counter, and grabs a lamp with a thick built-in lens.

"Damn it!" she mutters to herself, bringing the lens closer to where she was working.

"Don't tell me you've ruined the panel!" Bassi jumps up, visibly alarmed.

"Ruined?" Edna hisses, mortally offended. "Do you really think I could be so foolish and inept as to ruin a fifteenth-century panel?"

"No, no, I didn't mean that…" he stammers, taken aback. "But if you are going to curse at random…"

"It wasn't 'random,'" she huffs, adjusting the lens. "This is the wrong yellow."

"Is there a right kind of yellow?" Bassi asks.

"Yes and no. I was convinced it was lead-tin yellow, a pigment based on lead oxide, quite popular at the time and well-known since the days of the Egyptians and Assyrians."

"And instead?" the PP exhales, showing signs of wear and tear on his previously positive attitude.

"And instead, it's most likely orpiment,"

"Come again? You say that like it's a problem."

"Not necessarily a problem, but it's unusual. And that opens up possibilities, unusual possibilities." Edna explains, removing her glasses and sitting down. "As we were discussing, the choice of colors was never arbitrary or based solely on aesthetics. So you didn't just grab the first yellow pigment you had on hand, and especially if using it might get you killed."

"What do you mean? I don't understand."

"I mean, in ancient times, people believed, based on alchemy, that orpiment contained a mineral form of gold, referred to as 'arrehenicum' by Pliny. Does that word remind you of anything?"

"Uhmm, arsenic?"

"Exactly. Even the Romans knew how dangerous arsenic could be. Cennini, a painter known for his famous treatise on painting, which is still respected and used in the art world today, mentions this color 'which resembles gold,' obtained through an alchemical process that seems to echo the search for the philosopher's stone."

"And why does it seem strange to you that they used this kind of yellow?"

"Well, for starters, it's highly poisonous. So much so that once a suitable substitute was found, it was rarely used anymore. It wasn't a color you used on a whim. But more importantly, it's a color that is 'similar to gold,' and therefore, it's the type of yellow that is least associated with the usual baggage that goes with yellow. So it strikes me as strange to find it here."

Edna moves the magnifying glass over the panel and continues to work with the swab, utterly indifferent to Bassi's growing frustration.

"If you could share your concerns with me, I would greatly appreciate it, Dr. Silvera," Bassi fidgets on the stool. She must be doing this on purpose, he thinks, consciously clamping his jaws shut so that he will not say something he should not. It would only encourage her.

"Well, what can I tell you," Edna eventually responds, dipping the swab into the bottle. "It's curious that they specifically chose to use this pigment on Judas. And not only that. To avoid any confusion, the artist even took the trouble to write 'Judas Iscariot' on the figure. He knew what he was doing and he had a good reason for it."

"And, as you explained earlier, it's not plausible that the artist used this pigment simply because he ran out of the usual yellow, correct?"

"Correct. And this opens up other interpretations regarding our enigmatic friend. Using this particular color for the figure of Judas implies that he was being revered."

"Judas?" Bassi blinks. "But even today, 'Judas' is an epithet for being a despicable traitor!"

"True. But there are other theories about where the name "Iscariot" comes from. One of them is that it is related to the Persian phrase 'Isk Arioth,' which roughly translates as 'the one who serves' or 'the one who knows.'" Edna gets up, disappears through the door, and returns with several volumes in her arms, placing them on the table. Then she goes to the wall where Bassi had been standing earlier, puts on her glasses, removes several of the photos, and sets them down next to the books. "Let's see if I can give you a summary without boring your socks off," she says as she sits down, takes off her glasses, and massages her forehead as if trying to organize her thoughts. "So, we have the Judas described in the Gospels: a figure who, all in all, appears rather infrequently. He is always mentioned last in the list of the twelve disciples, and each time he is labeled as Iscariot. He has his only moment of celebrity in the grand finale, during and after the Last

Supper. I don't know about your relationship with the Catholic religion, Mr. Bassi, but the story is pretty well known so I'll assume you are following me so far."

Bassi nods.

"Very well. Then we have the matter of the payment for the betrayal of Jesus, the famous thirty pieces of silver which, you will remember, Judas didn't keep. And finally we come to the even more famous kiss, the apotheosis of betrayal, to indicate the guy that was to be arrested. And I'm sure you are familiar with that as well."

Bassi continues to nod, wishing she would get on with it.

"So here we come to the first crucial question: How did a close friend of Jesus, one of the twelve disciples chosen by Jesus himself, end up betraying him to such an extent?"

"Well, because he was a 'Judas,' after all," Bassi says, shrugging his shoulders.

"Perhaps," Edna acknowledges. "Indeed, the elusive and ambiguous nature of Judas gave rise to numerous dark medieval legends that depict him as increasingly sinister and wicked." She pushes a book in front of him, open to a page with the image of a painting.

"Ah, a Last Supper, if I'm not mistaken," he observes. "And a particularly creepy version, too."

"Exactly. It's a German altarpiece from the early 16th century, just a few decades after our panel: *The Last Supper* by Jörg Ratgeb. It's quite creepy, yes," Edna chuckles. "Do you recognize anyone?"

"Not really. But I am going to go out on a limb and say that the one dressed in yellow is Judas." Bassi deadpans. "Now that I look at it, Ratgeb was quite heavy-handed. This Judas looks really ugly…" he brings the book close to the magnifying lens and examines it closely. "Good heavens! Is that a fly?" He points at the black dot flying straight into Judas's wide-open mouth.

"A fly, indeed! Symbolizing Satan entering him, coincidentally right after he took the Eucharist. And that's not all. Look there, between the yellow folds of his tunic…" Bassi looks closely and nearly falls off the stool. "You are kidding me." he gasps, clearly embarrassed.

"I'm not, maybe Ratgeb was, but yes, that's an erect, ahh, member." Edna confirms. "An unequivocal sign of his moral indecency. Our poor Judas was also being portrayed as a pervert. Ah," she points with the nail of her little finger, "let me also draw your attention to the icing on the cake: the playing cards popping out of his pockets, the vice of gambling. In short, a true catalog of depravity. In Germany, you can name you child Adolf if you want but it is actually against the law to name your child Judas."

Bassi shakes his head. "Honestly, I fail to see how it's possible to envision Judas as ever being revered by anyone."

"So you can see the problem. Our artist was painting Judas with precious orpiment yellow, giving him delicate, refined features, and depicting him holding a Resurrection egg and a white rose of Paradise. But at the same time, the rest of the world was picturing Judas like this!" and she taps Ratgeb's image.

Bassi narrows his eyes. He is getting a glimmer of where this is going.

"Have you ever heard of the Gnostic Gospels?"

"Vaguely," he admits.

"They were lost with the decline of Gnosticism, a kind of religious philosophy that flourished in the first five centuries of Christianity. And, among these gospels, was the Gospel of Judas, rediscovered in Egypt in the late seventies. According to this text, the presumed 'betrayal' of Judas, referred to by the Latin term *traditio*, meaning 'surrender,' allowed Jesus to fulfill God's plan. Therefore, the disciple's action was not a betrayal as traditionally understood but rather the fulfillment of an order from Jesus himself, setting in motion the events prophesied in the Old Testament. In short, Judas becomes a sort of *deus ex machina*."

"Ah…" says Bassi, deeply perplexed.

"And there's more. According to the Gospel of Judas, the most profound truths were not imparted to all the disciples, but… drum roll… only to him, to Judas, the most worthy disciple, surpassing even John, the traditional favorite."

"So it would mean that Judas, how should I put it… had no choice." Bassi muses.

"In a sense, yes," Edna puts on her glasses. "And then there's the kiss. Advocates of this theory consider the kiss to be a crucial point. After all, Jesus had just entered Jerusalem triumphantly, greeted by the waving of palm leaves and giving a real show. He had spent years performing miracles and teaching the masses, not to mention that everyone in the Temple knew him. Forget the Temple, everyone in

Jerusalem knew him. So why was there a need to identify him with a kiss?"

Bassi is about to release another "Ah," but he refrains, although Edna can see it in his eyes.

"Of course, as you can imagine, the matter is highly controversial," Edna peers at him over her glasses. "In fact, there is another less extreme and more widely accepted variant, which suggests that Judas, by handing Jesus over to the priests, intended to compel him to reveal himself as the Messiah, something that ultimately did not occur and caused Judas immense remorse. In fact, the Church regards Judas as damned not so much for his betrayal (since all the apostles, sooner or later, were guilty of some form of betrayal, starting with Peter), but for not believing in God's infinite forgiveness and for taking his own life by hanging himself (interestingly, from a fig tree, known as the treacherous tree *par excellence*). As you can see, Mr. Bassi, it's a constant succession of symbols, allegories, and metaphors."

"So you believe that our Judas, here..." he narrows his eyes, attempting to untangle the avalanche of information she has presented to him.

"... Our Judas, here, is taking us into much deeper waters than we anticipated, yes," she exhales wearily. "And we might not be done yet. We still don't know who the person painted next to him is."

Chapter Forty-Three

"Summing up," PP Bassi closes his eyes in an attempt to gather all the pieces of information rolling around inside his skull like tumbleweeds. "We have a panel from the fifteenth century, undoubtedly depicting Judas duly dressed in yellow. However, the artist used a type of pigment unsuited to the negative nature of the aforementioned hateful and treacherous disciple, possibly due to adherence to the Gnostic – by which we mean heretical – view that Judas was actually the best of the disciples and acting at the request of Jesus himself. And as if we didn't have enough irons in the fire, we are now going to discover who the guy is standing next to him. I can see that you've just about finished, ahh, disrobing him. So who is he?"

"The Albedo, I suppose," Edna shrugs, as if the matter were obvious.

To Bassi, it is anything but. "And who, or what, is the Albedo?" he asks cautiously, suspecting that he will not like the answer when he gets it.

She lets go of the swab with which she was finishing cleaning up the figure's lower edge, takes off her glasses, and sits down, as if expecting this to be quite a lengthy explanation. "As you can see, Judas's companion is dressed in white. Nothing peculiar in itself, but in the Middle Ages, white was the color of lovers, symbolizing purity. On particular religious occasions, such as those dedicated to the Virgin Mary, the pope wore white. Our character is certainly not the head of the Church, since he lacks accessories like a tiara, miter, pallium, cloak, slippers, and other defining details. Therefore, unless he is Judas's lover and, consequently, one of the first openly LGBTQ individuals in church history, he is dressed in white for a very specific reason, especially when we consider what we find in the tray he holds in his hand and the figure of Judas next to him."

"Um, they appear to be large nails, some kind of pliers, a hammer," he pauses and contemplates, as if struck by a sudden illumination, "but… are they the tools of crucifixion?"

"Bravo, Mr. Bassi, excellent!" she grants him a small round of applause that seems somewhat mocking. "They are the symbols of the

Passion of Christ. This follows a certain logic, given that, most likely, the missing part of our panel features a deposed Christ. But you should know that in alchemy, the 'raw' matter is transformed into the smooth and perfect Stone only after the long and painful 'martyrdom' of the alchemical process." Edna points to the sphere on the left. "A Stone that is round here, but is often oval."

"Our egg?"

"You catch on quickly," Silvera nods, satisfied, giving him a surge of pride. "And here we enter the realm of Gnostic philosophy, which goes hand in hand with alchemy: the arduous alchemical process that liberates the essence from the raw material, just as the suffering of Christ's Passion frees him from the 'raw' imprisonment of human physicality."

"So, we return to our Judas, then?"

"In a way, yes," Edna admits. "But, as I never tire of telling you, colors also hold significant importance in this case. And to tie it back to the egg, perhaps you recall that yesterday I mentioned its three components – shell, albumen, and yolk – which corresponded to the three fundamental alchemical stages: Nigredo, Albedo, and Rubedo, the stages that lead to the culmination of the Great Work, which is the attainment of the philosopher's stone. However, sometimes, the Citrinitas is inserted between Albedo and Rubedo. In alchemical theory, four is almost as important a number as three: four seasons, four humors, four elements." She looks at him, with an expectant air, awaiting an appropriate response.

Bassi inhales, feeling tense, as Silvera has a knack for creating performance anxiety, something he hasn't experienced since high school.

"Citrinitas, like… yellowness?" he guesses, holding his breath.

"Of course!" confirms Edna, as if his answer were so obvious that it required no effort. "So here we have our guy, dressed inappropriately in white per the fashion of the day, but correctly if this is a message intended for initiates of alchemical science. Because white is associated with water, spring, childhood, and the phlegmatic humor, as well as the second alchemical stage, Albedo, followed by Citrinitas, which symbolizes air, summer, youth, anger, and here, on our panel, the attire of Judas."

"So, you think this is some sort of guide?" he asks hesitantly, aware that he has followed a line of reasoning very similar to an Indiana Jones script.

"Guide, clue, map," Edna shrugs, "or perhaps simply a display of cultural knowledge by an artist who wanted to showcase his expertise. It could be anything. Throughout the history of art, we have many examples of this." Edna rummages through the scattered books and pictures on the table, pulling out a few. "Michelangelo, Leonardo, Giorgione, Titian, Bosch…" she shows him paintings and sculptures that he knew he had seen before but had never struck him as 'messengers' or 'maps' of anything.

"Look, for example, at Parmigianino's *Madonna of the Long Neck*," Edna says, placing in front of him a classic Madonna with baby Jesus in her arms, accompanied by a group of little boys (or little girls, as it's not easy to distinguish them) on the left. Parmigianino was someone who lost everything in pursuit of alchemy, from work to health to sanity. And take a look here," continues Edna, pointing to the left side of the painting, the side crowded with small children. "The angel in the foreground offers the Virgin a vase, an oval-shaped vase, as it happens, over which, if you look closely, you can glimpse a certain shape."

"It looks like a cross," he says, focusing on the image with the help of a hand lens. "A cross carried by two… little angels?"

"Yes, little angels who stand there to evoke the winged putto representing Mercury, who in alchemical treatises represents the 'spirit' inserted into the ampulla-egg from which the Stone is obtained. So, a vase-egg, indeed. Even the Madonna, with her swollen and elongated figure, is a kind of 'mystical' vase from which Christ emerged. Because the central figure of Christian alchemy is precisely the Christ-Lapis, that is, the Christ-Philosopher's Stone."

"But why associate the figure of Christ with something as material as a stone capable of transmuting metals into gold?" he asks, because this is the aspect of the whole affair that immediately struck him as the most out of place.

"That is only *one* of the three extraordinary properties attributed to the philosopher's stone, which became the most well-known because it appeals to people's greed. The other properties of the Stone characterize it as a catalyst substance capable of healing the corruption of matter. And these properties mirror the figure of Christ: to provide the elixir of long life, capable of granting immortality by curing all diseases, and – listen closely! – to bestow omniscience, or knowledge. Does that remind you of anything?"

Bassi now has a certain deer-in-the-headlights quality about him so Edna decides to be merciful and not wait for an answer.

"We always end up back at Gnosticism and the pursuit of absolute knowledge of the past and the future, of good and evil. Hence the attribute of 'philosopher' attached to the stone. It possesses a triple power that, in a way, elevates even its most mundane property of transmuting metals into gold. Gold was considered an 'immortal' metal, and understanding how to produce it from base metals meant, simply put, knowing how to make a mortal body immortal."

"If I'm following correctly, none of this is adding up to anything good."

Edna sighs. "It's because of when these robes were painted," she points out somberly, "which seems to coincide with a period of systematic looting. A period in which thieves targeted works from private, often uncatalogued, collections. And when these works came to the attention of the wrong people, people with a real obsession for certain types of research…"

"You're referring to the Nazis, I suppose…"

"Yes," confirms Silvera harshly, "and I think primarily of Himmler, but not only him. The matter of immortality and the Aryan-Christ held a deep fascination for the Nazi upper echelon. It wouldn't surprise me if they were responsible for this, although I still don't understand why they bothered with this pantomime of the robes, unless Himmler, or someone like him, tried to keep this panel all to himself using this subterfuge."

Bassi gets off the stool and stretches to regain circulation in his limbs and joints. He hadn't realized that he had remained compressed and contracted all that time.

"Ah, you've finally taken human form again," Edna looks at him, "I was wondering how long you would last perched on that stool like a bird of prey!" And suddenly she stops and looks at him, perhaps because he narrowed his eyes at the words 'bird of prey', as if recalling something.

"Speaking of birds of prey, I forgot to show you something," Silvera resumes, reaching out to gently turn the panel. "See here? If you bring the lens closer, you can see it better."

"A bird? But I can only guess that because you mentioned a 'bird of prey.' With the best will in the world, the best I can make out is a vague stain that could vaguely resemble something with wings," he confesses.

"Wait!" she disappears into the other room and returns with an A4 sheet, which she places on the table. "I have a print of the photo enhanced to define the contours."

"And how, pray tell, did you get this?" he blinks, astonished. "Honestly, you didn't seem to possess such technological skills." If he remembers correctly, Edna didn't seem very adept even at managing the settings on her cell phone.

"Forget about it for now," she waves her hand dismissively. "Let's concentrate on the image. Do you know what it is? And don't tell me it's a bird again."

"An eagle?" he tries, feeling the same anxiety he used to feel when his high school physics teacher questioned him.

"Almost. It's a kite."

"Excuse me!?" he exclaims, almost choking on his words.

"A kite. Why do you make that face?"

Instead of answering, he goes to retrieve the leather briefcase he left propped up at the entrance, opens it, and takes out a folder that he begins to sift through with clenched jaws. When he finds what he was looking for, he answers. "Because Folli had the habit of associating telephone numbers not with a first or last name, but with places, food, animals," he explains, showing her the printouts, "and among the names saved in Folli's cell phone address book was… well, guess what? 'Kite'! That's why I made that face," he exhales, feeling exhausted.

Chapter Forty-Four

Carlo Kowalski, aka "The Pole," passed away on the same evening as Nando Folli. That's what the coroner noted in the post-mortem examination. The building porter discovered Kowalski's body yesterday, but it seems that he had already been deceased for a few days by that time.

Bassi taps his pen on the desk, attempting to organize his messy thoughts. Despite consuming two coffees and going for a morning jog, his mind remains foggy. He had a restless night, tossing and turning through strange dreams involving eggs, yellow demons, and crucifixions carried out with cotton swabs instead of nails.

This is unfortunate. Inspector Guerci had just informed him that Folli's yellow van had been in the Famagosta car park in Milan a week ago between 9:40pm and 11:53pm. There is no doubt. The car park attendant vividly recalls it, describing it as "so yellow it hurt your eyes."

The Famagosta car park is located six hundred feet away from Kowalski's residence.

A coincidence?

Bassi drops his pen and leans back in his chair.

No, there were too many coincidences in this case. And he hated, *hated,* coincidences. It violated every professional instinct he had to just assume that all the odd and unfortunate events in this case were merely *coincidences.* Consequently, he must assume that a week prior to their nearly-simultaneous deaths, Folli and Kowalski crossed paths in Milan, most likely at Kowalski's house on via Bonghi. And being an antiques dealer, Folli probably went there to view or purchase something.

Did Folli get the infamous panel that now haunts his dreams from Kowalski, or was Kowalski a potential buyer?

How long did Folli have the panel? A year? A month? Or did he get it from Kowalski last week? And if he did, did Kowalski know that it was a potential masterpiece from the fifteenth century?

That seems unlikely. If he did get it from Kowalski, and if Kowalski knew what it was, Folli probably wouldn't have been able to afford it.

He reviews the meager collection of papers containing the scant information they gathered about Kowalski. Apparently, he was, indeed, originally from Poland, despite having resided in Italy for over fifty years. He worked for an international shipping company, had a clean criminal record, and no relatives or dependents. The only item remotely noteworthy was that he owned his own apartment and that apartment included an attic. Perhaps, he muses, he should have a look at both.

He's also thinking about loose ends. About the deceased Pole and the peculiar coincidence that aligns his time of death with Folli's. About the "Kite" number on Folli's cell phone, a number that is now "disconnected or non-existent." And the infamous Franka, who relentlessly stalked the unfortunate antiques dealer until his demise. Now, Franka has turned off her phone, rendering any attempts to reach her futile.

Is that just another "coincidence?" Hmm.

Bassi stands up and walks over to the window. A bright, vibrant September day greets him, with a sky of clear, brilliant, and uniform blue reminiscent of the lapis lazuli skies Silvera spoke of.

Silvera.

He lets out a sigh and settles back into his armchair. He rakes his mind, hoping to extract something useful from its depths.

He reviews all the information that Silvera managed to extract from a simple, if ancient, piece of painted wood. It's absurd, almost too much to believe.

There is no denying that alchemy and heresy would be pretty unusual motives for murder in the twenty-first century. What if the panel had no connection to Folli's death at all?

And what about the elusive "Kite" discovered on Folli's cell phone? If it weren't for the bird stamped on the back of the panel, he wouldn't have given it a second thought.

His ruminations are interrupted by the ringing of his cell phone. And speak of the devil, it's Silvera.

"Dr. Silvera, good morning!" he exclaims, more boisterously than he intended. Silvera is talking now and he listens intently, in silence.

Chapter Forty-Five

Barbara Stanwyck plants herself in front of Edna, visibly annoyed by the rudeness and neglect she has endured over the past few days. She has no intention of letting it slide.

"Well, I'm here now, aren't I?" Edna retorts, placing her fists on her hips. "So drop the attitude and get lost."

Edna is not helping her case. Stanwyck stands her ground and begins voicing a series of peevish and guttural reproaches, riling up her loyal girlfriends who promptly rush to besiege Edna's shins.

"Look, the world doesn't revolve solely around the seven of you," Edna snorts, pushing them away with her hands while slipping on her rubber boots. "So get over it and stop protesting every time something doesn't go your way."

They may have a point, Edna grudgingly admits to herself as she starts cleaning up the manure. Yesterday, after Kalina's interrogation and the meeting with Bassi to work on the panel, she finally bedded them down in their coop at an unseemly hour with no more than a hasty "goodnight." And this morning, a phone call had delayed their release until long after their usual breakfast.

Well, two phone calls, actually. The first was from Councilor Repetto, and once Edna heard what Ornella had to say, she had no choice but to call Prosecutor Bassi and tell him everything she had just learned.

Bassi had initially remained as silent as a squid, but once he found his voice, there was no stopping him.

So here she is, managing the disappointment of seven birds that, over the course of twelve hours, have been deprived not only of their highly anticipated evening disco session but also of their ritual morning greetings.

Edna sighs, knowing that they will hold a grudge until at least All Saints' Day. In fact, upon a quick inspection of the coop, she realizes there is a complete absence of egg production, a tangible sign that the retaliation has already begun, and with full force.

Edna straightens up and brushes off her pants. It's a beautiful September morning, with colors that remind her of the bold and dazzling splendor of a Gothic stained glass window, and a sparkling breeze that still carries the scent of dew and salt. Magnificent.

Edna wishes she could sit there, on this low wall, until evening. Alone with the seven deeply offended hens, the olive trees, and the indigo stripe of the distant sea, beyond the glimmering roofs. She would like to forget all about painted panels, public prosecutors, Judas, robes, and, most especially, the niggling and, she suspects, critical detail that she can't quite remember.

Today, she wants to think of nothing. She simply wants to stay here in silence and contemplate existence like a Tibetan monk.

"Good morning, Edna!" Leonardo's voice cuts through her thoughts like the lash of a whip.

Well, *that* didn't last long. Edna squints, and only out of a latent respect for good manners, does she refrain from covering her ears to shut him out.

"Edna, are you alright?" Leonardo approaches, his tone not one of concern for the well-being of a fellow human, but rather as an apologetic excuse for disturbing her when she would clearly rather be left alone and in peace. Edna remains still, attempting to contain and suppress the very unneighborly impulses that Leonardo's voice (and presence) have stirred within her.

A lengthy silence ensues. But Edna is no match for her inner misanthrope. "Mmh... arghh... Oh, well, damn it!" Edna finally bursts out with a sort of roar, rising from the low wall. Her resolute intentions for contemplation have evaporated along with the morning dew and her patience. But, trying to look at the bright side, perhaps he can assist her in ferreting out the elusive detail buried in her mind she has been fruitlessly chasing since yesterday. "Are you busy, Leonardo?" she asks directly, wasting no time. After all, she admits to herself, if she had wanted to dedicate her life to contemplation, she wouldn't have become the person she is now. Instead, she would have secluded herself within the confines of the Carmelite convent up the road rather than live with such annoying and talkative chickens.

Chapter Forty-Six

Once again, it all comes down to the color yellow. In broad terms this is the dénouement of perhaps the most surreal half-hour of his entire life.

Bassi closes his eyes and clasps his hands under his chin, attempting to bring some meaning or, at the very least, some order to everything. And he is not done yet.

Councilor Orietta Repetto casts him a sympathetic glance, realizing that she has introduced the equivalent of the Oracle at Delphi into a murder investigation. Except that the cryptic pronouncements of the oracle always made sense, in the end.

They are currently in Gattorna, in the cramped dining room of the Leverone residence, accompanied by Signora Marlena, whom Bassi has deduced to be a kind of maid-housekeeper and practically a member of the Leverone family, along with Mr. Omero Leverone.

The fact that only a fig tree and a road separate the Leverone residence from Folli's shop means that someone would have conducted this interview eventually. But there is something more.

"So, Omero, if I understood correctly, you claim that you entered the van solely to move it from its current location, is that correct?" Bassi asks patiently, to confirm his understanding.

Omero shifts restlessly in his chair, opening and closing his knees with the bored impatience of a child forced to sit still in the presence of guests but yearning to be outside playing.

"Did you hear what Mr. Bassi asked you?" Signora Marlena startles him with her gruff voice. "Well, then? What do you have to say about this blasted van?" she presses on.

Omero squints as he sinks into his chair, retreating into his shell like a snail faced with an approaching bulldozer.

"If the offer of that coffee still stands, Signora Marlena, I would gladly accept it," the councilor interjects, clearly aiming to divert her attention from Omero.

Bassi contributes to the effort with one of his charming smiles, which proves successful. Marlena promptly scurries off to the kitchen, instantly lightening the atmosphere in the dining room.

"Now, Omero, let's talk. Everything is fine, and you did a great job with that yellow van. Care to explain how you managed it?" Bassi addresses him calmly.

Omero opens one eye, just one, and regards him cautiously.

Bassi offers an encouraging smile, though apparently it's not quite enough, as Omero remains silent.

Councilor Repetto observes them both thoughtfully, rummages in her bag and places a candy on the table. Omero quickly snatches it and pops it into his mouth with the speed of a chameleon's tongue.

"It was because of the yellow," Omero mumbles in a low voice, sucking on the candy and casting furtive glances towards the kitchen, where Marlena is bustling with plates and cups. "Yellow isn't a good thing, you know. Lemons are yellow, dead leaves are yellow…" He lowers his voice even further and whispers, "Marlena has yellow hair too… shh," he places his index finger over his lips and sinks his head between his shoulders. "And the van, yes, the van that almost ran over Berta the other day, that was yellow too. Yellow. Yellow like the sulfur of the Devil and Hell. *That soul up there which has the greatest pain' the Master said, 'is Judas Iscariot; With head inside, he plies his head without'.*" Unexpectedly and precisely, Omero quotes Dante, his tone serious. "Because, yes, yellow is bad. I had to keep an eye on it," he concludes, crunching loudly to put an end both to the matter and the candy.

"Ah…" Bassi narrows his eyes, "and who is Berta?" He certainly doesn't need a woman nearly run over by Folli's van.

"Berta, she's in the chicken coop," Omero explains, bending his elbows and tucking his fists under his armpits to mimic the flapping of chicken wings. "And later I almost crushed her too, Berta. It's not like I did it on purpose, you know. It's just that my wings didn't work properly, the tree branch broke, and… and I fell. That's why the window is now sealed tightly. Marlena even secured it with the padlock from OMG's bicycle, so I couldn't get out. But the yellow van was always there, long and yellow like a banana. I could see it even at night." Omero falls silent abruptly, distracted by a fly that dares to challenge the flypaper hanging from the ceiling.

"And you told me that, from the window, you can keep an eye on everything, because one must never get distracted!" Councilor Repetto nods, using her finger to push another candy towards Omero.

Omero swiftly makes it disappear in his mouth, nodding in agreement. "OMG always says it: 'A moment's distraction, a lifetime's destruction,'" he explains with great seriousness. "Yes, sir. And I could see the rectangle of light on the street. And at that hour, there shouldn't have been any light, no. A light in the shape of a rectangle... a quadrilateral in which opposite sides are parallel and in which each interior angle is 90 degrees. It was on the street, and above it was written..." He ponders for a moment, then opens the table drawer, retrieves a yellow pencil stub and a small notepad, and writes "ANTIQUES" in capital letters because expressing it verbally seemed a bit challenging for him. "And I saw people," he continues, grinding his candy with his teeth. "People entering and exiting. At first slowly, and then running. People with wheeled suitcases. And also people with pans like Marlena's pan for making fried meatballs. And people with red hair and furry coats that resembled the skin of a jaguar, a carnivorous mammal of the *Felidae* family whose name derives from the Tupi-Guarani word for *Yaguar*, which means 'he who kills with a leap,'" he solemnly specifies. "And the gray car with the dented fender screeching angrily as it hit the brakes. The car stopped there, in the rectangle of light, and then drove off whistling, not from the brakes but from the wheels. And then, silence, yes," Omero nods eagerly. "The yellow van was still there, and so was the rectangle of light that was all wrong because there should have been only darkness there. Light is life, yes, but it was all wrong there. And that wasn't good. It wasn't good at all." He suddenly falls silent, as if someone had switched him off.

"Do you remember what car it was?" Bassi asks cautiously.

Omero oscillates his head between yes and no, then looks expectantly at Councilor Repetto, who once again rummages in her bag and retrieves yet another piece of candy, placing it in the center of the table.

Omero quickly snatches the candy, leaving Bassi to realize that practically everything comes with a price, even crucial information he needs, though he hopes to extract it before the witness falls into a diabetic coma.

"A Clio," Omero says, happily chewing.

"Well done, Omero," Bassi applauds softly. "And by any chance, do you remember the license plate? Just a few numbers or letters would be enough…"

Omero tilts his head in small jerks, resembling a pheasant, and gazes at Bassi with his round eyes. Then he retrieves the notepad again, turns to a fresh sheet, and diligently writes the first two letters using the pencil stub. He follows with three numbers, then the second two letters. With his tongue protruding from the corner of his lips, he also draws precisely on the right side, the vertical rectangle with the circle of twelve stars above the 'I' for Italy. On the other side, he draws a continuous circle with the year of registration inside and the initials of the province below. The only missing detail from that perfect drawing is the license plate's screws.

Bassi blinks, taken aback, wondering how Omero could observe these details with such precision from a such a distance in the dark through a closed second-floor window. Unless Omero possesses not only an exceptional memory but also some sort of superhero-level vision. He would have to ask if Omero's doctor happened to be named "Xavier."

"I saw it through my binoculars," Omero explains, apparently reading Bassi's expression of astonishment and confusion. "The binoculars I use to watch the birds that OMG gave me for Christmas… *Adeste fideles laeti triumphantes, venite, venite in Bethlehem. Natum videte regem angelorum.* They work at night, too, even with a fig tree in the way. But the fig tree is a traitor, eh, and one must never climb its branches. Never! And there was also the kite."

"The kite?!" Bassi exclaims, nearly falling off his chair. Omero stops and blinks his round eyes, resembling a perplexed owl.

"Sorry, Omero, it's just that I didn't expect you to mention a kite. Please continue," Bassi offers an encouraging smile.

"It has been a long time since we last saw a kite around here, and that, in itself, is a sign. Even though OMG claims that only the flaws in your mind bring bad luck, I believe it's not true because things have their own way of speaking. That's why I took flight. I escaped through the door below, the one that leads to the vegetable garden and passes under the fig tree. Marlena only closes it when she goes to sleep. That's why I took flight," he spreads his arms and flaps them up and down like a one-hundred-and-seventy-six-pound pterodactyl, "to make the van and all that wretched yellow vanish. I hopped inside to keep an eye on it, as

OMG suggests. Things can't sneak up on you when you're sitting right on top of them. Then, I pushed it down the hill, far away from here. The kite also disappeared, swoosh, a Luftwaffe reconnaissance aircraft, a Blohm und Voss BV 141, fallen from the sky. Ta-ta-ta-ta-ta-ta," he points his two index fingers, mimicking a submachine gun, "shot down by anti-aircraft artillery. That's when I got distracted," he shrugs his shoulders and shakes his head. "That's when Marlena spotted me, and that's when she called Mr. Doctor who insisted I tell him about the yellow van." Then he scrutinizes Bassi with his round, pheasant-like eyes, leans forward, and breathes out petulantly, "And that's precisely why you're here, Mr. Bassi!"

Chapter Forty-Seven

"It's simply a matter of yellows, figs, vans, and kites." sighs Bassi, rolling his eyes sarcastically. "Why can't I get a nice simple gang murder or an old-fashioned serial killer?"

He makes a mental summary. There's Nando Folli, an antiques dealer, who died within a few hours of when Carlo Kowalski, known as "the Pole," died. Folli had almost certainly met with him in Milan a week before their deaths. Then there is Dr. Edna Silvera, and a councilor for tourism and entertainment for the Municipality of Fontanabuona, Orietta Repetto. They both end up in Folli's shop/laboratory the morning after he's killed, and find his body.

Silvera, who just happens to be a world-renowned art expert, accidentally stumbles upon a painted panel from the fifteenth century that may be an incredibly valuable masterpiece. Bassi recognizes there's a whole different investigation there but, for the moment, he'll concentrate on Folli's death. Then there is Kalina Dumitrescu, who, as it happens, is Silvera's mother's former housekeeper. And she receives a job offer at a pizzeria in Gattorna. That's where she was headed the night Folli died but she accidentally gets off at the wrong bus stop and ends up inside Folli's shop/laboratory where, through a series of unfortunate coincidences, she hits him with a frying pan on his forehead and runs off.

And finally, we have Omero.

And, believe it or not, this is where all this gets *complicated.* Bassi pauses for a moment and decides to separate Omero's story into sections. Omero Leverone is about fifty years old and, in many ways, is like a child of six but gifted with phenomenal knowledge, memory, and powers of observation. Councilor Repetto, who, for all her quirks, really knows her constituents, told him that Omero has always been like this, and that everyone in the village knows him. Omero has a special bond with a local pensioner with a passion for ornithology who often takes Omero with him when he goes bird watching. At the registry office, this pensioner is registered as Luigi Curotto, but his frequent exclamations of "Oh My God!" have caused Omero to nickname him

"OMG." Omero often uses nicknames for people and things and has named his personal physician "Mr. Doctor." Despite Omero's quirks, however, he has proved to be an important witness.

Bassi opens the notebook where he outlined the main facts he has managed to extract from Omero's story, a story that often seems to cross into the realm of fantasy.

The central point is the yellow van parked in front of the antiques dealer's shop. Then there is the light in the shop window, from the moment of the arrival (in life) of Folli until the following morning when he was found dead by Edna Silvera and Councilor Repetto. Then there's Kalina's (slow) entry and (rapid) exit, with a wheeled suitcase and a frying pan. Finally there is the still-mysterious red-haired woman with a jaguar-patterned jacket and an old gray Clio with a dented bumper, registered at the DMV in 1999. Thanks to Omero's photographic memory, Bassi hopes the mysterious red-haired woman won't stay mysterious for long.

Ah, and last but not least, there is also a kite. A kite that, somehow, falls from the sky as if it had been shot down like a Nazi bomber. No, that's not quite right. That's odd behavior for a bird. He's missing something. Omero's observations are always accurate but his interpretations could be whimsical. So not a bird. Bassi would know if there had been a plane crash… a drone, maybe? That might be worth thinking about.

And there are also various quotes from Dante, delightfully shared by Omero, about Hell, Judas Iscariot, the color yellow, and treacherous fig trees.

The councilor informed Bassi that Omero's father, a former high school teacher, was already elderly when he found himself a widower and solely responsible for the young Omero. Between the two of them, they couldn't have survived a week on their own, as Councilor Repetto opined with her usual colorful take on things. Omero had his head in the clouds and Professor Leverone, his father, had his head in his books which, when you think about it, isn't all that different. That's where Marlena came in, the only person in the household with even one foot on the ground – and Marlena, the soul of practicality, had two. She was the maid who entered their service when Omero's mother fell ill and stayed on after her passing.

Professor Leverone entrusted his son, his finances, and his home to her before departing for the Creator fifteen years ago, after celebrating his ninety-eighth birthday with a mind still firing on all cylinders like a finely-tuned race car.

And Marlena remained at her post, still caring for Omero. According to the councilor, this was not simply a financial arrangement and she would have done so regardless, even without the promise of the house and the annuity.

Bassi fidgets with the sheet on which he has written the license plate number that Inspector Guerci is attempting to match with the owner of the mysterious Clio.

In short, it is now clear that the van was not moved by the presumed murderer or by someone seeking the valuable panel, as initially suspected, but rather by Omero alone, with the sole purpose of removing that wretched yellow excrescence from his sight.

"Always that damned yellow," Bassi sighs.

Because now, in spite of himself, he's got yellow fever, too. When he thinks about the white light in the shop window and the new entry, the red-headed woman wearing a jaguar-patterned coat, he can't help but connect these elements to all those medieval concepts of Judas-yellows, Albedo-white, Rubedo-red, death as a necessary condition in order to be reborn, and all their various corollaries. This is clear proof that he needs a break from both Silvera and that cursed panel.

His cell phone vibrates. It's a text from Inspector Guerci.

Apparently, they have identified the owner of the Clio that Omero mentioned. Finally, something concrete and tangible. With his index finger and thumb, he enlarges the image and reads the message. And then he reads it again three times because he can hardly believe it.

The famous 1999 Clio, the car spotted in front of Folli's shop on the night the antiques dealer died, belongs to one Franchina Bottaro, a resident of Carasco.

This wouldn't be particularly noteworthy on its own, if not for her cell phone number, a number that Bassi now knows by heart. It's the number of the infamous Franka, the woman who bombarded Folli with messages ranging from saccharine to psycho-killer on the day of his death. She must have abbreviated her name, adding to it a slightly exotic consonant – Italian never uses the letter "k" – because she found the name "Franchina" insufficiently cool. However, her driver's license photo portrays her with jet-black hair, not red, as Omero had reported.

Which could simply indicate that Franka is someone who enjoys changing her hair color. She strikes Bassi as the sort of person who would.

So why did he immediately think of Nigredo-black, the initial stage of a process of death and rebirth that has begun but remains unfinished, and which precedes the stages of Albedo and Rubedo?

He tosses the pen onto the desk and sighs.

Yes, it's official. He needs a break. His next case would definitely be a serial killer.

Chapter Forty-Eight

"It's merely a detail," Edna shrugs, slouching in the chair next to Leonardo. "but it was right in front of my eyes. I'm a fool."

"I wouldn't call you a fool," Leonardo says while swiftly typing on the keyboard. For the past ten minutes, he has been filling the screen with bars, letters, and characters. "I would never have thought of it, and instead, thanks to you… here we are!" he exclaims, satisfied. "Welcome to the digital archives of Christie's, Sotheby's, Phillips, Dorotheum, and most of the other major auction houses in the world."

"Wow, that's incredible!" Edna puts on her glasses, increasingly convinced that digitization has made everything less private than a urinal at a football stadium. "Aren't you worried about them tracing your computer?"

"Me? Nah," he reassures her, laughing. "It would be easier for them to find a particular piece of hay in a haystack."

"Look at you…" she peers at him over her glasses. "A computer whiz, a whisky connoisseur, a skilled cook… and even a sense of humor. One might think you're the result of a successful genetic experiment, Leonardo. Or am I collaborating with a cyborg?"

"No, but I'll take it as a compliment," he chuckles, returning to tinkering on the keyboard. "So, explain to me what we're looking for now."

"Something struck me when I heard someone talk about a frying pan with precise measurements. Measurements that define it as a *palacinka*. If it has any other measurements, it's just a frying pan."

"I'm not quite following you, Edna," Leonardo looks at her perplexed. Leonardo has a decent opinion of his own intelligence and yet, he is unable to fathom the connection between a frying pan and the need to tunnel into Sotheby's archives.

"It's because of the *size*, Leonardo." Edna takes off her glasses and leans back again. "Sometimes the size of a thing can specifically identify it without any possibility of confusion. Remember when we assumed that our panel was part of a polyptych? That's a work composed of multiple parts, varying in number from two to as many as the artist chose. Now I am fairly certain that our panel was part of a triptych – a polyptych made up of exactly three panels. Because of the precise dimensions of our panel, I don't think it can be anything else." Edna reaches out and grabs a piece of paper and a pen from Leonardo's desk. "May I?"

He nods, leaning forward curiously.

"You see," Edna draws two rectangles, "whenever we 'frame' something, we tend to center the most important object. There's a reason for that." she explains, inserting a horizontal line in the first rectangle to divide it symmetrically along with two diagonal lines from corner to corner. She draws a small boat right at the intersection of the two diagonals.

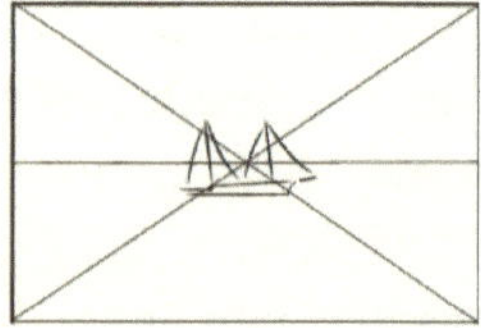

"See? Now, look at this." Keeping the horizon line unchanged, she draws in another boat in the second rectangle, this time positioning it to the right and towards the bottom.

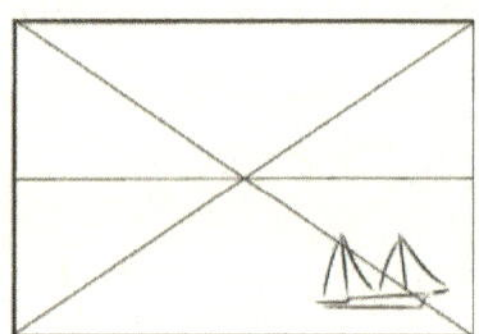

"OK. Which of the two drawings appears to you more... stately, more structured?"

Leonardo immediately points to the one with the boat perfectly centered.

"Exactly. Centrality conveys a sense of calm, of something firmly rooted and solid, almost immovable. It also signifies commitment: centering something is always the result of effort, a will to extract order from chaos. The little boat veering to the right," she points to the second drawing, "on the other hand, is more dynamic, but also unstable and somewhat restless. We make use of this, more or less unconsciously, when we take a photograph. Those who work in the media know this very well, and artists knew it perfectly from the moment they established 'boundaries' within which to enclose their representations."

Edna takes a second sheet and sketches a sort of throne in the center with a Madonna holding the body of Christ on her knees. "Centered compositions confer solemnity, completeness. Centering freezes the moment and crystallizes it, setting the subject apart from the ordinary random events of life." She looks at him. "Do you understand, Leonardo? It's all in the details. Our two figures in robes are positioned in a three-quarter view, they are shifted all the way to the right side. They are looking at something 'off screen,' but what? It's as if they are looking at a central composition that, however, is missing. In other words, they are the 'left slice of something.' A slice that was cut vertically. And this brings us to the precise measurements I mentioned." Edna draws a new rectangle, dividing it with perpendicular lines so that the central portion is twice the size of the two lateral ones. "This is most likely our panel," she says, outlining the narrow left portion.

"So you're saying that..." Leonardo begins to understand and resumes his typing.

"I'm saying that we need to search for panels on poplar wood, painted with tempera mixed with oil, dating from the late fourteenth century to the first half of the fifteenth century. So you'll need to look for panels that have the same exact height as ours but are either the same width or double the width. Since these are rather specific dimensions – another important detail that I've missed, although, again, it has always been right in front of me – this should narrow down the search significantly."

"Wow. And what do we do when we find some matches?" Leonardo asks, thoroughly caught up in the hunt now, his eyes fixed on the screen that continues to display lists of data.

"We'll cross that bridge when we come to it." says Edna, realizing that she has no idea.

Chapter Forty-Nine

Franka, aka Franchina Bottaro, sits stiffly upright in the waiting room, while Bassi observes her through the glass. She arrived accompanied by her husband, indicating that she has no idea why she was summoned. Bassi is aware that there are such things as open marriages, but even the most liberal arrangement must draw the line at casually chatting about deranged, obsessive text messages sent to a murdered lover. That's true even if the husband happens to be a little man with chubby cheeks, a potato-like nose, protruding ears, and the tender, soft physique of a Smurf. Even his color was a little off. Anyway, if she knew why she was here, she would have brought a lawyer, not a spouse.

Bassi glances at Inspector Guerci, who has been leaning against the door frame for ten minutes with his arms folded. Normally, Guerci would be in charge of conducting the interview, but he's thoroughly familiar with this suspect's text messages and he's not eager to begin.

Mrs. Franchina Bottaro, squeezed into a pristine trouser suit, with a helmet of red hair atop her head like icing on a cupcake, sharp, darting eyes, a determined snout, and the disdainful arrogance of a baroness whose tea someone has served cold, does not strike Bassi as someone who will be a cooperative witness, even without her history of colorful communications. In fact, she exudes "pain in the ass" from every pore of her body. "Pain in the ass" lacks elegance, and it is a term he usually reserves for the private confines of his mind, rarely crossing the threshold of his lips. However, it seems to have found an unintended escape this time, as Guerci turns around and dryly nods in agreement, remarking, "A pain in the ass indeed."

They call her in.

"I still don't understand the reason for this summons," Franka enters the room with a Valkyrian stride to stand just inside the doorway. "Come, Sandro," she tosses over her shoulder to the Smurf, who obediently trots up and stand behind her.

"Hello, I'm Prosecutor Bassi, and this is Chief Inspector Guerci," Bassi says quickly, noticing Guerci's momentary hesitation as he appears captivated by Bottaro's shiny red boots with toes capable of crushing ants in the corners, boots complete with the iron studs you would see on a Rottweiler's collar. "We need to ask you a few questions about Mr. Nando Folli."

Franka instantly falls silent, narrowing her eyes, not so much with dismay, but rather as if she were charging a laser beam in order to incinerate them all.

"Folli? Who is Folli?" the Smurf breaks the silence, speaking in such a "smurfy" voice that Bassi has to suppress a gasp.

"The antiques dealer," Franka promptly explains, fixing Bassi with a glare in an effort to discourage any further clarification. "I was complaining about a chest I wanted to buy for your mother. I'll take care of this, Sandro. You can wait outside." She dismisses him imperiously, turning back to her husband and firmly planting the studded tip of her boot between the door jambs to mark the impassable boundary. The Smurf doesn't object, as if adoring obedience was the cornerstone of their relationship. He trots back towards the plastic armchairs in the waiting room, seeing no reason to deviate from his modus operandi.

Franka closes the door and sits down haughtily in front of the desk, unclear which of the two, Guerci or Bassi, is responsible for this affront. With impartial fairness, she decides to direct her anger towards both of them. "Well?" she snaps, thrusting out her chin.

Guerci rolls his eyes, slides a Department of Motor Vehicles form in front of Franka, and with a visible effort, forces a smile of gentle condescension. He begins to explain, and Bassi recognizes the titanic struggle in Guerci's expression. "We know this car is yours. We would like you to clarify the nature of your relationship with Mr. Folli. And before you answer, please be aware that we have access to Mr. Folli's phone and are aware of the contents of your text exchanges."

"I fail to see why I should explain anything to you. Who I talk to is my business." Franka retorts. Then she leans forward, narrowing her eyes like sharp blades. "And what do you mean by 'you are aware of the contents of our text exchanges?' Who authorized you? This is a gross invasion of privacy, my dear sirs. There will be consequences for this!"

Guerci maintains the same fixed smile, though he is clearly struggling. "No, there won't, at least not for the police. This is a murder investigation." he clarifies.

"A murder investigation? What do you mean?" Franka blurts out, still seething with anger.

Bassi and Guerci exchange a glance.

"Exactly what we said. Have you read the newspapers, Mrs. Bottaro? Are you aware of what happened involving Mr. Nando Folli three days ago?" Bassi asks.

"No, I haven't read the newspapers, and frankly, what that idiot does is no longer any concern of mine." she retorts, crossing her arms, clearly annoyed.

"The issue isn't what Folli may have done, but what was done to him," Guerci brusquely specifies, his patience wearing thin and making no effort to conceal it.

"Did he kill one of his girlfriends? It wouldn't surprise me." Franka raises her chin, shaking her icing-like hair. "So if you brought me all the way here to vouch for that piece of shit, you can forget it," she hisses furiously.

Bassi looks at Guerci, and Guerci looks back at Bassi. Given the direction the conversation has taken, there doesn't seem to be much of an opportunity for subtle interrogation. The only thing to do is to let her have it and see what happens.

"Nando Folli's body was found three days ago in his laboratory with a pool of blood around his head," Bassi drops the bulldozer bucket sharply. "And this," he says, pushing forward the Department of Motor Vehicles form, "tells us that *your* car was seen in front of Folli's shop on the night he died. Do you have anything to say for yourself, Mrs. Bottaro?"

Franka's facial expression undergoes a drastic change. Her jaw drops, her eyebrows arch so much that her forehead disappears beneath her hair, and her eyes bulge out, with an equal and opposite force to that which sucks her lips inward to reveal her teeth down to the gums. She reminds Bassi of one of Francis Bacon's portraits. It doesn't flatter Bottaro's already less-than-delicate features, but it does suggest that she might be in a different position than they had hypothesized. Because either Franka is an incredible actress, or she truly had no idea that Folli is dead.

"Let's rephrase the question, Mrs. Bottaro," says Bassi. "Who was driving this car on the evening of September 15th?"

"I will only speak in the presence of my lawyer," Franka says hoarsely, looking at them with absolute and visceral hatred.

"We are not in an episode of CSI, Mrs. Bottaro, and nobody is formally accusing you of anything," the prosecutor reassures her with a smile. "Of course, if you prefer, we can continue this interview once you have contacted your lawyer. But for now, you are here as someone informed about the facts. Nothing more. Can you tell us what happened that night? Because you were there, right?"

Franka gazes at them silently.

"Even though you didn't know Folli was dead, you can still be a valuable witness," Bassi flashes one of his charming smiles. "Just tell us what you saw, and then you can go home with your husband. However, if you prefer to have a lawyer present, no problem at all. It would certainly complicate things a bit. More bureaucracy would be involved, the formal interview would need to be recorded, and you would naturally need to provide many more explanations to your husband and to anyone else wondering why Mrs. Bottaro is such a regular guest at the police station after the death of Mr. Nando Folli, a well-known lady's man..." Bassi shakes his head, expressing regret at causing her such discomfort.

"He was ghosting me, that pig," Franka declares after weighing the pros and cons and deciding to bring this matter to a swift conclusion. "And yes, we had an affair. It lasted almost three months. In fact, we were planning a little vacation to celebrate our anniversary."

"Anniversary?" Guerci interjects, perplexed.

"Yes, anniversary," she reiterates, displaying the irritation of someone attempting to explain etiquette to a chimpanzee. "The anniversary of our first three months, of course."

Guerci nods stiffly, attempting, and largely failing, to maintain his fixed smile.

"And then he started ignoring me, not answering calls or messages," Franka continues. "Because he's an idiot. You can see if someone has read your messages on WhatsApp! But that jerk tried to pretend he hadn't seen them." she growls, raising her voice. "I knew that he was trying to cut me off, to let things fade out so he could move on to someone new. But damn it, Franka is not someone you can just shove in a corner like one of his junk dressers." she remarks grimly.

Bassi is not yet sure if Franka actually killed Folli but he is sure she would have liked to. From Guerci's expression, it's clear that he and Bassi are both on the same page.

"Let's get back to the evening of the 15th," Bassi nods sympathetically, prepared for anything now.

"I followed him," Franka shrugs, as if it were the least a woman in her situation could do. "He had even stood me up for dinner, just a simple and stupid dinner I had asked for. He claimed he wanted to stay at home, that he was tired, had digestive problems, and all sorts of nonsense. And what does he do instead? He goes out. He takes his dreadful van and drives out to his shop." she says, pursing her lips and squeezing her handbag on her knees as if it were a voodoo doll representing Folli. "At first, when I saw him park in front of his shop, I gave him the benefit of the doubt, thinking he had some work he had to take care of. But when I saw that slut in the flowery dress with the suitcase sneaking inside… I understood. I realized that he was going on vacation with her!" she exclaims.

"But what made you think she was a new lover? Couldn't she simply be a customer?" says Bassi, spreading his arms.

"Yeah, right, a customer!" Franka raises an eloquent eyebrow. "She went in all cheerful and practically skipping and hopping like an Easter Bunny. It's true that they must have had a fight because she came out pretty fast and I could tell that she was really angry."

"I repeat, why were you so sure she was a new lover and not a client?" insists Bassi.

"Well, for one thing, she brought a suitcase with her. To top it off, once she left, I made a U-turn — I had parked on the opposite side of the street — stopped in front of the store, entered, and there, in the laboratory, behind the curtain where Folli and I used to fool around, I caught him with his pants down and on his knees. That's why!" Franka roars in exasperation.

Guerci turns to look at Bassi, who clasps his hands under his chin to better evaluate his next move.

"Finding your lover like this, in *flagrante delicto*, let's say, and so close to your anniversary…" he shakes his head sympathetically, "must have been a terrible blow for you, Mrs. Bottaro."

"Yes," she sticks out her chin, "but not as terrible as the blow I gave him," she smiles fiercely, clearly pleased with herself.

Bassi stares at her silently, unsure if he has heard correctly.

"A blow, you say?" Guerci articulates slowly, probably just as afraid of not having heard correctly.

"Sure," she nods, "one blow with this very purse," she lifts her big leatherette bag, "right in the face. The recoil sent the bastard flat on his flaccid ass. What could I have possibly seen in him, I wonder," she shakes her head in amazement. "He's certainly no Brad Pitt. In fact, it's hard to imagine anyone less like Brad Pitt. He looks like he's eight months pregnant and he belches like a camel. And to think that now he is…" she blinks as if she's having a second epiphany, "now he's dead!" and with a howl, she bursts into tears.

"So you hit Folli with your bag," Bassi repeats, handing her a tissue, "and knocked him to the ground, if I understand correctly."

She blows her nose loudly and nods her head yes.

"And then? Where was Folli when you left?"

She stiffens, as if she's swallowed a shovelful of quick cement. "There was no 'and then.' When I left, he was alive, if that's what you mean," she spits dryly. "He had his hands over his nose, because in this purse I keep my phone, diary, wallet, beauty case… About seven pounds of stuff. But come on, you can't kill someone by swatting them with a purse. Not even a wimp like Nando, may his soul rest in peace."

"Perhaps not," Bassi smiles conciliatorily. "And the young lady who had entered before you, the one with the suitcase and the flowered dress…"

"You mean the slut?"

Bassi makes a vague gesture to confirm that yes, he meant her, but he's not sure he shares her opinion about the woman's moral conduct. "Do you, by any chance, remember if she also had a frying pan with her suitcase?"

Franka narrows her eyes again. "So you know who the slut is!" she hisses, with the face of someone who has begun to suspect she has been taken for a ride, and she doesn't like that at all. "Because she did have a frying pan, yes."

Bassi leans back with his hands clasped under his chin.

So, the scenario went something like this: Kalina enters, Folli emerges from around a corner with his pants down, she hits him with a frying pan, and the antiques dealer falls to the ground. A few minutes later, just enough time for her to leave the parking lot on the other side of the road, make a U-turn, and stop in front of the shop, Franka Bottaro gets out of her car and goes inside. Folli is recovering, although he's still on his knees and still probably disoriented. Franka finds him like this, half-naked and in a compromising position, and hits him with a seven-pound handbag with enough power to knock him down for a second time.

Nonetheless, Folli survives. Mrs. Bottaro, if she is sincere (and Bassi is inclined to believe she is), claims he is still alive when she leaves. On top of that, the coroner found that Folli had been killed by a sharp blow to the temple, a blow that could not have been inflicted by a handbag, even if it did weigh seven pounds.

So what happens next? How does Folli die? Because if there is one fact that has always been clear in this mess of a case, it's that Folli is indisputably dead.

If Kalina didn't kill him and Franka didn't kill him, who did? Omero claims that from then on, it's just stillness and silence.

Was anyone else in the shop? That mysterious "someone" who perhaps held him back, as Kalina had implied when she acted out her encounter with Folli? But no one, not Kalina, not Franka, not Omero, had seen this someone. Could they have waited in the shop and slipped out in the morning, perhaps while Omero was eating breakfast? It couldn't have been earlier than that since, according to Omero, he hadn't left the window all night. "A moment's distraction, a lifetime's destruction."

So, where was he? He was back on square one, that's where.

Nando Folli was no more and they had run out of possible suspects. The one other promising person of interest, Filipponi, has an alibi that's so solid it's almost suspicious. At the time Folli was killed, Filipponi was in Genoa having a very long phone call with the mother-in-law of the president of the region to negotiate a price for restoring an important painting from the Genoese Baroque school.

So everything had cancelled out and the only "leads" Bassi had left were a report of a "kite" crashing on a mountain and a slice of a panel from the fifteenth century.

At the moment that was looking worse than having no leads at all.

Chapter Fifty

It's useless. Edna lets go of the mouse and takes off her glasses. She's been racking her brain for more than half an hour while staring at the same page of her research on Bosch. She knows she's missing something, something obvious, but she can't figure out what. Well, there's no point in continuing to beat her head against her laptop screen. It will come to her, eventually. Or not.

She picks up the empty cup from the top of a pile of papers, gets up, and heads to the kitchen, unsure whether to make another coffee — which would be her third — or to listen to common sense and give up for the moment. She shrugs and unscrews the moka pot. She's spent almost fifty years ignoring common sense. It's a little late to start now. She places the refilled pot on the stove and turns on the gas.

Then she gathers the books she left open on the table from the previous night and goes back to the living room to return them to the bookshelf. It's not as easy as it sounds because removing a book from her shelves does not create an empty space. It merely gives the remaining volumes a bit more elbow room, room which they will fight to keep, so putting every book back in its place is a struggle. She rolls her eyes, sets the volumes on the arm of the sofa, and begins fighting to clear an opening. It really is amazing. She can remove a six-hundred page tome from her shelves and the rest of the books, like some sort of art-historical gas, expand, leaving no trace of the slightest opening.

Speaking of gas… She sniffs the air, now saturated with the scent of overcooked coffee. In her haste to rush back to the stove, her elbow collides with a wooden photo frame, causing it to land on the carpet with a dry thud. She steps over it, hurries into the kitchen, and turns off the flame beneath the moka pot, hoping she has arrived in time. It would be the second one she's managed to ruin in just three months. The pot has survived but the now-boiled coffee has not and she pours it into the sink. She returns to the living room and bends down to pick up the frame. She thanks God it didn't break, considering the way her day has been going. But maybe God had nothing to do with it and she ought to be thanking the carpet for cushioning the fall. She runs the corner of her sweater over the black and white photo of her father, removing the dust. It was a picture she had taken herself, just a week before his fatal heart attack. It shows him gazing at her with his open smile and inquisitive eyes that never ceased asking questions, while waving his hand in the air in what could almost be seen as a blessing, if it weren't for the cigar he's holding between his raised fingers.

"What were you doing? Blessing me with tobacco?" Edna whispers, gently caressing his face with her fingertips.

As Edna gazes at the photo, she thinks back on her father's endless thirst for knowledge and the conversations they used to have. Even once, she recalls, on the imagery of blessing, an odd thing to discuss with an eleven year old! She hasn't brought up that memory for years but now she can recall it as if it had happened yesterday. The image of her younger self resurfaces, a slender eleven-year-old with hair escaping from a crooked braid, absorbed in the study of an anatomy treatise open to the page depicting the upper limbs alongside the reproduction of the mosaic of *Christ Pantocrator* of Monreale. Her father's soft voice narrates the significance of the blessing gesture and how it has been depicted in ancient works of art: palm forward, with thumb, forefinger and middle finger straight and the others fingers bent, with the three outstretched fingers apparently representing the Trinity.

But there was a twist to the story. Her father had told her that the first pope, Saint Peter, could not extend all his fingers in the traditional Jewish blessing gesture – the very same gesture that Mr. Spock stole to use as his "Live Long and Prosper" Vulcan greeting – due to a problem with his ulnar nerve. As a result, his ring and little fingers curled up involuntarily. Subsequent popes, out of respect for the founder of the Church, adopted the same gesture for their blessings. Thus it became a recurring motif in mosaics, frescoes, paintings, and religious representations, even those depicting the Child Jesus. Her father had laughed at how a minor medical condition could alter the course of art history.

Edna blinks, her breath catching in her throat as she focuses on yet another seemingly irrelevant detail. It has always been right there in front of her, an image she has witnessed countless times. She knows it by heart.

Butt Music.

Without a moment's hesitation, she grabs her jacket and phone and rushes out of the house as if propelled by a cannon. Perhaps now, finally, she knows.

She knows who killed Folli.

Chapter Fifty-One

"Is this a bad time?" Leonardo rubs his kneecap, emerging from the hydrangea bush where he had dived to avoid a head-on collision with Edna.

"Yeah, I mean, not really bad but…" she hastily brushes the leaves off his shoulders, apologizing for not watching where she was going. "By any chance, were you looking for me?" she asks as she fiddles with her cell phone. She realizes that this is a stupid question the second the words have left her mouth as Leonardo is standing in her front yard.

"I didn't want to disturb you by calling on the phone, so I was leaving a note on your chicken coop," he smiles, waving a piece of paper. "I knew that was the one place you would be sure to see it."

"A computer expert who disdains digital communication in favor of old-school paper?" Edna looks at him with respect rather than amazement, rummaging in her pockets for her car keys.

"Yes, but I see you're in a hurry, Edna… We'll talk later."

"Well, at least tell me what you wrote in that note."

"'Eureka.'"

"What did you find?" Edna asks distractedly, throwing her jacket on the car seat while jamming her cell phone between her shoulder and ear. "Orietta? It's Edna, call me back as soon as you can. Sorry, Leonardo, I'm trying to reach the councilor, and I always get her voicemail. You said that you found…?"

"Your missing panels. I also found out something new about the kite seal, if that's still of interest."

Edna looks at him, torn. She will have to choose… or maybe not. "Are you busy now?" she asks him point-blank.

"Not really, it's Saturday, and I'm not work…"

She cuts him short. "Do you need your computer to explain what you discovered?"

"Not really." he pulls some folded papers out of the back pocket of his jeans, "I even printed some stuff to give to you. I was going to leave them on the coop."

"Perfect. Get in. You can tell me about it on the way to Gattorna. Be prepared, though, I'm off to do something that's possibly illegal."

"Illegal how?" he asks. But this is clearly persiflage rather than a serious inquiry as he has already opened the door and gotten into the passenger seat.

"Like tampering – well, not exactly tampering – with evidence to make sure of something before involving the prosecutor and potentially making a fool of myself, or worse." Edna releases the clutch, smoothly exits through the gate and then rapidly accelerates in the direction of Gattorna.

"Let me guess. You intend to secretly sneak back into Folli's laboratory," Leonardo deduces, gripping his seat with both hands as Edna takes a curve with unnecessary enthusiasm.

"More or less," she remains vague.

"I assume the panel has something to do with whatever it is you have in mind?"

"For once, no. It's something less fascinating and decidedly more prosaic."

"If your concern is that I might report you to the police, that boat sailed when I broke into the auction archives for you. I'm a co-conspirator now, wouldn't you say?"

"When you put it that way, I suppose you have a right to know what I have in mind," she says, honking loudly as she barrels around another curve. "The thing is, I got the idea that maybe I know who killed Folli."

"Huh? And how?"

"Ever since my mother's former housekeeper recounted her version of the events at Folli's shop, something has been bothering me."

"Your mother's former housekeeper? And what does she have to do with the antiques dealer's death?" Leonardo turns to her in amazement.

"Nothing, as it turns out. But she happened to be there by pure chance and, uh, had a 'brief interaction' with him."

"I don't quite follow…"

"Sometimes I can't follow myself, believe me," Edna sighs. "To put it briefly, I got the idea of what must have happened when I saw a painting by Bosch that I know by heart, and bam! There it was. But while I'm pretty sure, even I admit that it's an odd notion so I need to personally check on something before I stick my neck out." Without taking her eyes off the road, she tosses the cell phone onto Leonardo's lap. "Would you mind calling Councilor Repetto? We're going to need her help if this is going to work. Just hit 'redial.'"

Before Leonardo can obey, Edna's phone explodes with its usual cacophonous ringtone, causing Leonardo to wince and Edna to swerve dangerously into the lane usually reserved for oncoming traffic.

"Damn it!" she snaps, getting the car back on the correct side of the road. "I should really change that. It was really amusing when it went off in faculty meetings but now I'm just annoying myself."

Leonardo glances at the phone. "It's the councilor. What should I tell her?"

"Tell her that in fifteen minutes, I'll be in front of Folli's laboratory and that I need a little help that only she can provide. I'll explain everything when I get there."

"The councilor says it's fine," he reports, hanging up. "But she also suggests that while you're up there, you should drop by and have a chat with Santi Niboni about the Dante event."

"Very well…" Edna rolls her eyes and sighs. Considering that the councilor has committed multiple felonies on her behalf, it seems a small request. "From your expression, I gather that this thing about Santi Niboni and Dante wasn't in your plans." Leonardo observes.

"You have a gift for understatement." she snorts. "I'd rather schedule a recreational root canal. So let's change the subject. Would you care to explain to me why you are sitting in my car?"

"Because you made me? I didn't get out of bed planning to spend my day in Gattorna!"

Edna chuckles. "That's not what I meant. You said you had discovered something important about the panel."

"Okay," he chuckles, in turn, smoothing his notes over his legs. "Let's see: there are two panels that correspond in height to our 61 centimeters, but only one is the same width as Folli's panel: exactly 30.5 centimeters. It passed through Sotheby's London on March 21st, 2016, lot 65, classified as 'Italian school – Early 14th,' and it was sold for eleven thousand pounds, although the starting price was four thousand."

"So, no description of the item," Edna mutters. "Which could mean that, just like our panel, the depicted figures had either been disguised or held little significance when taken out of the painting's overall context. However, eleven thousand pounds is not a small amount for a relatively anonymous panel with a nebulous attribution. Unless, of course, the buyer knew something that made the painting particularly attractive. By the way, do you happen to know who bought it?"

"Indeed I do," Leonardo answers with a satisfied smile. "The receipt is made out to a company called A.r.t., with its registered office in Switzerland. But A.r.t. also bought another piece, the one that matches in height but is double the width. It was sold at Neumeister in Munich, lot 145, on October 26th, 2018. The item was classified as 'Italian Gothic school,' with a starting price of eight thousand and sold for fifteen thousand."

"Excellent. Those must be our missing panels."

"But how did you know exactly what to look for? How did you know our panel was part of a triptych? It could have been part of anything. And what does all this have to do with frying pans?"

"I didn't know, exactly. But size matters, or at least it did in medieval art. Kalina's frying pan was a specific size because it had to be a specific size. The same thing is true with our triptych. The detail that I couldn't remember, that was bothering me for so long, is that the dimensions of our panel were not chosen at random."

"Thirty and a half centimeters isn't random?" asks Leonardo, unconvinced.

"Well, of course, they didn't use centimeters in the fifteenth century. And our panel artist loved him some symbology. That was very common in medieval art but our artist was more attuned to symbology than most. Even the measurements of his work encoded hidden knowledge."

"Well, it's certainly hidden from me! You're going to have to do better than that."

"Have you ever heard of the *Mensura Christi*?" she asks. A quick glance reveals that he has not. "OK. Measurement was not just for engineering and commerce. Back then, it had religious significance, too. The *Mensura Christi*, the 'measure of Christ,' was thought to be the exact height of Jesus Christ. And before you ask, it was 183 centimeters."

"I thought you said they didn't use centimeters," Leonardo teases.

"They didn't. You're thinking of it the wrong way. It was its own length and defined itself. Even today, in the Basilica of St. John Lateran in Rome, there is a *Mensura Christi* – four pillars holding up a slab – that was the religious equivalent of the standard meter in Paris, at least when it came to measuring Christ.

"You could buy prayer books that had a *Mensura Christi* based on this. Typically, there would be a line in the prayer book that was exactly one-twelfth of the standard one. You would be instructed to measure out that line twelve times 'to know the height of the body of our Lord.' The act of the measurement itself was a species of prayer. Even looking at the line in the prayer book was thought to provide protection and carrying a piece of string of that precise length was the equivalent of wearing a St. Christopher medal."

"That is fascinating, I admit, but what does that have to do with our panel?"

"Because the lengths of the sides of our panel aren't random. One-twelfth of a *Mensura Christi* is 15.25 centimeters. Do you see?"

"Well, our panel is 30.5 centimeters wide, so that's one-sixth of one. And it's twice that high, so that's one-third. But so what?"

"This is the fifteenth century. They took their religious symbology very seriously. You can't have a fractional Christ. If you are using a measure like that, it had better add up to a whole number. In our case, since our 'base unit' of measurement is one-twelfth of a *Mensura Christi*, that means a multiple of twelve. Our triptych is twenty-four of our base units, or two *Mensurae Christi*. In other words, the perimeter of our triptych is 183 centimeters multiplied by two or 366 centimeters. And that's what all this has to do with Kalina's frying pan and our panel."

Leonardo remains silent for a moment, processing this flood of information and then begins to applaud enthusiastically. Edna smiles briefly and says, "But we'll have to pick this up later. We've arrived at our destination!" Edna switches off the engine. "Although I still don't see the councilor."

She unbuckles her seatbelt, opens the door, and turns abruptly towards Leonardo, who has done the same and is stretching his leg out of the car. "And what do you think you're doing?" she asks dryly.

"I'm coming with you and the councilor," he explains calmly. "You weren't thinking of leaving me here to play lookout, I hope. And before you start, it's useless to try to change my mind with 'you'd better stay out of it' or 'I don't want to involve you.' Apart from the fact that you've already involved me, I've come clean with you but you've told me nothing about your incredible discovery that caused you to spontaneously run out of your house and drag me out into the middle of nowhere. So save it. I'm not waiting in the car while you go off and have an adventure."

Edna, for once, knows when she is beaten. "Very eloquent." she concedes, looking around. "Ah, there's Orietta," and she waves her arm towards the councilor who, for some reason, is half-hidden in the branches of a hazel tree and appears to be shooing flies away from her face.

"Does she always act like that?" Leonardo asks, perplexed.

"No. I'm not sure what she's doing. Is she trying to…" But the realization dawns too late and Public Prosecutor Bassi appears in the doorway of Folli's shop, fixing them with a stern eye before turning to look at the councilor whose cherry-colored bob clashes unmercifully with the hazel leaves in which she is vainly attempting to hide.

Finally, he shakes his head and calls out, "My first question would be 'what the hell are you doing here?' but since I prefer not to know, I won't ask. Come inside. Don't just stand there, come on!" he says as he waves them over before disappearing through the glass door.

"Oops…" splutters Leonardo.

"Waiting in the car doesn't look so bad now, does it?" hisses Edna between her teeth.

Chapter Fifty-Two

"That went well!" Edna snorts to herself. She had arranged everything so she could privately verify her hypotheses and avoid potentially embarrassing herself in front of the public prosecutor. Yet here she is, carrying out her investigation while Bassi, who is clearly not amused, is eyeing her like a dyspeptic hawk. While the state of Bassi's digestion doesn't concern her, she can't deny that his presence is disconcerting.

"So this fellow you have in tow is your famous neighbor?" the councilor whispers in a low voice, sidling up to Edna and swiveling her head like an owl to keep him in sight.

"Yeah," sighs Edna, realizing that she has yet another problem. "And how am I going to justify his presence to Bassi?" she hisses through her teeth. "I can hardly explain that he came along to help me break into a crime scene, can I? That doesn't seems fair. The only reason he's here at all is because I was in a hurry."

Orietta shrugs and makes a mental note to find out exactly what the hell Edna is talking about once they have successfully avoided going to jail. "You can always pass him off as your personal secretary, I suppose." Orietta glances back, yet again, at Leonardo. "Bassi already suspects you two are involved so a simple work relationship would be much more believable. I'd hire him in my office in a heartbeat!" she chuckles. "By the way, I still have no idea why we're here or what we're looking for."

"Leads and corroborating details," Edna explains grimly.

"Regarding that painting?"

"No, regarding Folli's murderer."

"What?" the councilor's eyes widen, but she isn't able to inquire further because Bassi abruptly halts in front of a bookcase. It's not just any bookcase, Edna realizes, but the one to which a curtain is attached dividing the shop from the laboratory, the bookcase only a few paces away from where Folli's body was found.

"Well, now, before we proceed, I'd like to know two things," the prosecutor says, arms crossed, as he stares at them. "First, what led you to come back here, Dr. Silvera? As for the presence of the councilor, I'm not going to ask. The Land Registry should probably decide to clear out the warehouse at the back. Right, Councilor?"

"I will certainly suggest it to them, Prosecutor Bassi," Orietta replies, unfazed.

"Great. Second question: Who is this gentleman you brought with you, Dr. Silvera?"

"Hello, Mr. Bassi. I'm Leonardo Sacco," he introduces himself, extending his hand. "Dr. Silvera's neighbor. We've already spoken on the phone."

"Ah, the famous neighbor, as well as Dr. Silvera's alibi for two consecutive nights…" Bassi examines him with narrowed eyes, shaking his hand. His expression displays a mix of surprise and incredulousness, leaving Edna uncertain whether to laugh or be offended. "And why are you here?" Bassi continues to scrutinize Leonardo.

"I asked him to come along," Edna interjects. "Engineer Sacco is a skilled computer scientist, and he's helping me with my research." It is partially true, after all.

"Ah…" Bassi nods. "And this research was supposed to be conducted here?"

"Don't be ridiculous, Mr. Bassi," Edna rolls her eyes. "I was in a hurry, and Leonardo was kind enough to update me along the way. He's providing assistance with some research for my upcoming meeting with the Dante Committee. Isn't that right, Councilor Repetto?"

"Indeed it is," Orietta nods. "In the council room. As you know, Mr. Bassi, the event commemorating Dante is less than a week away, and time is running out."

"Very well, Dr. Silvera. So you chose to park here, instead of in the square in front of the municipal hall, just so you could take a little stroll along the highway…" Bassi's sarcasm clearly indicates his diminishing patience.

"Not at all, Mr. Bassi," Edna exhales. She ran out of her own stock of patience two days ago, so she decides to confess and get straight to the point. "We, or rather, *I* am here for the same reason, I assume, as you. Or at least, I believe so, considering you stopped right in front of this bookcase. It's because of Kalina's little performance, isn't it?"

"Yes," Bassi admits. "And also because of what another witness, Franka Bottaro, Folli's most recent girlfriend, told us this morning. She might be the last person to have seen him alive."

"So, according to this other witness, she left Folli here," Edna concludes, "behind where the curtain would be."

"Exactly, and this…"

"And this is not where the councilor and I discovered the body," Edna nods. "We found Folli here, five or six steps away. You can still see the bloodstain."

"Are you suggesting a *third* person was involved? Because there is another witness, one I tend to consider reliable," Bassi glances at the councilor, who nods in agreement, "and he claims no one else came or went that evening."

"Not a third person, but a third element: bad luck."

"Luck doesn't exist," Bassi declares firmly, leaving no room for argument.

"I tend to agree with you, Mr. Bassi. That's why I would have preferred to come here and clarify any doubts on my own before offering you such a, ahh, creative theory."

"And what would that theory be?" Bassi stares at her seriously. He has, reluctantly, learned to respect these creative theories of Edna's.

"Well, my doubts arose when I observed Kalina's re-creation. You'll recall that when she was acting out Folli's part, it was as if someone had a hold of his leg and was trying to pull him back into the alcove behind the curtain. Remember?"

"Yes, that's why I initially thought there might have been someone else here. But as I was saying, the witness…"

"No, Mr. Bassi, our focus on another person was due to an error of perspective. We should have considered *something* rather than *someone*."

"I don't follow," Bassi admits.

"Not surprising," Edna sighs, realizing how insane she sounds only as she begins explaining her reasoning. "You see, I have made a particular study of the works of Bosch. As you know, Bosch is famous for his surrealistic paintings that often involve naked bodies and torture by demons. It's believed that he suffered from ergotism, a disease caused by a fungus called ergot that is the precursor of LSD and causes, among other things, very bad hallucinations. I was studying one of his paintings, *The Garden of Earthly Delights*, one I had seen countless times before, when all the pieces fell into place and the theory came to me."

"Will you be sharing it with us, Edna, or would it be quicker if we all got our own PhDs in medieval art history and figured it out for ourselves?" Leonardo asks. Even his patience has worn thin after waiting for an hour and a half and being bounced over twenty-five miles of winding roads.

"Tell me about the trousers Folli was wearing, Mr. Bassi." She asks, regally ignoring Leonardo's sarcasm.

"Well, let me see," Bassi tries to recall. "It was a regular pair of jeans with a black leather belt. Both the pants and the belt, as we know, were undone and…"

"Do you happen to know if the right leg had a small hole or any signs of fraying?" Edna persists.

"Not really, but if it's important, I can have it checked. But what this has to do with Folli's murder…" Bassi says, spreading his arms.

"It has everything to do with Folli's murder… because Folli wasn't murdered."

"You're suggesting this was suicide?" Bassi asks in disbelief.

"Not suicide. Just bad luck. Think about it: Folli suffered from heartburn, right?"

"Tremendously so. He was popping antacids like peanuts." Bassi confirms.

"Well, in my experience, people with chronic heartburn loosen their belts whenever they can, especially in a private place like this." Edna explains.

"OK. Go on."

"Well, let's imagine this scenario: Folli is here with his belt undone as usual. It's late at night, long after business hours. Suddenly, he hears Kalina's voice and hurries to check who it is. However, he gets hooked on something with the leg of his jeans, causing his trousers to slip down when he takes his next step. So, when Kalina sees him, he is standing in front of her without his trousers and struggling to move. She hits him with the frying pan, and he falls to the ground. Kalina then rushes out, and when Folli regains consciousness and stands up, he is still dazed from the blow, confused, and doesn't realize that his trousers are around his ankles. He takes five or six wobbly steps forward, stumbles, hits his head somewhere, and dies where we found him. Does that explain the facts as you know them, Mr. Bassi?"

Bassi blinks rapidly, never taking his eyes off Edna. "No… it couldn't have happened like that," he shakes his head, firmly convinced.

"Oh. Well, it was just a theory and I recognize it seems unlikely." says Edna, abashed and furious that she was unable to disprove her theory on her own before making a fool of herself.

"No, your theory is preposterous enough to be true. But it doesn't account for what we know. After Kalina left, Franka, his girlfriend, entered the shop, found Folli on his knees, jumped to an unfortunate conclusion, wound up, and struck him in the face with her seven-pound purse, knocking him flat on his back and rendering him unconscious… again."

"Ah," Edna swallows, "poor Folli. What a way to go! Usually, 'he never knew what hit him' is just an expression."

"So, your theory may be correct except that it all happened after Franka hit him, not Kalina. After he regained consciousness, he staggered to his feet, took a few steps, still completely out of it and…" Bassi waves his hand and lets out a tired sigh. "I suspect I'm going to be sorry I asked, but how did you come up with this?"

"Again, it was thanks to Bosch… and St. Peter." Bassi raises an eyebrow skeptically as Edna continues. "In Bosch's painting, the right panel is a vision of hell that includes several unclothed people being tortured. In one particularly famous detail, one of these tortured souls has a musical score tattooed across his, ahh, butt. It's actually music you can play. Just google it. Anyway, that image stuck with me and when I put it together with the idea that a minor health condition can have major repercussions, it all clicked with Kalina's story."

"St. Peter?" asks Leonardo, still looking confused, but Orietta interjects, with her usual practicality, "That's all very interesting. But it's still just a theory. What do we do now?"

"Now I'll have his pants examined closely. In the meantime, we need to find a nail, a protrusion, or something that could have caught Folli's jeans. We also need to find where Folli struck his temple — if that's what happened. It would have to be somewhere between here," decides Bassi, pointing, "and about here. Well, there are four of us, and there should be some latex gloves at the entrance. Let each of us take a quarter of this space and search!"

Edna breathes a sigh of relief. For once, things are going better than she'd feared. So she puts on her gloves and begins searching.

Chapter Fifty-Three

Dr. Silvera made a big deal about the importance of details. But, at least in this case, details had nothing on chance, fate, or plain old bad luck. Because that's precisely what caused Folli's death. Bassi clasps his hands together under his chin and admits to himself that the unlikely series of events that ended with Folli's demise probably wouldn't have occurred to him. He understands himself well enough to realize that he prefers to see a world with some order and intention in it. But Folli was killed by nothing more than bad luck and worse heartburn.

Bassi rests his elbows on the desk, lost in thought in the gentle half-light of his office. He thinks about Folli, who had survived frying pans, insane lovers, and heavy handbags only to succumb to the corner of a marble pedestal that, upon impact with the antiques dealer's skull, toppled and disappeared behind a large trunk.

He also ponders the role of chance. The coroner has just confirmed that the filaments found on a metal hook protruding near the famous curtain dividing the shop matched Folli's torn trousers. And perhaps the most spectacular intervention by the Goddess of Randomness, the appearance of a former Romanian housekeeper wielding a frying pan who really, really needed to pee. By God, Bassi shakes his head, what were the odds that Mrs. Dumitrescu would quit her job that very day? And that she would receive another job offer in Gattorna? And that she would alight from the bus at the wrong stop, coinciding with Folli's return to his laboratory? And what about the hook snagging Folli's trousers, provoking Mrs. Dumitrescu's reaction, and subsequently Franka's? All of this already appears extraordinary to him. But chance, not yet finished with Folli, orchestrated his collision with a marble pedestal. Yes, details matter. But fate matters more.

Bassi switches on his desk lamp and arranges the papers on his desk. The case is closed. After all, the investigation was launched to establish the cause of Nando Folli's violent death, and that cause has been unquestionably determined and confirmed by the autopsy report. The verdict is "Death by Misadventure." Legally speaking, there's nothing to see here.

But the matter of that painted panel still lingers in his mind. While they aren't really his department, there are still a lot of questions about that panel that need answering. And then there's the matter of Kowalski's death. Again, it's not his problem. He died – or was killed? – in Milan. But he has questions, all the same.

He is unsure what to do about the panel. The correct answer is nothing. Since Folli wasn't murdered, there's no case and, so, the panel isn't evidence. In fact, it's legally a part of Folli's estate. But sorting out estates in Italy can take years and something tells him that the mystery of the panel won't wait that long. Not that long ago, someone wanted that panel very badly, badly enough to hide it and disguise it. And his nose tells him someone still does. The worst thing he could do would be to simply chuck the panel back into Folli's shop where he found it. Perhaps he ought to hand it over to the Office for the Protection of Cultural Heritage. It was certainly more their responsibility than his. But…

He reaches for his phone, weighing it in his hand for a moment, then lets out a sigh and dials a number. "Dr. Silvera, I hope I'm not interrupting," he blurts out in a single breath, while a neon sign flashes in his head: DANGER! STUPIDITY AHEAD! "I've been thinking about our infamous panel, and… well, here it is: Folli had saved a number on his phone under the name 'The Pole,' it's someone he met in Milan just a week before his death. The number belongs to a man named Carlo Kowalski. I was wondering if by any chance that name rings any bells, perhaps it's a name you've come across in the art world… Dr. Silvera, are you still there?"

"Did you say Kowalski?" she responds after a too-lengthy silence, her voice strained.

"Yes. Do you…"

"Perhaps it would be better if you came to see me in Chiavari," she interrupts. "I'll explain when I see you." And with that, she abruptly hangs up.

Bassi remains sitting at his desk, staring at the phone in his hand. Why hadn't he listened to himself? But he never could take good advice when it came to leaving well enough alone, not even from himself. It was too much like that earlier art smuggling case. He had gotten his teeth into it now and, to mix a metaphor, he couldn't just walk away without tripping over all those loose ends. He was still an idiot, though.

Chapter Fifty-Four

"Kowalski…" Edna muses. "That name opens up a lot of avenues for your investigation. Some of them you'd probably prefer to close, lock, and drop the key in the ocean." she continues, handing Bassi a bottle of fruity white wine called Bianchetta Genovese. She doesn't know if Bassi can drink on duty – most of the experience she's had with police involves old *Law & Order* episodes – but, under the circumstances, offering Bassi tea didn't feel quite right. Since Bassi had reacted with an enthusiastic "Bianchetta Genovese!" when he saw the bottle, however, she uncorked it without further inquiry.

"So, if I understand correctly, the Rose Kowalski you know could be the same Rose Kowalski who left her apartment to our Polish friend. According to the documents that Inspector Guerci just managed to track down," he says, enlarging the images on his mobile phone's display, "Carlo Kowalski inherited the apartment from her as her sole surviving family member."

"She was probably his aunt." Edna sips the wine thoughtfully. "If it's the same Rose, and the age seems correct, my father often spoke about her. They met in high school, where she was a year behind him. My father hailed from a small town in the Friuli region, but my grandfather wanted his son to pursue an education. So my father went off to high school and if it weren't for the war and everything that happened, he would have enrolled in a university when he graduated." Edna lets her gaze wander for a moment into the straw-colored, aromatic wine because digging up these memories isn't easy. "Well, as you may know, after the racial laws of 1938, one of those infamous Centers for the Study of the Jewish Problem was established in Trieste in 1941," she continues solemnly. "These laws were only loosely enforced until the Germans took over Northern Italy in September 1943 and began persecuting Jews in earnest. They set up the Risiera di San Sabba to serve as a transit camp for Jews from Friuli, Veneto, Istria, and Dalmatia. My father ended up there in November of 1943. The surname Silvera leaves no doubt about one's heritage, especially when your high school gym teacher happens to be one of the leaders of the local fascist chapter. He was eighteen when he was loaded onto the convoy to Auschwitz."

"And then what happened?" Bassi asks, his tone expressing genuine sympathy for forcing her to revisit such memories.

"He managed to escape from the convoy thanks to a raid by the Resistance," Edna continues after taking a generous sip of wine. "It was March 1944. He and the others with him managed to force open the door of the rail car and escape in the confusion." Edna laughs bitterly, toying with her glass. "My father made his way to a rural area, far away from cities and German troops and hid out there for quite some time, eventually joining the partisans."

"I can imagine that it wasn't easy for a Jew to hide, even with the protection of the partisans," Bassi sighs.

"It was not, especially after the summer of 1944 when thousands of Cossacks were transferred to Friuli by Hitler's order. They were actual Russian divisions under the command of the Wehrmacht, who established an occupation regime with an anti-partisan mandate. And this is when Rose comes into the picture again."

"Rose Kowalski?" Bassi blinks, surprised.

"Yes, Rose had become the very young secretary of an official at the Office for the Superintendence of Fine Arts in Udine. Her father was a diplomat, so she had lived in several countries and spoke fluent German and Italian as well as a little French and, of course, her native Polish. That made her very useful, especially given the constant 'artistic' requests from Hitler and the Third Reich. They were constantly on the lookout for fine art they could plunder and the homes of deported Jews were searched thoroughly for anything that might interest the Nazis. However, this seemingly impeccable and unassuming secretary, much like her namesake Rose Valland from the Paris museum Jeu de Paume, was actually working for the partisans and against the regime. She found the perfect allies in my father and his friend Pietro Calligaris who helped her prevent as many works of art as possible from falling into German hands and passed information to Rodolfo Siviero's men."

"*That* Pietro Calligaris?" Bassi asks cautiously.

"Yes, the very same," Edna exhales heavily. "He was my former mentor. He is also the reason I risked going to jail for damaging private property – an overreaction, to say the least."

"If I remember correctly, you broke into his cellar and destroyed his entire collection of champagne with an iron bar – it was several thousand euros worth of damage, not to mention the criminal waste of good champagne which went down Pavia's sewers. Definitely an overreaction…"

"Perhaps you don't fully understand the situation," Edna says flatly, leaning forward. "That man was a friend of my father, and my father trusted him." Edna gets up and walks to the window. "*I* trusted him."

"And it was in fact thanks to him that you became a widely-respected art restorer. True, you had a suspicion that he was…"

"It. Was. Not. Just. A. Suspicion," Edna punctuates harshly. "Calligaris always played a double game. Even back when he was 'fighting' to protect artistic treasures with my father and Rose, he was collaborating with Himmler's henchmen. And he didn't stop because the war ended. Who knows how many stolen Italian works of art he managed to launder through Christie's, Sotheby's, or directly into the vault of some wealthy, unscrupulous collector before he…"

"Before he what?" Bassi stares at her, his eyes piercing like blades.

"Why are you doing this? You're nothing if not thorough." Edna snorts. "You've known the whole story since we discovered Folli's corpse. So you can stop pretending."

Bassi nods his head slightly, and relents. "It wasn't your fault, Edna, if that's what you think," he says in an indulgent tone.

"You still don't understand!" she raises her voice. "All those paintings that Calligaris gave me to restore, all those works 'rescued' from the basements of museums, art galleries, and estates, which he claimed he would re-introduce to the art world, the exhibitions that never materialized, the forged documents, documents that *I signed*! He used me. He used me for years. I trusted him and he made me into an accomplice, a criminal! And you want to talk about champagne!" She was furious now.

"No, Edna." he says, sympathy in his voice. "You're right. He used you. You weren't an accomplice. If anything, you were a victim. And perhaps you jumped the gun. Calligaris has never faced formal charges…"

"Don't make me laugh, Mr. Bassi," Edna scoffs bitterly, as if he could in her present mood. "You, of all people, know how the game is played. Calligaris had friends, both powerful friends and dangerous friends.

Some owed him favors. Some wouldn't have wanted to see him charged because he could have dragged their names into it. It certainly wasn't a question of evidence. There was enough hard evidence to build a pyramid. And yet, he was never even charged."

"Apparently, the evidence was all circumstantial." explains Bassi calmly.

Now Edna really does laugh. "Is that what the report said? They had names, dates, transactions, as many leads as they could have wanted. Did they ever actually investigate any of it? Oh, no! It was all 'circumstantial' so why bother?" she shrugs, feeling the weight of it as if it had happened twenty minutes ago instead of almost twenty years. "I quit and never went back. I couldn't bear to stay a minute longer. I couldn't even continue doing elsewhere the kind of work I had done for him. It sickened me. That's why I abandoned the field of restoration and turned to teaching."

"So, in your opinion," asks Bassi, trying to get the conversation back on track, "Calligaris was a dealer in stolen art?"

"And a traitor as well," Edna sighs, pouring herself another glass of wine and wishing she had brought the scotch back from Leonardo's before remembering that it was empty. "After all, he was and is an expert on Judas. As I've said, nothing ever happens by chance."

"And that's why you…"

"That's why I knew so much about the Iscariot."

"But Calligaris withdrew his complaint against you, regarding the shattered bottles of champagne…" Bassi looks at her.

"Yes he did. And I'm sure he had very good reasons for doing so. He wouldn't have enjoyed the publicity, for one."

"Or maybe he cared about you," he suggests, still staring at her.

"Oh, Mr. Bassi. And you, a prosecutor! Whose side are you on?" she rolls her eyes.

"I'm on yours, it's clear. That's why I'm trying to understand."

"There's really nothing else to understand. Calligaris is a slimy opportunist, plain and simple. The only thing that comforts me is that my father died before it all came to light."

"Your father eventually obtained his university degree, right?" Bassi asks, happy to change the subject.

"After the war, yes. In medicine," Edna replies, getting up and walking over to the bookshelf. She retrieves an old black-and-white photograph of a tall, dark-haired, handsome man in a white coat, accompanied by a determined-looking blonde little girl engrossed in a thick tome on comparative anatomy. "He was a very good doctor. He had a talent for it."

"What happened to Rose?" Bassi inquires.

"She was reported to the police shortly before the end of the war. I now suspect it was Calligaris who did it because the informant was someone very close to her, someone aware of her work and movements. However, thanks to her father's connections, she managed to escape before being arrested. My father and Calligaris learned that she had ended up in Switzerland, but then they lost track of her. It's possible that, not knowing who had betrayed her, she chose to sever all ties with her past. But let's return to the matter at hand: do you think Folli acquired the panel from Kowalski?"

"In the van, we found something like a receipt, with a signature that could be Kowalski's and dated on the day the antiques dealer went to Milan. The receipt mentions 'five pieces' for a total of one hundred and fifty euros. Although the items are not clearly identified, it's possible that one of them was our panel." Now Bassi is musing out loud. "This suggests that Carlo Kowalski knew as much about art as I know about raising caribou. So even if he was Rose's nephew, she didn't pass down any of her knowledge to him, that's evident."

"Perhaps he only discovered he had an aunt when he inherited the apartment," she shrugs.

"Among the documents Guerci sent me, there is also something related to the apartment in question," Bassi says, enlarging the display on his phone. "It's a report of a break-in dated April 12th, which is two days after Rose's death. Apparently, someone ransacked the house. But the police couldn't confirm if anything was missing or not."

Edna raises her eyes to look at him, and he falls silent, staring back at her as if they both had the same thought.

"Do you think they were searching for the panel that ended up with Folli?" he asks quietly.

"Maybe. And maybe it was just some petty thieves who checked the obituaries to know where to burgle undisturbed," she suggests.

"True," admits Bassi, drumming his fingers on the arm of the chair, looking disappointed.

"Now, don't be like that, Mr. Bassi," Edna urges him in a conciliatory tone. She's tempted to give him a pat of encouragement on the shoulder, but refrains, deeming it a bit too disrespectful. A ring from her doorbell rescues her from any further attempt at sympathy.

"Sorry, Edna," Leonardo greets her apologetically as soon as she opens the door, "but I thought you'd want to know right away, otherwise I would have just left a note on your chicken coop. I found something related to the kite and…" He stops abruptly, puzzled by Edna's wide-eyed expression and her attempt at what appears to be a bizarre version of charades.

"The kite, you say?" Bassi pokes his head into the entryway. "And what do you know about a kite?"

Edna rolls her eyes and exhales irritably. She had managed to keep Leonardo's investigations out of her conversations with Bassi. Now, all her efforts had come to nothing in less than three seconds.

"Ah, Mr. Bassi…" Leonardo smiles uneasily, realizing too late why Edna had reacted to his presence by having a minor seizure. "What a pleasant surprise."

"A surprise, certainly." observes Bassi dryly.

"You didn't really think I managed to obtain all those enhanced photographs on my own, did you?" Edna spreads her arms. "So don't even think about picking on this young man, who simply showed great kindness to a neighbor in distress. You ought to give him an award for services to the police."

"Certainly not. God forbid!" Bassi nods, wearing an expression that indicates he believes Edna's explanation about Leonardo's involvement as much as he believes in the Easter Bunny. But he decides to let it go as he wants to hear about the kite stamp on the panel. Kites were turning up far too frequently in this investigation…

"Excellent! Take a seat, Leonardo, and tell us everything," Edna invites him inside, while wordlessly attempting to communicate that he should do no such thing. Bassi had already looked the other way so often he would probably need a neck brace. She did not think tossing computer hacking and various other felonies onto the pile would improve his mood.

"Um, sure," Leonardo takes a seat hesitantly, feeling embarrassed. Discussing his extra-legal efforts to interfere in a police investigation with a public prosecutor had not been on his bingo card this morning.

"Before you start, Article 615 of the Penal Code punishes anyone who illegally enters a computer system protected by security measures," Bassi calmly addresses him. "But I am sure that you have done no such thing. Isn't that correct? Because if you *were* to tell me that you had broken into a computer system, I would be legally required to arrest and charge you." Leonardo nods slowly without taking his eyes off of Bassi's face. "That being said… based on your perfectly legitimate research, is there something I should be aware of that could be useful in shedding light on this infamous kite, Mr. Sacco?"

"Perhaps." responds Leonardo cautiously. "It might be worth having a look at a lot of paintings that passed through a London auction house a few years ago."

"A lot of paintings? Could you be more specific?"

"Not a lot of paintings," explains Leonardo, "a lot of paintings."

"That's what I said."

Leonardo sighs. "I don't mean a lot of paintings. I mean one lot of paintings. As in a lot at an auction. This lot consisted of twenty paintings.

Bassi nods skeptically, signaling for him to continue.

"It was quite peculiar… this entire lot consisted of twenty separate works, including panels and canvases. They were all from different periods but they all bore a distinctive mark or stamp on the back…" Leonardo nods towards Edna's computer, and she nods in return.

Before Edna can even figure out what he's trying to do, he has somehow interfaced it with his own computer and is scrolling through a series of images. "A stamp like this," he says.

"Ah!" exclaims Bassi. "And when did these paintings arrive at the auction house? Don't worry, Mr. Sacco," he reassures him with a smile, correctly interpreting the computer engineer's reticence, "I'm not going to ask you any questions about how you got this information and who I learned it from will remain within these four walls." Even as Bassi says these words, he knows there is no going back. He's in it up to his neck now. But that was already the case, really, when he had made the decision to dial Edna's phone. "April 19th." replies Leonardo.

Edna meets Bassi's gaze, one eyebrow raised.

"Yes." he nods thoughtfully. "That's less than a week after someone ransacked Rose's house."

"I'm not quite following you but, all things considered, it's probably better that way," Leonardo remarks, looking both relieved and perplexed.

"Mr. Sacco," Bassi gets up and joins him at the computer, "would you have a look and see what your... unique skills can turn up about Rose Kowalski... Yes, spelled like that, let's say around the date of April 10th. In the meantime, I can't wait to examine Edna's fascinating library." instructs Bassi as he deliberately wanders off and leaves Leonardo at his work.

He needn't have bothered. Leonardo types quickly, and within a few seconds, he's turned up a wealth of information using nothing more nefarious than Google. "Is this what you're looking for? This was in the Milan edition of the *Corriere della Sera* dated April 10th: *"Rose Kowalski, the elderly woman hit by a bus two days ago, died today at Niguarda Hospital without ever regaining consciousness..."*

"You, who don't believe in chance, Mr. Bassi," Edna mocks, "tell me, how do you explain the fact that a woman who had handled countless works of art in the past ends up under the wheels of a bus, that her house is burglarized not even two days later, and that the following week an entire lot of paintings with dubious provenance arrives in the warehouses of a well-known London auction house, all with a similar mark?"

"This isn't chance." answers Bassi grimly. "'One death is bad luck. Two deaths are coincidence. Three are enemy action.'"

Chapter Fifty-Five

"Now tell me the rest." demands Bassi staring at them intently.

Edna keeps her eyes fixed on her glass, while Leonardo feigns indifference by absentmindedly caressing his keyboard. Both remain silent.

"Come on! I can see it in your faces! There's something more. I thought I had made it abundantly clear from the start: whatever is discussed here doesn't go beyond these four walls," the prosecutor scoffs. "Do I need to put it in writing?"

"Well… It might be that we've stumbled upon two missing pieces that go with Folli's panel," Edna grudgingly admits.

"And after all this, it didn't occur to you that this was something I ought to know?" snaps Bassi, clearly annoyed

"What would have been the point? It maybe interesting, but it's a dead end." Edna shrugs.

"What do you mean, a dead end?" Bassi furrows his brow, not yet appeased.

"They were both purchased in 2018 by the same company, but from two different auction houses," Leonardo explains. "The company is called A.r.t., and is registered in Switzerland. However, when I tried calling them, I got a recorded message saying that the number is out of service."

"Oh, that's new. Even I didn't know that." Edna leans forward, intrigued.

"I found out after we returned from Gattorna. I've done some freelance research on my own." He admits with a guilty smile. "That's one of the things I had come over to tell you. I also printed out these." He rummages in the back pocket of his jeans and hands Bassi a folded sheet of paper.

"And what is this?" Bassi asks, frowning.

"Names, contact details, email addresses, and mobile numbers of all the members of A.r.t.; they all have one very interesting thing in common."

Bassi looks up sharply from the sheet he is perusing. "And what is that?"

"They don't exist. Not a one."

"What!?" Edna and Bassi exclaim in imperfect harmony. "Are you absolutely certain?" asks Bassi.

"Yes, I'm sure. These are all fake identities. The whole company has been set up just to make these purchases untraceable."

"Don't be like that Mr. Bassi," Edna interjects, noticing the look of disgusted defeat on his face. "You're like a wilted lettuce left out in the sun..."

"Well, it's just that... Oh, it's nothing," the prosecutor passes his hands over his face. "For a moment, I had hoped to be able to connect this with an old case of mine, one that I had to walk away from." It's clear from Bassi's face what he thinks about unfinished business.

"Why? Did it involve Switzerland?" Edna asks.

"Not exactly, or at least not exclusively. It was a major investigation into an organization that, at first glance, appeared to be beyond suspicion, comprised of entrepreneurs, bankers, restorers, shippers, even government officials. But they were dealing in stolen and smuggled Italian artworks, purchased through offshore companies specifically created for this purpose... including in Switzerland. This elusive A.r.t. company has their fingerprints all over it. Their meticulous attention to detail is what derailed my earlier investigation and it looks like it's happened again." explains Bassi shaking his head.

"I wouldn't say it's a complete dead end, Mr. Bassi." Leonardo demurs.

"And why not? Is there something else you haven't told us?"

"Not exactly. It's something I haven't shown you. As for what it means, I'll leave that to you." responds Leonardo, typing rapidly. "You see, there are more ways than one to search the internet. Most people think about search terms, but it's possible to do something similar with images. And if you construct a proper search around the image of the kite stamp, you get this!" he finishes, flipping the laptop around so that Edna and Bassi can see the screen.

"But those are..." gasps Edna.

"Yes." smiles Leonardo. The screen is displaying a series of engravings, stamps, seals, all on different media, but undeniably linked to the drawing of the kite they discovered on the back of Folli's panel and the lot of artworks from the auction house.

"And what does this mean?" Bassi asks, intrigued.

"Again, I have no idea," Leonardo shrugs. "But it must mean something. These images seem to be associated with nothing in particular. This one, for example," he clicks to enlarge an image, "is linked to a Chinese restaurant in Érd, a Hungarian city near Budapest. But only in the 'background,' I guess you'd say. It doesn't appear on the menu or in the logo or in pictures of the restaurant."

Edna puts on her glasses and carefully examines the images. "It's clearly intentional," she says, shaking her head, "these images are too similar to be just an endless series of coincidences. But they are also hidden, unless you know what you are looking for and how to look for it." muses Edna, thinking out loud. "I don't know… Maybe it's the internet version of a secret handshake?"

"You mean something like a secret society?" Bassi asks thoughtfully. Some of the facts surrounding his old art case are stirring in his subconscious. There's something there but it's too elusive for him to fully grasp.

"Well, I don't know what I mean. I can only see what you see, Mr. Bassi." Edna rolls her eyes. "But the idea of a secret society choosing a kite as its emblem – according to my friend Ottavio, there's a Japanese order that did exactly that – isn't necessarily ridiculous. And it's undeniable that it's turned up on a lot of paintings, including the one we have here. What's more likely? That there's some connection or no connection at all?"

"So, you think Rose Kowalski could have been part of this society or whatever it is?" Bassi ponders, while Leonardo simply shifts his gaze back and forth between the two as if he were watching a ping pong match.

"How do I know?" Edna snorts. "'Think' is a big word. But since you ask it like that, she *could* have been, I suppose. And I can already guess what you're going to ask me next, so the answer is *no*: my father never mentioned kites, let alone secret societies." Edna laughs at the look of disappointment on Bassi's face. "Oh please! Did you think it was going to be that easy? Do you think my father left a sealed letter in his desk laying out your case for you?" she scoffs.

"I suppose not." sighs Bassi. "And while we're on the subject of kites, and in the spirit of putting our cards on the table, it seems there's another kite in this case. This one appeared in the sky over Val Fontanabuona. A witness saw it flying several times over Folli's shop… even at night, which is rather unusual for a diurnal bird of prey. A kite that, incidentally, seems to have fallen from the sky and crashed into the woods on the mountain in front of Gattorna."

"Fallen from the sky and crashed? That doesn't sound like a bird. Are you sure your witness isn't making things up?" asks Leonardo.

"Very sure. Observations by this witness are incredibly reliable. You can't always rely on his interpretation of those observations, though. I am absolutely certain that he saw what he said he saw. But it wasn't a bird. It was a drone."

"I assume you've been searching for it?"

"Indeed we have. Our witness was able to provide us with an excellent idea of where it might be. So excellent, in fact, that Inspector Guerci's team managed to find it. Unfortunately, it's in quite a sorry state, not so much from the impact of the crash, but because whoever was operating it had some sort of explosive device on board. It blew up when it crashed. My guess is that it wasn't meant to be a weapon, but rather a way to make sure that no one could extract any information from it and trace it back to the operator. In short, we're ruling out that it belonged to a hobbyist who wanted to take nature photos." concludes Bassi dryly.

"But you must have been able to determine something from the wreckage." Leonardo probes, clearly intrigued.

"Apparently, it's a professional drone made of carbon fiber, designed for aerial video surveillance. It's capable of flying even in the rain and has a range of several miles. It has high-performance engines and is extremely quiet during flight…"

"Well, for someone to mistake it for a bird of prey like a kite, silent flight would be a basic requirement," Edna comments, raising an eyebrow.

"It certainly would." Leonardo nods with a slightly feral smile. For the last twenty minutes, he has been constantly on the back foot, not knowing whether he was going to be arrested by Bassi or obliterated by Edna. But now the case isn't about art or international criminal societies. It is about technology and he is the big cat in this jungle. "Were they monitoring or tracking something specific?"

"Possibly. Our witness observed the 'kite' flying over Gattorna and the surrounding areas frequently, for several days. The fact that it was often seen near Folli's shop could be very suspicious, but it could also be completely irrelevant…"

"Come now Mr. Bassi. This drone was equipped to self-destruct. Its activities were very relevant to something. We need to analyze the data from the drone." remonstrates Leonardo, spreading his arms.

"But he just told us it exploded!" Edna frowns.

"A drone as sophisticated as that would have a fairly complicated computer system on board. These aren't like radio-controlled cars that children play with. This is a complex system that flies itself. It almost certainly carried several gigabits of memory so it could record its flight path, store images, etc. So where are those memory chips? Even if they were damaged, something is probably salvageable." Leonardo really has the bit in his teeth now.

"You're right!" nods Bassi. "There should be an internal log where all the flight data, and possibly other data, has been recorded. We'll try to recover it. But I don't want to get my hopes up too high."

"Your optimism is an inspiration to us all, Mr. Bassi," Edna observes dryly while pouring herself another glass of wine. "In any case, the investigation doesn't end here. Find a way to use the evidence we already have. Anything you can get out of your mystery drone is icing on the cake."

"And what evidence do we have?" he sighs skeptically.

"To begin with, we have evidence that a lot of twenty artworks, comprising panels and canvases from the 15th to the 17th centuries, is connected to art smuggling. Perhaps they were stolen from Rose Kowalski's house, but let's avoid speculation and stick to the facts for now," Edna crosses her legs and continues. "We are at an impasse with Folli's panel for the moment. But we now have the name of an auction house, a suspicious lot of artworks, and a specific date of purchase. From there, we have a lot of questions we can ask. Questions about buyers, sellers, and what questions were asked – and weren't asked – when these works came up for sale. My guess is we'll find that this auction house wasn't chosen at random and that, whoever these people are, one of them is working at the auction house itself. All this might even be connected to the old investigation that you mentioned earlier. Of course, I doubt if this one transaction will be enough to bring down what appears to be a very sophisticated organization, but you have to start somewhere, don't you think, Mr. Bassi?"

"True. Although this is all going to be a lot more complicated than you make it sound. But I grant you that we could give it a try…" says the prosecutor, nodding thoughtfully.

"Poor Folli. He died in about the most undignified way imaginable. But for all his faults, I think he genuinely loved good art. And he would be pleased that his death, however comical, would start a series of events that would save some of the art that he loved. To Folli!" Edna concludes, raising her glass.

"To Folli, yes," smiles Bassi, pouring himself some Bianchetta to join her and Leonardo in the toast. "Regarding our theory, though," he continues, "assuming our antiques dealer did indeed purchase the panel from Rose Kowalski's nephew, why wasn't it stolen with all the other art works?"

"Hmm," Edna sets down her glass. "It's hard to say. It could have just been overlooked. It was a burglary, after all. And the kite stamp was also almost erased. It would have been easy to miss in bad lighting if you were in a hurry. We only noticed it when Leonardo enhanced and magnified the image of the back of the panel."

"That would make sense," agrees Bassi.

"What will happen to the panel now?" Leonardo asks.

"Good question!" Edna exclaims. "Surely you're going to keep it securely stored in a police archive as evidence?"

"The official procedure is to turn it over to the Office for the Protection of Cultural Heritage and let them decide how to proceed." sighs Bassi. "Although, to be honest, I was tempted not to say anything to anyone and entrust it to you. But I've already been sailing too close to the wind lately. If I want to keep my job, I've got to start making more, ahh, conventional decisions." He puts down his glass and clasps his hands under his chin, "Tell me this. If that lot of paintings that was sold at auction really was stolen from Rose Kowalski's apartment, what on earth were they doing there in the first place?"

"I was wondering that too," Edna shakes her head. "And the answer is that I haven't the slightest clue." She snorts and pours herself another glass of wine. She has come to realize that the past is not a nice neat parcel you can tie in a bow, throw in the back of the closet, and forget about.

Chapter Fifty-Six

"And you would be…?"

"The daughter." Edna replies, perplexed, standing on the landing of her mother's apartment. For a moment, she wonders if she's in the right place since she has no idea who this surly woman whose bulk completely blocks the doorway might be. She seems formidable enough and Edna carefully eyes her floral apron, flesh-colored knee-highs, and tweed skirt.

"Ah, here you are!" Ottavio sails toward the entrance, draped in a large cashmere dressing gown that makes him look like an oversized marron glacé. "Ada, this is Edna, Zara's daughter!" he says, waving his hands in an enthusiastic introduction. "Edna, this is Ada Garibaldi, Flora's cousin," he winks with the smug pleasure of someone pulling Kim Kardashian out of a hat.

"Good evening. My apologies." Ada grants Edna a brief nod of the head by way of greeting, while examining her with ill-concealed distrust. "But you know how it is. You've never come to visit your mother so, of course, I had no idea who you were." Her tone makes it clear that she has no reason to be embarrassed, as opposed to the degenerate daughter standing before her who couldn't be bothered to occasionally visit her own mother. "The Mistress is in the good living room," she announces as if she were a particularly snotty English butler and then marches into the kitchen.

"Good living room?" Edna snaps, grabbing Ottavio by the sleeve. "Were you aware we also had a *bad* one? Who the hell is this woman and is that our mop she's apparently sat on or did she bring her own?"

"Instead of thanking me for solving all your problems, you're quibbling over how to describe the living room?" Ottavio rolls his eyes. "Or did you imagine that I would be your mother's caretaker forever? In the last few days, you've dealt with all sorts of stuff, from finding corpses to impersonating Miss Marple and sniffing around fifteenth-century panels while rubbing elbows with state officials and fascinating techno-savvy young men… But I've got fifty bucks that says you didn't bother to spend a minute looking for a new housekeeper for Zara."

Edna takes the hit, shaking her head and mumbling apologetically. "I wouldn't take that bet. Is Miss Congeniality here to stay or is she just here on trial?" she inquires. Obnoxious she may be, but Edna is coming around to the idea that she might be just the person to go toe-to-toe with her mother and live to tell about it.

"I would never presume to make such important decisions without consulting her AWOL daughter first," he raises his hands defensively. "But considering that I have a life of my own, when I found this great opportunity, I didn't hesitate. You don't find people like Ada just hanging about. Ada – who adores me, by the way – is here because my Flora has explained to her why I, an esteemed musicologist, was forced to take care of my neighbor, and she was moved to tears by my sorry plight." Ottavio lowers his voice to a whisper and looks around conspiratorially. "I am already subliminally working on her, leveraging her Christian piety and, above all, the congenital trait of the Garibaldi family, which is the urge to jump in feet first when they see someone making a hash of things – or at least not performing up to their exacting standards – and it seems to be working." he looks smugly in the direction of the kitchen where industrious banging can be heard. "So, *please*, for once, try not to ruin everything just for the pleasure of being difficult." he sighs, pushing her towards the living room. "And go say hello to your mother because if Ada finds you here at the entrance chatting, she will encourage you to fulfill your filial duty by means of a rolling pin."

"You look awful!" Zara greets her daughter cheerfully as soon as she sees her enter. "Jonah spat out of the whale would seem to have just returned from a two-week stay at the spa compared to you. How *do* you do it?"

"Nice to see you too, Mom," Edna exhales, flopping on the sofa. "You always find the right words to cheer me up."

"Don't be sarcastic with me," Zara waves her jingling bracelets. "If your mother won't tell you the truth, someone else will. The way you dress, I'm surprised people on the street don't try to give you spare change."

"Here we go." Edna grumbles. "It's a mystery why I'm not here sixteen hours a day," she says, turning towards Ottavio. "Remember this next time you feel a lecture about filial love coming on."

"Piffle. You're always so melodramatic," Ottavio crosses his legs, patting his pockets hunting for his pipe. "It's just Zara's way of showing affection and letting you know she cares about your well-being. Is this the first time you two have met?"

Edna gives him a pregnant look. Then she gets up and goes to a large shelf where her mother has piled up decades of photographs. She grabs one at random, where her father and Zara, looking like Gregory Peck and Lauren Bacall in *Designing Woman*, smile at the camera with the lighthearted complicity of two friends playing at being lovers, or vice versa. Seeing her father's face prompts her to ask, "Do you remember Rose Kowalski, the woman Dad used to talk about?" without even stopping to ask herself if that was a wise move.

Zara remains silent for a long time.

"Of course, I remember her," she finally nods, "the Polish woman who was a secretary at the Superintendence of Fine Arts during the war," she replies, staring her right in the eyes, her curiosity piqued by the question. "Why are you bringing it up now?" she asks with disturbing directness.

"I found out she died not too long ago," Edna tries to appear noncommittal. She now regrets starting this conversation with Ottavio in the room, who is now scrutinizing her with narrowed eyes.

"It's not really so strange, is it? She could hardly have been a spring chicken. She must have been about fifteen years older than me," Zara shrugs.

"She was run over by a bus in Milan. She didn't die of old age," Edna points out, piqued. "Though she was not, I admit, a spring chicken, as you say. Do you know if Dad ever heard from her after she fled to Switzerland?"

"She wasn't in contact with your father, no," Zara shakes her head, still drilling Edna with her sharp, icy-green gaze. "Perhaps she was in contact with Pietro, although he never mentioned her either. It's a pity you didn't bring it up before, I just spoke to him two weeks ago and I could have asked." She drops this bomb with the casual nonchalance of someone commenting on the weather.

"By Pietro, do you mean *Pietro Calligaris*?" Edna leans forward, tense.

"Of course! How many other Pietros do you think I know? I don't know why you look so surprised, he was your father's closest friend. I talk to him on the phone a couple of times a month." she jingles her bracelets in exasperation. "Pietro has always been a gentleman. Even after what you did to him… all that lovely champagne…" she shakes her head pityingly. "Any other man would have destroyed you, professionally and otherwise. Instead, he protected you. He never fails to ask me about you and he follows your career. Such a gentleman!"

"I can't believe it!" Edna roars, leaping out of her seat. "Just to spite me, you defend that slimy, criminal bastard! That's insane…" she stares at her incredulously. "Your husband and his friend Rose risked their lives to preserve art and culture, and yet you defend Calligaris, who has betrayed them all his life, maneuvering behind their backs – and mine – to do the exact opposite? Can you hear yourself?" Edna has seldom been so furious. And that's saying something. She can barely stand to breath the same air as her mother.

"Your father and Rose risked their lives because of the war, my dear. That's all," Zara shrugs, as if Edna had just been reading her poetry rather than barking at her like a pit bull. "The fact that they were obsessed with saving works of art does them credit, of course. Your grandfather had instilled in your father the idea of culture as a form of freedom, which in many ways is commendable… But let me say that if Pietro hadn't been there to bail him out, your father would have certainly gotten himself killed, I would never have met him, and you wouldn't be here putting on a Greek tragedy in my good living room. So stop behaving as if it's all about you, Edna. You're almost sixty, not sixteen!" concludes Zara calmly, apparently more interested in removing lint from her pale blue sweater than in her daughter's distress.

"Uh, if this is where the Chorus comes in," coughs Ottavio, trying to ease the atmosphere, "it would be nice to know why we are discussing Rose now and how you found out about her death."

"It may be that the dead antiques dealer got the famous panel from Rose's nephew," Edna snorts. "He had inherited her apartment and everything inside, including the paintings. But after her death and before her nephew could get access to the property someone else paid Rose's apartment a little visit and, apparently, removed a lot of old paintings. And all the pieces had a kite-shaped stamp on the back."

"And how do you know this?"

"They all ended up being sold on through a famous auction house in London."

"Uh huh. This is getting more and more interesting," nods Ottavio, chewing on the stem of his pipe. "It's even more interesting that someone threw an octogenarian under a bus instead of waiting for nature to take its course."

"Nobody ever said that someone threw her under a bus!" Edna interjects.

"Nobody said that. But you thought that. I know I did." he looks at her sideways. "And if you haven't been thinking that, why the trip down memory lane?"

Edna nods her head in half-admission.

"Strange that they all had this stamp, while it was almost erased from perhaps the most valuable piece of all, don't you think? As if…"

"As if someone was trying to hide it, yes," Edna nods. "But the question is, what was it doing in Rose's attic in the first place?"

"It seems unlikely she was part of this ring, or whatever it was. Perhaps she was trying to protect it," he opines. "If I understand correctly that would be in line with the kind of person she was."

"It's true she died suddenly in a bus accident. But when you are over eighty years old, you should give a little thought to arranging possible legacies, material and otherwise, don't you think? But there was none of that. Instead, everything ends up in the hands of a slightly ne'er-do-well nephew who knows nothing about art and who sells off an extremely valuable painting to Folli for a pittance. I don't know what Rose had in mind when she was collecting all this art, but I'm pretty sure it wasn't that."

"This is also true," Ottavio admits with a sigh, while Zara, bored, fiddles with the three strands of pearls she wears even with her pajamas. "And so?"

"So nothing," Edna shrugs. "Bassi said that the panel will go to the Office for the Protection of Cultural Heritage, and that's the end of it."

"Dinner is ready for the lady of the house," interrupts Ada, marching in. Ada seems to march quite a lot and she is clearly fanatical about precise mealtimes as only a committed cook can be.

"But it's only half-past six!" Zara protests, annoyed.

"It's the perfect time for dinner," Ada replies. "So you have time to digest before going to bed."

"And how long do you imagine it will take me to digest dinner? I'm not a python…" sighs Zara, ignoring Ada's offer of a robust forearm and standing up by herself.

"If you're a good girl, after dinner, we'll also watch a little TV because tonight there's that show with the nuns," Ada steers her towards the dining room. "Well, what's with that gloomy face? Is it that you don't like nuns, or is it because of the leek soup? Come on, Signora Zara, leeks are nature's candy, they detoxify and make your skin beautiful," she explains hastily, putting a spoon in her hand. "As for the TV, we'll see. Perhaps we can take turns picking out our favorite program."

But Zara, with the spoon tightly squeezed between her knuckles and the air of someone who hopes this is just a bad dream, turns towards the living room and cries out in a shrill voice, "Leeks?!? Where is my Romanian? I want my Romanian housekeeper…" Ada closes the door, mercifully silencing her diatribe.

"Perhaps Zara has found just what she needs." Edna admits grudgingly, settling back on the sofa.

"I'd say it's a good match," nods Ottavio. "And I take all the credit for it. I'll also take that etching by Pietro Negri that you haven't given me yet, if you recall."

"It's impossible to forget, since you remind me of it every time I see you."

"All in all, this outing to Siestri turned out to be more stimulating than you expected," he opines as he relights his pipe. "You thought you'd go there and be bored to death, and instead, look at what happened: the thrill of a whodunit with a corpse, the excitement of an unexpected find, the misdirection from a former housekeeper with a frying pan, and a final twist with a character re-emerging from the shadowy past," he ticks off raising his sausage-like fingers. "And now I even found you a new and promising housekeeper. Would you have ever imagined that?"

"No," Edna admits, "especially not the housekeeper thing."

"There, you see?" he spreads his arms in an explosion of cashmere. "Perhaps the same thing will happen in the matter of Rose, the kite, and the fifteenth-century panel. Now everything seems to have petered out and your investigation has reached a dead end. But…"

Edna contemplates his smoke-wreathed figure critically, unable to decide if his smile is reassuring or chilling.

Chapter Fifty-Seven

With a heavy sigh, Public Prosecutor Jacopo Bassi sets his phone down and leans back against the chair. It's done. He can hardly believe it, but it's finally over.

He shared all the information that Leonardo uncovered with his contact in the Carabinieri Art Squad, and it proved to be immensely useful. Combined with the squad's existing data, this information led them to identify the elusive "inside man" – who turned out to be a woman – that had been orchestrating these sales from inside the London auction house. And it looked like all this was connected to his former case. Though perhaps "former" was not the right word since it had never ceased to occupy his thoughts.

Now, at long last, he sees real progress. Arrests had been made. Artworks had been seized. New investigations had been launched. Naturally, he won't be the one personally leading the investigation, it's unlikely he'll even be directly involved. But that's alright. It's not the hunger for glory that drives him. It's his hatred for loose ends and things unfinished, especially when it came to seeing justice done.

Of course, as dramatic as these results were, they weren't going to end art smuggling, not even by this one organization. In reality, they've merely inflicted a minor setback on a major art trafficking network. One so large and so well-organized, that losses like these were just a normal cost of doing business. Nevertheless, it's a beginning. The difficult thing in these cases was finding the end of the string. Once you did, it was just a matter of pulling hard enough to make everything unravel. This case, by itself, wasn't going to unravel the organization. But, as Dr. Silvera said, one must start somewhere. All things considered, this appeared to be real progress on something that had stagnated for far too long.

Bassi rises from his chair and walks to the window.

The sun is setting behind the hill. Another day is ending. When Bassi thinks back it seems that months, rather than days, have passed since the morning Folli's lifeless body was discovered.

He moves away from the window and approaches his desk. Opening the folder that Guerci had brought him a short while ago, he finds the data extracted from the remains of the drone that was recovered from the grove of holm oaks on Monte Caucaso.

Bassi picks up the sheet and reads it for what feels like the hundredth time. Despite being able to recite those few lines by heart at this point, he can't help but go over them again. The drone had taken its maiden flight just two weeks ago, conducting a brief test near Wartau, a Swiss village located in the canton of San Gallo, just a stone's throw away from Liechtenstein. It made its appearance in the sky over Val Fontanabuona on the exact day when Folli returned from Milan after meeting Kowalski. It lingered in the vicinity of the municipality of Moconesi for a total of eight hours and forty-seven minutes. As Bassi does not believe in luck or chance, he is inclined to view the drone's sudden appearance and persistent presence as being connected with recent events. To Bassi, it seems likely that the drone is evidence that someone was aware of both the panel's presence in Kowalski's attic and its transfer into Folli's possession. Someone who had both the means and the motivation to equip themselves with a cutting-edge drone camouflaged as a bird-of-prey, specifically, a kite, complete with a camera featuring digital video transmission and autonomous flight capabilities. Chance and luck could take a hike. He just didn't believe that this was all the result of some Swiss hobbyist who had a thing for aerial nature photos. Bassi retrieves an image from the open folder, extracted from a few seconds of the only video recovered from the drone. It depicts a portion of a terrace adorned with a stone balustrade, a well-maintained lawn surrounded by trees, and a figure, seen from above, holding a control box, the face concealed by the visor of a blue cap.

He lets out a sigh, carefully places the papers back into the folder, and stares into space, thinking. He reviews all the pieces of evidence, the theories, and the speculations. This is not the first time he has done this but, unfortunately, he always reaches the same conclusion.

He sighs again and reaches for his cell phone. In for a penny, in for a pound, they say.

Chapter Fifty-Eight

The truth is always hidden in the details," Schiaffino solemnly concludes, his sigh echoing in Edna's ear.

"Wow. Very deep! Have you been reading takeout Chinese fortune cookies again?" Edna sits down, propping her legs up and resting her heels on the coffee table. "Oh, my apologies. I didn't mean to insult you. I forgot you only dine at restaurants with at least two Michelin stars."

"Do you sharpen your claws specially when you know I'm calling or do you always keep them that way?" he sighs again. "You have all the conversational bonhomie of a tax auditor with a toothache."

"Listen, Edoardo," she snorts, "I don't know what kind of days you've been having lately, but let me assure you that mine have been like a ride through a haunted house – and I mean a real one, not a carnival ride. So, if you're looking for sweet nothings, call your wife, lover, or whoever you like, but spare me and get to the point. And while you're at it, stop blowing like a sperm whale."

"I just wanted an update on Siestri and Dante's commemoration," he explains, repressing another sigh. "Does that little task ring a bell or have you erased it from your mind, just as you always do with anything that doesn't align with your fancies? Perhaps you have another fantastical excuse for not doing even the simplest thing that I asked you to do?" Schiaffino asks, annoyed now.

"Are you implying that the entire circus triggered by the death of the antiques dealer is my fault?" Edna rolls her eyes. "Let me remind you that it was *you* who sent me to Siestri a week before the event, and on a day when heavy rain was forecast. If it had been up to me, I wouldn't have been within fifty miles of the place that day. So, if we really have to find someone to blame for that mess, between the two of us, it certainly isn't me! And since you ask so nicely, I was, in fact, there today, and I'm happy to report that Councilor Repetto came up with some great ideas. They are excellent for highlighting the region's importance and, above all, perfect for pleasing all the literary trombones and wannabes. In short, I may admit, after it's all over, that maybe the event was not as terrible as I initially thought it would be."

"Excellent!" he comments, satisfied. "I'm glad to hear you're in such a good mood because I wanted to invite you to din–"

But Edna's doorbell mercifully rides to the rescue and interrupts him in mid-sentence.

"Someone's at the door, goodbye!" Edna hangs up. Having guessed what he was going to say, she prefers to cut him off. She opens the door only to find it completely blocked by a massive bouquet of flowers, ferns, ribbons, and cellophane.

"I'm sorry. You must have the wrong address. No one has died here." she says, trying to peer over the gigantic bouquet.

"No one died, well not today, anyway. They're for you, Edna!" mutters a familiar voice.

"Mr. Bassi?!" she exclaims, more astonished by the fact that someone as refined as the Public Prosecutor had chosen such a tasteless flower arrangement than by his presence. Ikebana, this was not.

"Will you be letting me in sometime today or shall I just stand here on your porch attracting attention?" Edna steps aside wordlessly and allows Bassi to wrestle the floral monstrosity through the doorway, losing a number of leaves and buds in the process.

"Don't say a word. Let me explain first." mutters Bassi, heaving his burden onto her kitchen table and beginning to untie the multitude of ribbons.

"Leave it, leave it, Mr. Bassi. I'm sure I can find a, ahh, vase for that." says Edna, finally getting a hold of herself. "And please excuse my, um, less than polite welcome, but… well, I didn't realize it was you." Her apology is abruptly cut off because Bassi has just extracted from the jungle of ferns, gerberas, carnations, and lisianthus a package wrapped in bubble wrap and then in wrapping paper. It's a rectangular package but quite long and thin, reminding her of only one thing.

"You didn't!" she approaches, incredulous.

"If you mean is this Folli's panel, then yes, I did." he nods, gently unwrapping it. "And as I was saying, let me explain first." Then he sits down and leans back with a sigh, looking more drawn and haggard than Edna has yet seen him. "You'd better sit down too."

***

"So you believe the kite-drone was there to study Folli's movements or, more specifically, this panel's?" Edna fidgets absentmindedly with a ribbon left on the table.

"I'm almost certain of it, yes," Bassi confirms. "Which leads me to believe that whoever's behind this knew the panel was at Kowalski's."

"But… if they were so interested in the panel, why not take it when they broke into Kowalski's apartment, instead of going through the trouble of monitoring its movements? Or do you think the drone people are a different group than the people who committed the burglary? Even then, why didn't they just break in themselves if they knew it was there?"

"I have no idea. But I'm starting to suspect that Kowalski's death may not have been a simple heart attack. Not only that, the device that was being mistaken for a kite was a very expensive, high-performance drone that someone brought in from Switzerland. My instincts are telling me that there is something going on here, something serious. But let's get back to the present. The drone crashed before I took the panel from Folli's laboratory. So at the moment, I doubt anyone knows that the police have it. But I can't be sure of that. These people seem both determined and resourceful and they may be monitoring things again. So, a good friend of mine in the Carabinieri Art Squad is receiving a beautiful, framed Klimt print as a gift. By an amazing coincidence, this framed print is just about the same size as this panel which seems to, somehow, have gotten tangled up with this lovely bouquet that I brought you to thank you for all your help. Life's funny like that sometimes." finishes Bassi, smugly pleased with himself in spite of the enormity of what he has done.

"Why here?"

"Several reasons. First, you're probably one of the best-qualified people on earth to study this panel and find out what secrets it still might hold and where it came from. But more importantly, you'd never agree to do it."

"You've lost me."

"You have a reputation for being serious, at least when it comes to art, to a fault. You would never agree to keep a priceless masterwork like this in your bedroom closet and risk it being damaged or stolen. The whole idea is ludicrous. And if I know that, the people chasing this panel know that. At the moment, your house is the safest possible place for it."

"Mr. Bassi, I must apologize. Clearly, I have had a bad effect on you. That is one of the most ridiculous, insane ideas I think I have ever heard."

"So you'll do it then?"

"Of course I'll do it. What do you take me for?"

Bassi, wisely, chooses not to respond to her question. Instead, he hands her a USB stick he has taken from his jacket pocket.

"I'll leave you with this as well. It contains a copy of the data we recovered from the drone. I wouldn't want your neighbor to feel left out. I expect great things from you both." Edna rolls her eyes at this but forbears to comment. "It has been… interesting getting to know you. Be careful." with that, he stands up, gives her a slight bow, and departs.

Edna sighs and then gets up herself, gathering the flowers to arrange them in whatever vases she can find, along with two large buckets. Cagliostro, who has just entered through the partially open window, approaches cautiously and begins sniffing a large amaranth gerbera.

"Now I have to find a place for this damn panel as well," she thinks as she rewraps it.

Perhaps hiding it in plain sight by hanging it with the rest of her artwork might be best. She'll think about it. For now, she'll put it in the back of her closet. She pours herself a glass of water and drinks it all in one gulp. She's unsettled by this whole affair – the kite-drone, Kowalski's death, which, like the death of his aunt Rose, may not be what it seems… Thoughts of her father and his heart attack come to her mind. He had always been extremely healthy and his death was so sudden and unexpected that it left everyone shocked and dismayed. She blinks back a tear. Why is she digging up all this? Her father passed away twenty-five years ago! *Stop it, Edna!* she tells herself. *Conspiracy theories don't suit you. Nor do murder investigations. You are an art historian, not Jessica Fletcher!*

The ear-destroying ring of her phone slashes through her reveries and brings her back to reality with a bump.

"Orietta!" Edna exclaims with genuine enthusiasm. "No, no. You're not disturbing me. You couldn't have called at a better time. Yes, I'm alone." she casts a fleeting glance at a clearly-offended Cagliostro.

"Dinner? Why not? I'm starving, and, today, I'm just not in the mood to cook. Perfect. We'll meet there, then."

She ends the call, gazes for a moment at the USB stick that Bassi left her, and with a sigh, inserts it into the center of the crowded pen holder on her desk. She's tired now, hungry, and still needs to lock up the chicken coop and bid goodnight to her seven sulking hens – an endeavor that requires a fair amount of commitment, both emotional and otherwise, especially when they feel they are being sent to bed early. She sighs. As that whiny Scarlett used to say, "After all, tomorrow is another day!" And tomorrow, she will think about it.

Sometime later, after picking a few feathers out of her hair and changing into something, she reflects wryly, that even her mother would have approved, she's finally ready to head out for the evening. But when she opens the door, she finds Schiaffino standing in front of her.

"Edoardo! What are you doing here? Are you stalking me now?" she stares at him in surprise, fists firmly planted on her hips.

"You've only got yourself to blame. If you didn't keep hanging up on me, I wouldn't be forced to drive all the way out here to talk to you," he explains.

"So what do you want?"

"To invite you to dinner, if I may."

"As you can see, I was just on my way out for dinner myself," she replies.

His crestfallen expression is both woeful and comical.

Edna contemplates him for a long moment, then rolls her eyes, sighs and decides to take pity on him. "I'm going to have dinner with my friend, Orietta, she's one of Gattorna's municipal councilors." she explains as she brushes past him and heads towards the gate. A sudden thought causes her to stop and turn around. "If you want, you can invite both of us!" she suggests. "You'll just *love* Orietta. I know the three of us will get along famously!" she pronounces, unable to hide a mischievous smile.

He opens and closes his mouth, at something of a loss. But he did not become successful in academic politics without being able to tell which way the wind was blowing. With a sigh, he walks towards his car, opens the passenger door and ushers Edna into the soft leather seat before taking his own place behind the wheel. The car starts with a gentle purr, he shifts into first gear and accelerates. A seagull hovers above them before, white and silent, gracefully wheeling to follow them into hills glowing in the light of sunset.

Chapter Fifty-Nine

"Remember that you are dust, and to dust you shall return," the caretaker sighs, setting down the shovel and brushing off his corduroy trousers. He lifts his head to gaze at the sky, where dusk is yielding to night. The calls of the thrush and the nightingale can already be heard in the distance. It's late, but there's no one at home to expect him. He prefers to get everything done tonight. In his business, he's constantly reminded that there may not be a tomorrow. Besides, digging a grave with people standing around waiting for the funeral to start can be quite uncomfortable. He has already prepared the temporary grave marker and attached the name tag to it: Carlo Kowalski.

Not a common name, that. He wonders idly if this Kowalski was somehow related to the other Kowalski buried along the west side of the cemetery. Chiaravalle was nothing like as big as the Monumentale in Genoa and having two Kowalskis here was an oddity.

Come to think of it, that other Kowalski grave was an oddity all by itself. It was untended. No one ever came to visit it. And yet, one day he found it marked with a gilded bronze sculpture in the shape of a bird of prey taking flight.

It's an impressive piece, one of the most impressive in the cemetery, which makes its sudden, unexpected appearance doubly odd. Sometimes, when he's finished his regular rounds of removing weeds and making sure everything is in order, he'll stop and visit that sculpture for a few minutes. He's not sure what it means, but it must mean something and the person who merited such a monument must have been quite extraordinary.

It's a mystery, but these little enigmas are what makes life interesting, especially in a place like this. He glances around a final time to make sure everything is in order. Then he picks up his shovel from the ground and slowly walks toward the shed to put away his tools. It's time to go home.

THE END

www.ingramcontent.com/pod-product-compliance
Lightning Source LLC
Chambersburg PA
CBHW060711190726
48289CB00002B/643